Gunshine State

"Part heist novel, part revenge tale, *Gunshine State* is a searing action story in exotic locales populated by fascinating grifters and unsavory characters. Add this to your must read list."
—Eric Beetner, author of *The Devil At Your Door*

"A tense, fast-moving, vividly-drawn thriller."
—Garry Disher, author of the Wyatt novels

"A gritty slice of Down-Under noir, served lean and mean."
—Wallace Stroby, author of *The Devil's Share*

"A phenomenal, hard-as-nails thriller with more tight corners than a maze and a double cross around every one of them. I loved it."
—Timothy Hallinan, award-winning author

"A lean, mean, hard-boiled knockout."
—David Whish-Wilson, author of *Old Scores*

"*Gunshine State* moves like a bullet. This novel firmly positions Nette as one of Australia's leading writers of hard-boiled crime."
—Alex Hammond, author of *The Unbroken Line*

"*Gunshine State* is magnificent. Taut, tense—a tremendous thriller."
—Andrew Grant, author of *False Witness*

"A breakneck ride from first page to last. Nette drags the reader into a sharply drawn world of dark motives and even darker morals. A must for lovers of hard-boiled crime fiction."
—Emma Viskic, author of *Resurrection Bay*

"This hard-boiled thriller comes at you like a furious street brawler and pins you to the wall with a white-knuckle plot and authentic characters. Like a vicious left hook to the ribs it will leave you breathless."
—Leigh Redhead, author of Simone Kirsch series

GUNSHINE STATE

ALSO BY ANDREW NETTE

Ghost Money

Girl Gangs, Biker Boys, and Real Cool Cats:
Pulp Fiction and Youth Culture, 1950 to 1980

ANDREW NETTE

GUNSHINE STATE

Down & Out Books
3959 Van Dyke Rd, Ste. 265
Lutz, FL 33558
www.DownAndOutBooks.com

Cover design by Zach McCain

ISBN: 1-946502-20-0
ISBN-13: 978-1-946502-20-9

To my mother, Judy Nette.
You are much missed.

IRON TRIANGLE

The high-pitched whine of the power drill tore through the confined space of the back office. Chance winced at the noise, worried it could be heard on the street outside.

'How much longer, Addamo?' he said, his voice edgy.

The man crouched on the floor with his back to him said nothing, his attention focused on a green metal safe the size of a three-drawer filing cabinet.

They'd agreed, no more than two hours for the job. Just over forty minutes left. Chance pulled at the smooth stump where the little finger on his left hand had once been, leaned against a battered wooden desk. He picked up a sheet of A4 from the mess of paperwork, held it to the glow of the portable halogen lamp, read an order for glassware. He let the paper flutter to the floor, sniffed, the aroma of their sweat mingled with stale beer and fried food.

'I thought all you needed was a stethoscope and a good pair of ears, like in the movies.'

Addamo cut the power, swore in Italian. He looked over his shoulder, the olive skin on his face stretched tight and beaded with sweat.

'We've been over this, already. All safes get shipped from the manufacturer with what they call tryout combinations. Ideally the owner resets it on delivery. Doesn't happen as often as you think, but unfortunately, these folks are the exception.'

'You said you might be able to guess the combination,' said Chance. 'The noise from the drill, someone might hear it.'

'I could try to manipulate the lock, old safes like this one, tumblers on the inside, sometimes you can hear them falling into place, listen to the clicks as they move over the levers. My old man would've been able to do it, but I'm not half as good as he was.'

Addamo ran a latex-gloved hand through his thick black curls. 'The quickest way to get into the safe is to drill into the wheel pack. Then I'll use this to watch the wheels as I spin the dial.' He fossicked in a blue canvas sports bag on the floor, came up with a short length of tube, some sort of eyepiece on one end, held it in front of Chance.

Chance didn't recognise the instrument, shrugged.

'It's a borescope,' said Addamo. 'You insert the tube in the hole I'm drilling now, lets you see inside. Hopefully, it's just a matter of lining up the notches and watching everything fall into place. Got it?'

'Yeah.'

'Good. So, let me get back to work.' He turned to face the safe, stopped halfway, looked back at Chance. 'And stop standing over my fucking shoulder. You're like a bad bloody smell. Go keep watch or something.'

The drilling resumed as Chance closed the door behind him. The noise remained audible as he moved down a wide corridor, rooms running off it, kitchen, toilets, a large public bar. He glided the torch beam over the refuse of Lawrence's farewell party, dirty glasses, strands of streamers draped over the tables. The street outside the large front window was empty.

He turned the handle on a heavy door at the end of the corridor, stepped into the square of uneven packed dirt used as a car park at the rear.

Chance stood next to a dumpster, strained to hear the drill. The only sound was the thrum of crickets and the night breeze passing through a line of gums nearby. The knot in his stomach unwound slightly; he savoured the humid air on his arms and face.

When Lawrence had first introduced them, Chance thought Addamo was a flashy Italian twentysomething male with too much attitude and not enough brains.

Lawrence had clapped Chance on the back after the Italian had left. 'Don't worry about him. When it comes to the job, he'll be a hundred percent reliable. His dad was a locksmith in town, a solid guy, taught the kid everything he knew.'

Lawrence was right. Addamo was good. He'd got them inside without any problems, calm and professional. Chance rolled a cigarette, chuckled. He was the one out of practice after eight months of low-key living, driving trucks around the Iron Triangle, the ore-producing region of South Australia bounded by the towns of Port Pirie, Port Augusta, and Whyalla, a part of the country that hovered in a no man's land between mining boom and rust belt.

He'd worked in a mining camp in West Australia before that, as far away from his previous employer as he could get. Good money, but Chance had quickly grown tired of the daily regimen of drug testing, limited alcohol intake, and strict rules, every move he made dictated by corporate margins and risk prevention.

Lawrence, a union organiser in Port Pirie, had tried to recruit Chance soon after he arrived. Chance said he wasn't interested. Didn't see the point. Told Lawrence as much. No hard feelings, Lawrence said, maybe another time.

'Not likely,' said Chance.

Lawrence had sought Chance out a few months later, found him drinking in his favourite Port Pirie pub.

'I'm still not interested in joining the union,' Chance said as Lawrence slid onto a bar stool next to him, ordered two beers. Lawrence's face was older, more grizzled, his eyes ringed with dark circles.

'To hell with the union, I've got a business proposition you might be interested in.'

Lawrence's wife, Port Pirie born and bred, had been diagnosed with cancer. The likely cause was the largest lead smelter in the world, its stack visible across town. It supplied a lot of jobs, also poured forty tonnes of lead into the air each year. The result was higher than usual incidences of asthma, kidney failure, brain disease, and cancer. You can't see lead poisoning, but you can see unemployment, the refrain every time someone questioned the wisdom of allowing the smelter to poison the air.

The doctor told Lawrence the cancer had started in his wife's liver, spread to her lungs and brain, gave her six months to live, a year tops. Lawrence quit his job to look after her full-time, needed money.

The annual conference of the South Australian branch of his union would take place in town in a week's time. They were going to throw him a farewell bash to mark his years of service. The venue was a large, family owned pub in town. Every conference delegate, union people from Port Pirie and surrounds, would be there. They'd drink the place dry.

The party would be on a Saturday night, the takings stashed in an old safe in the back office until they could be deposited on the Monday. Lawrence wanted Chance to help him rob it.

'You want to knock off your own farewell party?'

'Yeah, that's exactly what I want to do.' Lawrence stared at Chance with rheumy eyes. His lower lip quivered slightly. 'I've got bills to pay while I look after Faye, and my savings and superannuation aren't going to cut the mustard. The money in that safe will include bar takings, the bistro. If nothing else, it'll give me some breathing space until I can think of what to do next.'

'How come you know so much about this place?'

'Represented some of the staff there, job before this one.'

'So your information is old.'

'There were no alarms back then and the place has the same owner, old school, never thought he'd need to spring for electronic security, patrols, anything like that.' Lawrence grabbed a paper serviette from a pile on the bar top, took a biro pen from his shirt pocket, sketched the layout as he spoke. 'There's a window of opportunity between one and six a.m. when the money will be in the safe. All we've got to do is go in and get it.'

'Who's going to get us inside and take care of the safe?'

'Got someone lined up, son of an old mate. Knows his shit.'

'Sounds like you've got it sorted, why do you need me?'

'Mate, I'll hardly be in any condition to help, and the other guy can't do everything. Need you to keep an eye out, whatever else is needed.'

'Why me?'

Lawrence gave Chance a knowing smile, ordered two more beers. 'Something about you made me think you'd be open to the idea.'

Chance flicked the butt of his cigarette into the darkness, about to go back inside when he heard a noise.

He stepped into the shadow of the dumpster, was enveloped by the sickly sweet organic smell of rotting garbage. He held the long-barrelled flashlight parallel with his leg, ready to strike.

The sound came closer. Footsteps. A figure passed in front of him, a man, headed for the back door.

Chance stepped out of the shadows, the torch above his head.

The man wheeled around, arms outstretched.

Chance grabbed Lawrence's jacket, pulled him back into the shadows.

'What the fuck are you doing here?' hissed Chance. 'I could have hurt you.'

'Just wanted to see how things were going.' The words slurred as they came out of his mouth. His eyes had a glassy sheen and the alcohol on his breath cut through the stink of the rotting garbage. 'Jesus, Gary, relax, there's no one else around.'

Chance let him go. Lawrence swayed slightly, put a hand on the dumpster to steady himself. 'Calm down, mate. I put this job together, got a right to see how it's going.'

'This is not a union site visit. It's a bloody robbery.'

5

Lawrence belched, set his jaw defiantly.

'At least get out of sight,' Chance said, spinning the older man around and directing him toward the back door.

Addamo had stopped drilling, knelt in front of the safe, one eye pressed against the borescope, twisting the combination dial.

'We've got a visitor,' said Chance.

Addamo wiped away the sweat on his face with his forearm, did a double take at Lawrence's presence.

'This some sort of joke?'

'Dickhead here decided he wanted to check up on us.' Chance made no effort to control the irritation in his voice.

Addamo looked at Chance, one eyebrow raised.

Lawrence swivelled his head between the two men. 'I just wanted to see how everything was going, where's the harm in that? I put this job together, I figured—'

'Shut up,' said Chance.

Lawrence went quiet.

'I'm nearly there, Gary,' said Addamo. 'Ten minutes, twenty tops, reckon I'll be in.'

Chance shone a beam at the corner of the room, between the desk and wall. 'Sit there,' he told Lawrence.

Lawrence regarded the space sullenly, opened his mouth to speak.

'Don't say anything.' Chance cut him off. 'Another word, I swear, I'll knock you out, leave you here for the owner to find in the morning.'

After a few minutes of watching Addamo work, the tension in the small room felt unbearable. Chance flicked a dark glance at Lawrence, stepped into the corridor, paced up and down.

On his fourth or fifth pass by the doorway to the public bar he noticed a vehicle parked on the street outside. Chance moved closer to the front window, saw a mustard coloured Holden that had seen better days. 'Fucking Lawrence,' he whispered, just as another car pulled up behind it.

The second car was white, brand new, with a logo on the driver's door, a shield with a lightning bolt running through it. A man got out of the car. He wore black pants and a white shirt with a patch on the shoulder featuring the same logo as the car door.

Chance hated private security guards; in his experience, ex-cops or try-hards looking to prove something. He watched in horror as the man walked around the Holden, shone his torch inside and then into the front window of the pub.

Chance crept out of the public bar, jogged down the corridor, threw open the door to the back office. Addamo had the safe open, was scooping money into a green plastic garbage bag, looked up.

'We've got to go. Now.'

'What are you talking about?'

'Lawrence parked his car out the front. It's attracted attention, a security guard, he's coming in.'

'I swear, I didn't know they had security,' said Lawrence.

Chance didn't bother replying. 'Take what we have, leave the rest,' he said to Addamo.

Addamo glanced regretfully at the safe, grabbed the plastic bag and stood up.

They were a few metres from the back door when the overhead light came on and a gravelly voice behind said: 'Stop right there. Won't warn you again.'

Chance stopped, raised his hands.

'Turn around,' said the voice.

Chance and Addamo did as they were told. Lawrence didn't move.

The security guard stood at the far end of the corridor. He held his pistol in both hands, stepped slowly toward them.

Out of the corner of his eye, Chance saw Lawrence fumble with something in the belt of his trousers, realised it was a gun. Lawrence drunkenly turned.

Chance pushed Addamo to the floor, followed after him.

Three shots rang out. Two came in return, followed by silence.

Chance opened his eyes. Lawrence stared lifelessly at him across the threadbare carpet. Acrid smoke hung in the air above the corridor. The security guard writhed on the floor at the far end of the corridor, clutched a spreading red stain on his shoulder with one hand, grasped for his pistol several feet away with the other.

Addamo was already up and out the back door with the money.

Chance leaned over, felt the flaccid skin around Lawrence's neck for a pulse, got nothing. He cursed his former partner's stupidity, flew out the door after Addamo.

The Italian reached his vehicle parked behind a row of shrubs. A car engine coughed into life, headlights illuminated the stretch of dirt in front of it. Chance jumped into the passenger's seat.

Port Pirie would be too hot after this and whatever they had made out of tonight's job wouldn't last long.

It looked like he'd have to go back to work for the Chinaman.

GUNSHINE STATE

One

His plane landed in Brisbane mid-afternoon. Chance got a cab, gave the young Indian driver the address.

They tailed a white four-wheel-drive pickup for most of the freeway, its rear loaded with PVC piping, two stickers on the back bumper bar: 'Australia: if you don't like it, leave' and 'All is great in the Sunshine State'.

No sunshine today. Rain all morning, more forecast, the sky a slab of swollen cloud, the air thick and humid. Two and a half hours in the air and his entire world had changed. No red dust, no signs sprayed with shotgun pellets, no huge domed expanse of blue, far as the eye could see.

The taxi exited the freeway, plunged into a warren of inner city streets, refurbished buildings, sleek new apartment blocks, rows of cafés and bars, footpaths crowded with well-dressed, well-fed people. The taxi turned into a residential street, stopped in front of a block of red brick veneer flats, 'Ocean View Apartments' in curved metal letters next to the entrance. A large Pacific Islander man sat on the front steps, watched Chance walk up the cracked concrete path and disappear into the building.

Chance knocked on a door two flights up. He heard music on the other side, a sixties crooner, interspersed with moist coughing. The music stopped, the door opened. A woman in her sixties peered at him through the gap. She had sharp blue eyes, surrounded by mascara, a generous mouth caked with coral lipstick.

'With you in a minute, love.'

The door closed, more coughing, followed by the sound of the chain being taken off.

'Come in, love.'

Chance walked down a narrow hallway, brushed aside a curtain of plastic beads, stepped into a cramped living area. Weak sunlight came through the venetian blinds.

He stood in the middle of the room, hands behind his back. The woman was draped in a white kaftan patterned with lime green tropical flowers. Years of Queensland sun had turned her face and arms to leather.

'Been expecting you. Make yourself at home while I get what you came for.'

Chance listened to her move about in the adjoining kitchen. When he was sure there was no threat, he relaxed, glanced around the room. The decor was island kitsch, oil paintings of beach sunsets, a cane table and chairs, several half-coconut ashtrays overflowing with butts encircled with the woman's lipstick.

On the mantelpiece, framed back and white photographs, two deep. He recognised his host in one. Her taunt body, clad in fishnet stockings and a sequined bikini, faced away from the camera, her head cocked over her shoulder, a smile and a cheeky wink for the audience.

'Long time ago, love.'

Chance looked up. The woman stood in the doorway, a manila envelope in one hand.

'Not that long ago, I bet.'

'You're a dear, but no time for that now.' She handed him the envelope. She lit up, drew in deep, coughed as she waved smoke away from her face. 'Better check it's all there,' she croaked.

Chance cleared a space on the coffee table, shook the contents of the envelope onto the glass. Car keys, driver's license, folded bundles of cash, and a phone.

'The keys are to the red Toyota Corolla outside,' said the woman.

12

He looked at the details on the driver's license. Peter Jacobi, thirty-two. At least they'd got Chance's age right.

The woman leaned against the mantelpiece, tapped her cigarette into the nearest half coconut. She coughed hard, suddenly looked old and birdlike in the dim light.

Chance held up the phone. 'This clean?'

'Does a bear shit in the woods?' The woman gave him an offended look. 'Imported from Mexico where there's no reliable register of handsets, mobile numbers or users, and sellers are unregistered. Can't be traced.'

She stubbed her cigarette out, went back into the adjoining kitchen, returned with a brown paper bag. She placed it on the table in front of Chance. 'Almost forgot, the Chinaman wanted you to have this.'

Chance peeked into the bag and saw a silver pistol barrel.

'Registration papers are there, too, love.'

He gazed at the woman, eyebrows raised. 'Something tells me that's not my lunch.'

She lit another cigarette, peered at him through the curling smoke. 'Welcome to the gunshine state.'

Two

It rained the hour-long drive to Surfers Paradise. Water fell from the gunmetal sky at a forty-five degree angle with such force the windscreen wipers struggled to keep up.

The downpour turned to mist just as Surfers materialized around him, strip malls and new housing projects replaced on all sides by high-rise hotels and apartment blocks.

His hotel was a box-like building between a vacant lot and a double-fronted store that sold souvenirs, stuffed animals, UGG boots, and fake Aboriginal arts and crafts. Chance arrived just as a large tour bus pulled up and disgorged a line of middle-aged Asian tourists. They chatted excitedly as their female guide herded them toward the entrance.

The reception smelled of cleaning products, week-old Christmas decorations on the walls. Chance stood by a table, thumbed through a Chinese language travel brochure while he waited for the new arrivals to check in. The receptionist, a young Asian male with bad acne, informed him there was a prepaid reservation in the name of Peter Jacobi and otherwise served him with an absolute minimum of human interaction.

His room on the fourth floor was small, the décor minimal. How many places had he stayed in like this? Life stripped down to the basics, nothing that wasn't cheap or nailed down: a shower, TV, bed, a cupboard with an iron and a board. He couldn't remember the last time he'd ironed anything.

Chance heard screams outside his window, pushed the heavy curtain to one side. Above the adjoining building were two tall cranes to which two heavy cords were attached. The machine hurled people high like a reverse bungee jump. The wail of its passengers filled the air, a mixture of joy and terror. He watched the contraption for a while, then showered, changed and set off toward Orchid Avenue, Surfers Paradise's main drag, or the Glitter Strip as it was better known.

Night fell fast as he walked and it was almost dark when he merged with the crowded footpath. Damp Christmas decorations dangled from the streetlights. Luxury boutiques and restaurants mixed with two-dollar shops, takeaways, internet cafés, and massage parlours. Traffic crawled bumper-to-bumper, cars, an amphibious truck used as a tourist bus. Chance recognised the make from his time in the army.

Older couples and large multigenerational families from Asia, India, and Africa headed back to their hotels after dinner, giving the streets over to packs of young people. The men had an air of random aggression. The women, dressed in T-shirts, tight cut-off jeans, and high heels, hobbled behind their male peers, trying to keep up.

He headed toward the sound of the ocean but was stopped before the beach by a wire fence with a sign announcing construction. He rolled a cigarette, smoked as he listened to the surf, the waves faintly visible in the darkness.

He'd visited Surfers as a child, didn't remember much except his family had stayed in a fibro house, the beach only minutes across a hot asphalt road. He wondered if the house still existed. Probably carpet-bombed with steel and concrete like the rest of Surfers by overseas investors and local businessmen keen for a fast buck. What fifty years ago had been mangrove swamps and wooden shacks was now a city of almost a million people. Despite the luxury hotels and billion-dollar marina projects, it

still exuded an air of impermanence. The commerce felt tempo-
rary, everyone from somewhere else.

Chance wandered back to the Strip to find somewhere to eat,
decided on an Irish-themed tavern, found a seat at the bar, and
ordered a beer and a fisherman's basket.

As the night wore on he found himself sandwiched between a
group of middle-aged men and a table of drunk twentysomething women. The women all wore tiny red devil's horns. A
huge purple dildo sat in torn wrapping paper on their table,
along with several jugs of margaritas.

He gravitated toward the men, all contractors, one of whom
had just come into money. Chance hoped to pick up some local
intelligence on Surfers, maybe a lead to another job if this one
didn't pan out. All he got instead was a lot of whining about a
white man's burden of economic uncertainty, shit weather, and
marriage problems. Chance paced himself, one beer to their two
or three, ended up several hours later in a strip club that felt like
it had been assembled from a DIY kit, chrome finishing, black
leather, loud music, and watered-down drinks.

He felt his phone vibrate in his front shirt pocket, peered at
the solitary text message: Sea World underwater viewing gallery,
ten a.m. tomorrow, Dormer.

He pocketed the phone, said his goodbyes, and made his way
back to the hotel.

Three

The underwater viewing gallery was packed with exhausted-looking parents and their children. Chance watched the large grey shapes and multi-coloured smaller ones glide by as he waited for Dormer to make contact.

After a few minutes, two kids standing to his left were replaced by a man, a foot taller and several years older than Chance.

The man stared at the passing marine life, his face lit by the dappled sunlight filtered through the water.

'Show me your left hand,' he said, not taking his eyes off the gallery.

'What?'

'Your left hand, I want to see it.'

Chance raised his hand. 'Satisfied?'

The man made a show of counting off the fingers, gave a curt nod, straightened the cuffs of his pale grey suit. 'No hard feelings, Jacobi, just checking that I'm talking to the right person.'

Dormer returned his gaze to the tank, just as a large shark drifted on the other side of the glass.

'Ever wondered why the sharks in this tank don't eat each other?'

'No.'

'They only target the unhealthy ones. Sharks can tell, apparently, when one of their kind moves slower than usual or makes erratic movements. They'll go for the kill. It eradicates the weak, keeps the rest of the school healthy. A bit like humans, wouldn't you say?

'I suppose.'

'Not that there's anything unhealthy looking about you.' Dormer flashed him a sideways look, returned his gaze to the tank. 'I hear you're a veteran, Jacobi.'

Chance tensed, unsure what information the Chinaman had passed on.

'Yes.'

'Where?'

'East Timor for a couple of years, followed by a stint in Afghanistan.'

'Doing what, might I ask?'

'Driving trucks.'

'A truck driver? A cabin-dwelling creature, rarely seen, known for high speed, capacity to slack off and love of a cold beer.'

Chance took no offense, was more interested in what the statement betrayed about Dormer, his inside knowledge of the army.

'Where'd you serve?'

'Infantry. Iraq and Afghanistan, then I made a horizontal career move into the private sector.' Dormer reached into his jacket pocket, took out a slip of paper and handed it to Chance. 'We can swap war stories another time. Be at that address at seven sharp tonight, we'll take it from there.'

'The ticket to this place cost me nearly a hundred dollars,' said Chance. 'I thought I'd get a bit more information for my money?'

'You'll get more. Tonight.'

Chance watched Dormer disappear into the crowd, returned his attention to the sharks.

* * *

The Strip was packed with families and backpackers taking advantage of the break in the weather. A sprinkling of hard-core drinkers sat in the receding shadow in front of bars and cafés, nursing their first beer of the day or the final one of the night before.

On a whim, Chance paused at the entrance to a seedy arcade, a survivor of the city's relentless war against its past, stepped into the dimly lit interior: A kebab shop, a massage parlour that looked like it sold everything but, two cheap Asian restaurants, vacant shopfronts.

Chance entered one of the restaurants, ordered beef rendang and coconut rice. He ate half the oily, tasteless meal, left the restaurant, found a surf shop, and bought a pair of board shorts. He retrieved his car from the hotel's underground car park, drove down the Gold Coast Highway to Burleigh Heads.

Chance knew his unease was just part and parcel of the usual pre-job jitters, that he had no choice but to play along and wait until tonight when he'd find out more. In the distance the sky-scrapers of Surfers Paradise were silhouettes shrouded in sea spray. He dived into the water and let the surf pound the morning's events out of his mind.

Four

The house was hidden behind a high brick wall on a winding residential street twenty minutes' drive inland from Surfers.

Chance stood in the indigo twilight, pressed a buzzer. The gate slid open to reveal a red brick hacienda-style residence, metal bars on the windows.

The man who opened the front door had an aging bruiser's body, faded blue tattoos on his heavily tanned forearms, a generous head of grey hair, cut Rockabilly-style, mutton-chop side burns. He held a can of beer in his free hand, radiated the same air of unfocused aggression as the young men Chance had seen the previous evening on the Glitter Strip.

Chance followed him through a kitchen into a dining room. Full-length-glass double doors revealed a patio with a large hooded barbecue and a set of wrought iron table and chairs. Beyond the patio he could see one of the many manufactured waterways that snaked through suburban Gold Coast, a ribbon of liquid tar in the fading light.

The man kept going to the very back of the house, stopped at a doorway, motioned Chance inside, followed, and took up a position next to a life-size porcelain statue of a greyhound.

White shagpile carpet, wood-panelled walls, framed photographs vying for space with Australian rules football memorabilia and framed newspaper cuttings, a large flat-screen TV showing motor racing, the volume on mute.

Dormer, dressed in the same suit he'd worn that morning, sat on one of several black leather couches arranged around a glass-topped coffee table.

Next to him was a woman with straight shoulder-length hair, bone-white skin, an aquiline face with a large nose, and brown eyes surrounded by dark circles. A nametag, pinned to the front of her white shirt, read: Sophia. As she acknowledged Chance, she raised a cigarette to her lips, drew on it hard, exhaled the same way. Some people made smoking look pleasurable.

A second woman and an older man stood around a bar at the far end of the room. The woman looked at him from underneath a jagged fringe of blonde hair. A slim body accentuated by her choice of clothes: cut-off jeans, a faded Rolling Stones T-shirt and old cowboy boots.

The man had a nuggetty build, similar to Chance's, a generous head of silver hair, and blue eyes that flanked a cauliflower nose covered in tiny strands of red.

The man grinned, stepped out from behind the bar, gave Chance a double-pump handshake. A big man, at ease with the space he took up.

'Welcome to Surfers, Peter. My name is Dennis Curry. Good to have you on board. Can I get you a cold beverage?'

'Not for me, Mister Curry.'

'Mister Curry was my father, old bastard that he was. Call me Dennis.' He glanced in Dormer's direction. 'You've met Frank. The miscreant next to the greyhound is my flatmate, Mal Kerrigan.'

Mal raised his beer can in sullen acknowledgement.

'As for the females, the Mediterranean beauty on the couch is Sophia Lekakis. The lady propping up the bar with me is Amber.' Amber flashed a quick smile, her eyes lingering on him as if they were sharing a secret. 'Everyone else right for a drink?' Curry looked around the room with the air of a best man at a Bucks party. Getting no takers, he clapped his hands together. 'Right, let's get started.'

Curry steered Chance toward the leather couches. Everyone sat except Mal, who maintained his stance next to the greyhound.

Dormer reached for a manila folder on top of a pile of magazines on the coffee table, slid out an A4 colour photograph, handed it to Chance. It showed an Asian man leaning against the bonnet of what looked like a brand-new Dodge Charger.

'Meet Frederick Gao, Freddie to his friends, thirty years of age, son of prominent Filipino tycoon, Lucio Gao. Old man Gao is one of those hard-arsed self-made men, arrived a penniless migrant from mainland China just after World War Two, got where he is now through hard work and making himself useful to a certain Filipino dictator. In return for services rendered, said dictator gave Gao a large chunk of the country's north to run fairly much as he pleases.'

Chance studied the photograph. Freddie had straight dark hair, a large girlish looking mouth, surrounded by traces of baby fat. Chance tried to picture his old man, imagined a scrawny old Asian guy, his demeanour half patrician Chinese, half street hustler. Much like the man he'd reluctantly gone back to work for and who'd recommended him for this job.

'Nice car,' said Chance, handing the picture back. His knowledge of the Philippines was limited to the time he'd briefly dated the Filipina singer of a house band in Perth. Her name was Joy, an apt moniker.

'He has a hanger-sized garage full of them at home,' said Amber. 'Christ knows where he drives them, given the traffic in Manila.'

Her voice had a dry, throaty timbre, at odds with her youthful face, small pointed nose, and large, round blue eyes. Chance noticed her hands. They looked large and powerful, out of proportion to the rest of her body.

'Old man Gao probably bought him his own stretch of highway,' said Curry over his half-raised glass.

'Gao junior hasn't inherited his father's work ethic, smarts, or obsession with being an upstanding and patriotic member of the overseas Chinese community,' said Dormer. 'In fact he's a complete fuck up, no interest in the family business, kept on a short leash, and a very generous allowance.'

'Freddie only has eyes for three things: cars, gambling, and women,' Curry continued. 'He has a particular fondness for blondes.'

The old man leered at Amber as the innuendo sunk in. No one else spoke. She sipped her drink, unperturbed at being the centre of attention.

'In America the mecca for high rollers like Gao is Vegas,' said Dormer. 'In Asia it's Macau. In Australia it's Melbourne's Crown Casino, in particular their Aussie Millions Poker Tournament in a week's time. They have a whole department dedicated to identifying and tracking whales like Gao, knowing what they like, wooing them out here to play.

'Gao's attended for the last two years running and this year's no exception. And, as has been his past practice, he'll be stopping over for a week in Surfers. He might play a bit of poker at the casino but the real attraction, apart from Amber here, are the off-site games organised by Dennis.'

'What's an off-site game?' Chance pulled out his tobacco pouch, rolled a cigarette. He was relieved to be finally working again, his mind alive with the mechanics of putting the job together.

'Like the name says, a game that takes place outside the casino,' said Curry. 'I provide the venue, the security, make sure any palm that needs greasing is greased.'

'Sounds dodgy,' said Chance.

'Of course it's fucking dodgy. That's what Freddie likes about it. Gao's not like the American high rollers. Those boys treat gambling as a job, long hours, use math and other skills to find patterns and sequences. Freddie is a gambler in the true meaning of the word. He likes the life, being treated like a rock star, the thrill of playing a pro. Add a dollop of illicit glamour,

Freddie's there. He'll blow half a million, not even bat an eyelid, fuck off to Melbourne a happy man, ready to lose more money.'

'Gao arrives tomorrow and is scheduled to stay six days,' said Dormer, grim-faced, like a teacher trying to keep the attention of an unruly class. 'Only this time there's going to a slight variation to his itinerary.'

The old man's eyes gleamed. 'We're going to rob him of every cent he has.'

'Before we go on, I want to know whether he's in or out.' Dormer looked at Chance as he spoke.

'Frank, don't insult our guest.'

'You brought me in to help you organise this, including security. It's my job—'

'Let's get one thing clear.' Chance looked at Dormer as he spoke. 'I may have been recommended for this job, but it's my arse on the line if something fucks up. I'll decide whether I'm in or out, and I don't make the decision until I've heard more about the job.'

'I appreciate what you're saying, Frank, but I think we can trust Peter.' Curry turned to Chance. 'Freddie will have a large amount of cash. He'll carry a lot of it around with him. The rest he'll stash in the safe in his suite, which just happens to be in the hotel where Sophia here works nights on reception.

'We let Gao get re-acquainted with Amber, lose a bit of money, wait until he's relaxed. When the time is right, you and Dormer will go in, get him to open the safe, and the money's ours.'

Chance remembered his last job, the safe in the Port Pirie pub, old but still hard to get into. Whatever Curry was talking about was sure to be new and far more difficult to access.

'You just going to ask Gao nicely to open the safe, give us all his money?'

'Leave that to me,' said Dormer. 'Trust me. He'll give us the combo.'

'A place like that has got to have good security.'

'We're not talking Fort Knox,' said Curry. 'But that's where Sophia comes in. She'll give us a pass card to Gao's suite, rig the security cameras so that they experience a little malfunction that night. We'll also have Amber on the inside, so to speak, and she'll have you to help her keep an eye on Gao.'

'How so?'

'You'll pose as Gao's chauffeur. Drive him where he wants to go, take Amber to him, that kind of thing. Your boss has told me good things about you, Peter, that you're the man to have on the inside. I see what he means. You have a sort of everyman quality. Don't look too flashy or smart. No offence.'

Chance shrugged.

'With your considerable charm, you should be part of the furniture in no time. No one will give you a second thought and you can keep an eye on things. Help us decide when to move.'

'Will he have his own security?'

'If it was the Philippines he'd be travelling with a small army,' Dormer said. 'But he thinks Australia is safe, usually only travels here with one bodyguard.'

'I'm still not convinced about how we'll get into the safe.'

Chance detected a flicker of annoyance cross the old man's face.

'I'll wager Freddie's never seen the business end of a gun before. He should fold like a bad poker hand. Shock and awe, as you ex-Army lads would say.'

'Maximum terror in minimum time with minimum noise,' added Dormer. 'You and I get the money, get out, no one gets seriously hurt.'

Chance noted Dormer's qualifier, chose to ignore it. 'What happens when Gao goes to the police?'

'And risk the ire of his father?' Curry looked at Chance askance. 'Not bloody likely. He'll be too embarrassed to tell anyone.

'There's one other reason he won't make a fuss,' said Amber. 'What's that?

'His wife.'

Curry read the scepticism on Chance's face, leaned in close to him.

'Believe me, I know these people, spent time in the Philippines in the eighties. Marvellous bloody place, gone to the dogs after Marcos.' He lost the thread of what he was saying, paused for a moment to find it. 'I've had dinner with old man Gao and his eldest son, Jefferson. That boy is a major player, not like Freddie, but when his father's around, he won't say a word. All that deference to the patriarch shit the Chinese go for.'

'So now you've heard the plan, Pete, what do you think?' Amber flicked the fringe away from her face with one of her hands, fixed her blue eyes on him.

Chance rolled another cigarette, took his time. 'How much do you think Gao is good for?'

She didn't miss a beat. 'Rough estimate, I'd say we're looking at least two to three million dollars.'

'I'm in.'

Five

Chance was awakened by the sound of vacuuming in the corridor outside his room. He lay in bed, turned over the previous night's conversation in his mind.

He could think of half a dozen holes in the plan. He always could. Even with supposedly foolproof plans, something could always go wrong. But he liked the relative simplicity of what Curry had proposed, the absence of too many moving parts. With a bit of luck it could work.

Gao would arrive in Surfers that afternoon. Chance had to pick him up at the airport, take him to his hotel, wherever else he wanted to go. All he had to do until then was get into character, which included dressing for the part.

As last night's gathering broke up, Curry had put a meaty arm around Amber, pulled her to him, and whispered in her ear. Whatever he'd said, she'd laughed, whispered back. Chance wasn't sure how to read the exchange. Curry was old enough to be her grandfather.

'Is the red Toyota Corolla on the nature strip outside my house yours, Peter?' asked Curry.

Chance nodded.

'You can't chauffeur Gao and a lovely woman like Amber around in that piece of junk. Take the Volvo in the garage. One other thing, do you own a suit?'

When Chance said he didn't, Curry looked at Sophia, who

hadn't moved on the couch. 'No worries, Sophia here will help kit you out.'

The hotel restaurant was crowded with Asian tourists, a smattering of budget travellers taking advantage of the complementary Bain-Marie breakfast. Chance examined the food on offer: dried fried rice, noodles, greasy eggs, and bacon. He opted for toast and coffee, took his food and a copy of the local newspaper to the first available table.

He skimmed as he ate: three pages about flood damage in northern Queensland, an article about Surfers Paradise being the tattoo capital of Australia, pages of advertisements for tradesmen, live-in caregivers, phone sex, and escort services.

He turned back to a news story he'd passed over, another Australian Special Air Service soldier killed in Afghanistan. Politicians from all sides lined up to express their condolences and determination not to blink in the face of the enemy. Chance marvelled at the way the media made Afghanistan sound like a big-budget action movie while expressing shock and outrage whenever Australians got killed.

Chance had done a couple of years at Tarin Kwot, TK as it was colloquially known, Uruzgan Province, central Afghanistan. Most of his time had been spent behind rows of razor wire and sand bags. He'd only emerged behind the wheel of a Bushmaster as part of a heavily armed convoy, on the edge of his seat for the entire drive, scanning the Mars-like landscape for any sign of the Taliban.

For the most part, the worst enemy was the weather, the extremes of hot and cold, and the grit that got into everything. He'd never seen an SAS soldier his entire time in country and was lucky enough to have contact with the enemy only once. Chance had been driving as part of a convoy en route to a forward base in the Chora Valley. An improvised explosive device had taken out the lead vehicle. First Chance knew about it was a flash, followed by a loud clap that felt like it had gone off in his chest.

Not that any of it mattered now. It was a bullshit war that would soon be forgotten. For all their protestations about not giving in, the politicians had taken the majority of Australia's troops out, part of the West's withdrawal from Afghanistan. Soon the locals would be left to fend for themselves against a gang of religious extremists on one side and a thieving corrupt government on the other.

Sophia was waiting at the entrance to the shopping mall. She stood under the awning of a kitchenware shop to avoid the rain, a cigarette in one hand. She dropped the smoke when she saw Chance approaching, ground it with the heel of her shoe.

'Let's make this quick, I start work in a few hours.'

The mall was packed, families and young people drifted among shops with no apparent purpose but to escape the poor weather. Sophia cut a path through the sea of people, led him into a menswear store, one of a chain selling expensive but ubiquitous-looking clothes.

She dismissed an offer of help from the young, male shop assistant with a shake of her head. She looked Chance up and down, selected several white shirts, a dark blue cotton suit with a slight pinstripe.

'You need to blend in, so we need something sober, nothing too flashy.' She handed him the clothes and pointed toward the dressing room.

She circled him when he emerged five minutes later, smoothed the shoulders of his jacket. Her perfume had a musky aroma. A small golden crucifix hung from a chain around her neck, no wedding ring.

He wanted to ask her why she was involved with Curry, instead said, 'I bet you never thought this little gig would involve you having to select clothes for a strange man?'

'You and Curry remind me of my ex-husband and my good-for-nothing brothers back in Greece. Couldn't wipe your own arses.'

She wheeled him around to face the mirror. 'How do you feel?'

His suit-clad reflection looked back at him, small mouth, strong jaw, green eyes, short dark hair. He could count on his hand with the missing finger the number of times he'd worn a suit since leaving the army.

'Like a pimp.'

She flashed him a humourless smile. 'I'd say we've got it about right, then.'

Six

Chance stood with the other drivers at the arrivals gate. He held a piece of paper in front of him, 'Mister Frederick Gao and entourage' written on it.

Apart from being slightly thinner, Gao looked every bit the Asian princeling he'd come across as in his photograph.

A tall Asian male, cheeks covered in smallpox scars, pushed a trolley full of designer luggage a few steps behind him. The bodyguard.

It took Chance a moment to realise there was a third member of Gao's entourage, a rangy Caucasian with close-cropped white hair and a matching goatee.

Gao noticed the sign, walked toward Chance.

'Welcome to the Gold Coast, Mister Gao. My name is Peter Jacobi. I'll be your driver during your stay. Did you have a good flight?'

'Yes, thank you, very pleasant,' he said in a high-pitched American accented voice. Gao gave Chance a weak handshake. Chance noticed the chunky gold watch on his wrist

'My associates.' He waved at the man pushing the luggage trolley. 'This is Nelson. And this is Mister Tavener.'

Both men nodded but said nothing.

Gao spoke in a language Chance didn't recognise to the man pushing the luggage. Nelson stepped away from the trolley and Chance realised he was expected to take over.

'If you'll follow me, gentlemen,' he said pushing the trolley, 'the car is this way.'

Chance made small talk as he ferried the men down the Gold Coast Highway. Gao was polite but disinterested, his responses limited to nods and one-word replies. His two companions said nothing.

As they neared Surfers Paradise Gao fished a mobile out of his jeans pocket, cooed into the phone. Chance thought he heard a strident sounding female voice on the other end, guessed it was Gao's wife.

They stopped at a bank in the heart of Surfer's Paradise. Chance waited in the car while Gao and his associates conducted their business. When they emerged thirty minutes later, the bodyguard carried an aluminium suitcase.

Gao's hotel was six stories of glass and concrete on the Surfers Paradise beachfront, slender, curved, built for views. A half-circle driveway came off the street, led to double-fronted glass doors.

Chance offered to take their luggage up so he could check out the accommodation, but was beaten to the punch by the hotel staff, who could sniff out a good tipper when they saw one.

Gao paused at the entrance to the hotel. 'Bring Amber to the hotel at eight. You're free until then.'

Without waiting for Chance's response he disappeared inside.

Amber said nothing on the drive from Curry's house to the hotel.

Mal had answered the door, chaperoned her to the back seat of the Volvo. He gave her a peck on the cheek before she got in, stood on the driveway and watched the car back onto the street, like a protective parent sending their child off on a first date.

Gao and Nelson were waiting out front of the hotel when Chance pulled up. There was no sign of the other man, Tavener. Amber played her part well. She greeted the Filipino warmly as he climbed in, even managed a smile as his hand caressed the inside of her thigh. Gao told Chance to take them to the main marina, fell into an easy banter with Amber, mainly cars and the weather in Manila. Gao's bodyguard sat stony faced next to Chance in the front.

Chance waited by the car as the three of them had dinner in an expensive seafood restaurant. A cold breeze came in off the ocean. He smoked, watched the collection of million-dollar yachts bob up and down on the dark water.

The off-site game was located in a block of identical brown stucco apartments called Villa Costa Brava, just off the Gold Coast Highway, in the suburb of Miami. A sunken driveway provided low-key protection from prying eyes. The street on either side was lined with units, the occasional California bungalow and weatherboard dwelling. Bathers and towels hung from balconies, inflatable rubber toys littered the nature strip.

Chance leaned against the Volvo and wondered whose idea it had been to use names like Miami and Costa Brava. They might have lent Surfers a certain exotic touch back in the sixties when it was first getting started, but now they sounded mismatched and old-fashioned.

Gao emerged with Amber and the bodyguard just before midnight, directed Chance to drive them back to the hotel. Chance snuck a glance at the two of them in the back seat, saw Amber lean into Gao and nibble his ear.

He watched Amber and Gao walk hand in hand through the double-fronted glass doors of the hotel's brightly lit reception area, his gaze lingering on the taper of her back as it met her buttocks in the flimsy cocktail dress.

He parked the car across the street, got out and rolled another cigarette. The tobacco tasted bitter. The smoke mixed with the tangy remnants of a breeze that managed to thread its way from the beach a block away. The only noise was the swish of traffic in the distance and the hum of electricity in the cables above him.

* * *

The trill of the phone woke Chance. He grabbed it from the passenger's seat, stared at the screen, bleary eyed. A text from a number he didn't recognise: "Front entrance, five minutes."

The windscreen was beaded with moisture from a light rain. Chance looked at his watch. Half past five. Outside dawn was breaking, a grubby blue.

He stood stiffly by the car, still playing his part, held the passenger's door open. Amber avoided eye contact as she slid into the back seat.

Chance snuck quick glances at her in the rearview mirror as he drove. Amber sat very still, gazed through the passenger's window.

Halfway to Curry's house, she caught Chance looking at her, locked eyes with him.

'What the fuck are you staring at?' she said, her voice a mixture of tiredness and belligerence.

'I could ask you the same thing.'

'Whatever it is, wipe that fucking look off your face.'

'What look?' Chance diverted his eyes to the road, felt his face flush with embarrassment. Had he been that obvious?

'The look that says you feel sorry for me because I let Gao fuck me.'

Chance thought about possible comebacks, decided he didn't want to fight, just wanted to go back to his hotel room, grab what sleep he could.

'It's just a job, Jacobi. Believe me, Gao's not nearly as bad as some of the johns I've had and at least the hotel sheets are clean. Understand?'

'Loud and clear.'

Her large blue eyes, rimmed with exhaustion, held his stare for a moment before she looked away.

Seven

The reception area of Gao's hotel was cool and clean, grey slate-coloured tile work, hardwood finishing. A restaurant on one side, half occupied with the late breakfast crowd; on the other, a sleek reception counter, images of a waterfall beamed on the wall between them.

Chance asked the well-groomed twentysomething male at reception to be put through to Gao's suite.

'Mister Gao has left instructions that neither he nor the members of his entourage are to be disturbed.'

'Did he leave any message for me?'

'And you are?'

'His driver, name's Jacobi.'

The receptionist tapped a couple of keys on his computer.

'No, nothing here.'

Chance went back outside, stood by the car and rolled his first cigarette of the day. The mid-morning sky was clear, the chill slowly being replaced by the sun's warmth. With nothing to do, Chance figured he might as well wait for Gao to make an appearance.

He was on his third smoke when he saw the Filipino's white-haired associate, Tavener, walk toward him. Tavener was dressed in suit pants and a blue business shirt. He had a high forehead, dark eyes set deep in his craggy face. His skin, like his general demeanour, had a battered, weather-beaten look.

'Nice day,' said Tavener. He spoke in an easy American drawl.

Chance glanced at his cigarette, unsure whether he was supposed to be smoking in front of the people he was driving.

Tavener picked up his unease. 'Relax, don't make no difference either way to me whether you smoke.'

Chance took the pouch of tobacco from his pocket, offered it to the American.

'Gave them up, five years, six months, eight days ago, but who's counting.' Tavener smiled. 'What are you doing here? No one asked you to swing by this morning.'

'I thought you might want me on hand to drive.'

'Conscientious. I like that.' Tavener nodded slowly to himself. 'How long you been driving for Curry?'

Chance was supposed to be ingratiating himself with Gao and his people, knew this was a good opportunity, but suddenly felt suspicious of Tavener, where his questions were headed.

'A while.'

'Before that?'

'Various jobs, drove trucks in the army.'

'Well, that explains the work ethic. Ain't nothing like the military to instil a sense of conscientiousness in a man. Where'd you serve?'

'East Timor, then Afghanistan.'

'Afghanistan? Meet any of our boys over there?'

'A few.' The truth, he'd avoided American servicemen wherever he could. Word was they attracted enemy activity like flies on shit.

'Curry's a lucky man to have a good driver like you.'

'What about yourself, been working for Mister Gao long?' Chance dropped his cigarette butt on the footpath, stepped on it, met Tavener's gaze, aware he was crossing a line.

'Not so long.'

'What exactly is it you do for him?'

'This and that, you know how it is.'

'Do I?'

'Smart fella like yourself, reckon so.' Tavener stifled a yawn, bored with the conversation. 'You stick with what you do well and I'll do the same.'

Tavener made to go, stopped, turned.

'By the way, you can go, Mister Gao doesn't need you this morning.'

'I can wait. See if he changes his mind?'

'No, run along, go practice your golf swing or whatever. We'll ring when we need you.'

Chance drove to his hotel. He changed into casual clothes, swapped the Volvo for his red Corolla, returned to Gao's hotel, parked on the opposite side of the street to the half circle driveway, sat in the car, waited.

He couldn't explain what he was doing, just a gut feeling something wasn't right. He was no clearer two hours later, as he tailed a white rental car containing Tavener and the Filipino bodyguard, Nelson, along the Gold Coast Highway to Coolangatta.

The last Queensland town before the New South Wales border, Coolangatta had a quieter feel. There were fewer people on the street, the buildings were older and there was less highrise development.

The hire car slid into a gap alongside a strip of restaurants. Tavener got out, greeted two men sitting in the outside section of one of the restaurants. Chance looked for a place to stop, couldn't find one, had to go around the block twice before a space appeared half a dozen cars up from where the hire car sat. By the time he'd parked, Tavener was sitting with the two men, deep in conversation. Chance tried to get a better look at the American's lunch companions. Two men with bad suits and bad haircuts. Cops or ex-cops, Chance could pick them a mile away.

Perhaps Tavener had a little side business he needed to conduct. Or maybe he'd just stepped out for lunch with old friends. Except no one around the table looked friendly. And why had Tavener gone to all the trouble of hiring a car when he could have asked Chance to drive him?

The nagging feeling in Chance's gut went up a notch as the three men stood without ordering anything. Tavener got back into his hire car, the two men into another vehicle parked close by. Chance followed them back to Surfers, watched as they turned into the car park of an aging motel, the cream stucco chipped and faded, garden overgrown.

Chance hastily changed lanes, narrowly avoided colliding with another car, parked on the roadside a hundred metres or so up from the motel. He sat there, watched the entrance in the rearview mirror.

The vehicle containing Tavener's unknown lunch companions was the first to leave, followed five minutes later by the white hire car. Chance fingered the phone on the seat next to him, thought about ringing Dormer or Curry, dismissed the idea.

What they didn't know might help him.

Eight

Tavener said nothing to Chance on the drive to the side game, and apart from a brief greeting and instructions to bring Amber around midnight, Gao looked straight through him.

Kerrigan answered the door at Curry's house, the usual sullen bulldog look on his face. He grunted, escorted Chance to the back room.

'Wait here,' he said, and left.

As Kerrigan shut the door behind him, Chance examined the pictures on the wall. Curry posing next a large marlin, hamming it up with a group of Japanese Sumo wrestlers, handing a giant cardboard check to a group of gaunt-looking children in pyjamas and their smiling nurse.

One photograph was different from the others, a colour shot of Curry standing on a beach with a young male. The old man looked uncharacteristically stiff and uncomfortable, a blank expression on his craggy face. His young companion had a wild look in his dark eyes and a mane of long unkempt dark hair.

Interspersed with the images were framed newspaper clippings, tight newsprint on yellowed paper. Chance read the nearest article, "Waterside war claims another life." It was an account of the shooting of a dockworker called Les 'The Ferret' Newman in a Melbourne pub nicknamed the 'Blood House.' Although the place had been packed with drinkers, no one had seen a thing. An anonymous police detective said the slaying was part of an ongoing feud between rival factions of the Ship Painters and Dockers. The article was dated June 1970. A grainy photo of the crime scene accompanied it, beefy cops admiring a pool of blood on the floor.

Chance had heard of the Painters and Dockers, a trade union active on Melbourne's waterfront in the sixties and seventies, a front for sly groggers, gunmen, pimps, armed robbers, and stand-over men. So great had been the spoils from the union's illegal activities that factions had waged a prolonged and bloody battle for control. When civilians started dying in the crossfire, police launched a campaign to smash the union, sent its members fleeing across Australia.

'The good old, bad old days.' Curry stood in the doorway, a maroon dressing gown wrapped tightly around his frame, hands deep in its pockets.

'The cops ever find out who killed Newman?'

'That sly little cunt?' Curry stood next to Chance, squinted at the framed article. 'Nah, don't believe they did.'

He grinned, walked toward the bar. 'Amber will be ready in a few shakes. Did Mal offer you a beer?'

'No, not the friendliest chap.'

'Just wary of strangers.' Curry threw a can of beer to Chance, popped one for himself, drank deep. 'How's our Filipino mate?'

'I dropped him at the side game earlier this evening.'

'The rate he's losing, we won't need to rob the bastard.' Curry belched. 'Manage to pick up anything else of interest?'

A slight tremor of panic rippled through Chance at the possibility Curry knew about the morning's activities. He looked at the old man, detected nothing behind the statement.

'No.'

Curry nodded slowly.

'I've known your boss, Mister Long, for a long time. Had to count every penny when I dealt with him. He still like that?'

'He'd find a way to skin a maggot if there was a margin in it.'

Curry chuckled and drained his beer.

'Spent much time in Surfers, Peter?'

'Not since I was a boy.'

'What do you think?'

Chance hesitated.

'Don't give yourself an aneurism, son, just making conversation.'

'It's changed a lot.'

'Surfers may be having a few problems, but it'll bounce back, always does. Best city in Australia, despite what those Mexicans down south say. A city built by men of vision, men who were prepared to put their money where their mouths were.'

Curry ducked behind the bar, emerged with another beer.

'I remember the first time I visited. Wasn't much older than you are now. There was something about the place. It felt wide open, like anything was possible. No one gave a fuck where you went to school, where you were born, the only thing that talked was money. And the weather, compared to the shitty winters in Melbourne, sunshine all year around. Like the name says, it was a paradise. Still is.'

Amber entered, stood next to Curry. 'You finished reminiscing?' she said as she took the old man's beer, sipped from the can.

'You ready?' Her blue eyes regarded Chance from under her blonde fringe. Her manner was clear of any tension from the exchange in the car earlier that morning.

When Chance nodded, she pecked the old man on the cheek.

'Have her back safely and no funny business,' said Curry, a broad smile on his face.

Chance couldn't tell whether it was a joke or a threat.

Nine

Chance tried not to look at Amber, who watched him from the back seat, but instead focused on the music on the car stereo, one of Gao's CDs, a high-pitched female singer accompanied by a piano.

'Take that crap off will you,' Amber said. 'It's bad enough I have to listen to it when I'm with Freddie.'

Chance ejected the CD, turned on the radio, found a comercial station playing eighties music.

'That's not much better. Don't you have any real music?'

'Define "real music?"'

'Springsteen, John Lee Hooker, Muddy Waters, any kind of blues, jazz.'

'Afraid not.'

'Just turn it off then.'

As they neared the Villa Costa Brava, Amber told Chance to stop a block from the entrance. They got out of the car and stood on the nature strip. She held onto his shoulder with one hand to steady herself while she changed her sandals for black pumps that made her slightly taller.

'Sorry about the other night,' she said.

'Pre-game nerves?'

'Something like that. You got those rollies on you?'

Chance handed over the pack, watched her roll a smoke with surprising dexterity.

'Where did you get those big hands, holding onto a pole where you danced?

'Very fucking funny.' She leaned forward, accepted a light from him. 'No, from stroking the egos of insecure men.' Amber exhaled a stream of smoke into the night air. 'How the hell do you smoke these things? They taste like shit.'

'Each to their own.'

She leant against the bonnet of the car, held her cigarette smouldering next to her ear. 'Curry says you were in the army. Were you one of those super soldiers, a Green Beret or whatever they're called, same as Dormer?'

'Green Berets are American.'

'Interesting,' she said, making it sound anything but. 'But you were in the army?'

'Yes.'

'What did you do?'

'I drove trucks.'

'That all?'

'Pretty much.'

'So that missing little finger, you didn't get it on some dangerous secret mission?' She smiled, taking the piss now.

Chance laughed in spite of himself. 'No, somewhere much more dangerous.'

'Where?'

'I'll tell you about it some time. What else do you know about Dormer?'

'Not much. I don't know him or what his connection is to Dennis. He just sort of appeared one day. Dennis has a lot of business associates. They come and go.'

'What about Sophia? She doesn't seem like the criminal type. How did she get involved?'

'Dormer brought her in. Apparently she's got money problems, something to do with her family in Greece.'

Amber flicked the cigarette butt into a nearby hedge, shivered, her voice no longer playful. 'Okay, Mister Mystery Man, here's the drill. You're going to come in with me tonight. When we get inside, let Gao and his people scope you out, see that you're just doing a job.'

'What then?'

'There's usually a few spectators. Sit with them and watch until Gao gives you the signal to leave. Got it?'

'Yes.'

'Good. Let's go, it's bloody freezing out here.'

All the apartments at Villa Costa Brava were dark except for the windows on the ground floor. Two men stood outside the door. Both were solidly built. They smiled at Amber but looked at Chance with studied belligerence, before ushering them into a large, dimly lit room that smelled of cigarette smoke and sweat.

Poker was the game of choice, three large, green felt-lined tables, each one occupied by a female dealer and half a dozen or so people hunched over multi-coloured piles of playing chips. There was a smattering of females, including several elderly Asian women, but the punters were mainly male, a combination of men in flashy clothes and others who looked like they'd just walked off building sites and factory floors.

Two women tended a bar at the far end of the room. A thickset man in a black suit, the de-facto pit boss, constantly swept the room for any sign of trouble.

Gao beamed, put down his cards and stood when he saw Amber. She walked straight up to him, kissed his cheek. He signalled for another chair. Amber helped herself to a cigarette from a packet at Gao's side. He lit it with a gold lighter, said something that made her laugh, and returned his attention to the game. A couple of the other players at Gao's table looked at Amber blackly but said nothing.

Chance found a seat, watched the other spectators. They were mostly female, girlfriends and wives of men playing, tired looking brunettes and dishwater blondes with too much make-up and tight-fitting clothes. Tavener and Nelson sat in the row in front of Chance. Nelson sat stiffly in the chair, his face straight ahead, the aluminium briefcase Gao had picked up at the bank the previous day on the floor next to him. Tavener made no pretence of following the game, chewed on a matchstick as he read a newspaper. Neither man acknowledged Chance.

Gao lost solidly for four hours, the pile of chips in front of him getting smaller with each hand. Despite this, he maintained a jovial demeanour. Chance didn't know a lot about poker but even he could see what a careless player Gao was. He folded when he shouldn't have, raised when it was clear to everyone else around the table he had nothing. Amber sat beside him the whole time, allowed him to light her cigarettes, laughed in all the right places. Only when Gao was engrossed in the game did her eyes drift, but she never looked at Chance.

Curry appeared around midnight, swept into the room in a powder blue dinner suit, a red cummerbund and bow tie. He oozed an old school roguish charm, the smile on his face evidence he enjoyed his behaviour as much as the person receiving it, stopped by each table, backslaps and handshakes for the men, a gentle touch on the shoulder and a wink for the women. When he'd finished, he sat at the bar, sipped a highball and watched.

Just after two, Gao stood up, signalled his entourage it was time to leave. He shook the hand of the other players at his table, tossed one of his few remaining chips to the dealer. Chance followed the Filipino and the others out of the room.

Ten

Chance dozed in the front seat until he was roused by the sound of the text message saying Amber was on her way.

'Don't take me home yet,' she said as Chance started the car.

'Where do you want to go?'

'Wherever.'

Careful not to repeat the mistake of the previous night, he avoided eye contact in the rearview mirror, concentrated on the road.

He drove aimlessly for thirty minutes.

'Can you pull over somewhere?'

He swung into the car park of a strip mall, a dozen or so shops, takeaway food, laser hair removal, a vet. She let herself out.

'Roll me a cigarette, would you?'

Chance rolled two cigarettes, lit both, passed one to her. It started to drizzle.

They listened to the sound of surf beyond the houses on the other side of the highway.

'Rough night, Jacobi?'

'Not nearly as rough as yours, I imagine.'

Dark clouds moved across the sky, the drizzle turned to rain. The black cocktail dress clung to her like wet tissue paper, exposed the contours of her body.

'I can look after myself,' she said, taking shelter under the awning of one of the shops. 'Besides, you won't have to play driver for much longer.'

'What are you talking about? Gao's in town for another few days.'

'Change of plans, he told me tonight. He's leaving the day after tomorrow, going to stop off in Sydney for a few days before he heads to Melbourne.'

'Christ, you understand what that means?'

'We have to move the job up. Tonight.'

'We're not ready.'

'Don't be a bloody idiot, Jacobi.' Her heart-shaped face contorted in anger. 'You may have only walked in a couple of days ago, but Curry's been planning this for nearly a year.'

'With you as the bait?'

Her hand lashed out. He felt a sharp sting on his cheek, recoiled, surprise more than pain. She glared at him from under her sodden fringe.

'Don't let Curry fool you. He may come across as a harmless old man, but he even gets a whiff you're shaky he'll kill you, or have Dormer do it for him.'

Chance remembered the clipping he'd read about the murder in the pub in 1971, Curry's casual response when asked about it.

'Dennis needs money badly. He's made some bad business decisions, invested heavily in a new apartment complex, now there's a property slump. He owes money he doesn't have. Dormer is as keen as mustard, too. They'll do this job with or without you.'

'Tell me.' He massaged his cheek as he spoke. 'What do you get out of this?'

'Money, plus I owe Dennis. This pays him back.'

'What about Curry's flatmate, Kerrigan, what's his role in this?'

'Not much. He's a friend of Dennis's, shares his chequered past.'

Chance knew there was more to what she was saying, decided against pressing her on it.

Amber dropped the remains of her cigarette on the asphalt. 'So what do you think?'

'It stinks worse than a turd on a hot summer day.' Chance dragged on the last of his rollie, threw the butt into the darkness. 'But I need the money, same as you, so what the hell.'

She rolled her shoulders, yawned, looked at her watch.

'Christ, it's early. I need to get some sleep. Drive me back to Curry's. We've got a busy day ahead.'

Eleven

Chance grabbed a couple of hours of fitful sleep, was awakened by his mobile phone, Dormer telling him to get to Curry's house as soon as possible.

He showered, dressed, was about to leave, when he paused to rummage through his possession for the brown paper bag he'd been given the first day he arrived in Queensland. Chance tipped the contents onto the unmade bed, a loaded .38 snub-nose revolver in a leather ankle holster, license papers. He slid the gun out of the holster. It was new, not like the scarred, battered pieces he usually worked with.

His eyes burned from lack of sleep. He thought about last night's conversation, strapped on the holster.

He was the last to arrive, a familiar sensation as he scanned the room, fear laced with adrenaline. Everyone knew about Gao's change of plans, wanted to know what was next.

Dormer sat on the couch in the same grey suit.

Sophia wore tracksuit pants and pink T-shirt, ever-present cigarette smouldering in one hand.

Curry sat swaddled in his maroon dressing gown. His eyes were bloodshot, the white stubble on his face reminded Chance of mouldy fruit. Mal sat on the couch next to him.

Amber looked good despite the dark circles under her eyes.

She flashed him a quick half smile when he entered, a lingering trace of last night's shared confidence.

On the glass-topped table sat an overflowing ashtray, coffee plunger, half full cups, and a road map of the Gold Coast, a large piece of paper with a sketch in blue biro pen. Chance poured himself a coffee, looked at the sketch, a crudely drawn floor plan.

'We have to go ahead with the plan tonight,' said Curry, his eyes diamond hard. 'There's no telling when Gao will be back or if he's coming back at all. This could be our last opportunity to bag him.'

Dormer spoke next in what Chance was sure was a choreographed performance.

'The basic plan is sound. We just need to think through all the angles, make a few new adjustments for the new scenario we find ourselves in.' He turned to Amber. 'What has Gao told you?'

'Only that he was cutting his trip short, going to Sydney for business. He flies out tomorrow afternoon.'

'What else?'

'He's got plans today, business of some kind. He wants me to meet him at his hotel tonight for dinner, then the side game, then back to his suite.'

'What kind of business?' A hard edge crept into Curry's voice.

'And why isn't Jacobi driving him?' added Dormer.

'I don't know.' Amber looked between the two men. 'He doesn't talk to me about that stuff.'

'Whatever the reason, it's not a good sign,' Curry said calmly. He looked at Amber, forced a smile. 'The other members of Gao's entourage, let's go through them again.'

'Nelson is the muscle. He sleeps in the second bedroom in Gao's suite. He's always armed. The only time he ever leaves Gao's side is when I'm with him.'

'The American, Tavener?'

'Some sort of business adviser, helping Gao with a deal he's got cooking. He has a suite on the floor below.'

'The money, where is it?'

'There's spending money in a briefcase carried by Nelson. The rest is in a safe in Gao's bedroom. Only Freddie knows the combination.'

Dormer touched the tips of his fingers together, made a cathedral and rested his chin on it.

'We'll hit the suite tonight, after Amber and Gao return from the side game. Jacobi, you wait an hour after you've dropped them off at the hotel, call me. We both go in. Sophia will be on duty at reception, she'll give us a copy of the pass card that'll allow us to access Gao's suite. We'll get the combination out of Gao, get the money, and get out.'

Chance sipped his coffee. The brew was lukewarm and bitter. He put the cup on the table. 'And what happens if Gao doesn't feel like cooperating?'

'He'll cooperate because I'll give him no choice. Don't worry, if it's one thing I learned in the army, it's how to get information out of people who don't want to give it.'

Curry rubbed his meaty paws together. 'Shock and awe, right, Dormer?' Chance looked at the stub of his missing finger. Despite all the bullshit in the movies about people holding out under torture, the reality was that there was very little someone wouldn't do when faced with the threat of serious physical pain. Gao would fold.

'What about the police? What are our plans for a getaway?'

'We've already discussed this, he won't go to the cops,' said Dormer, irritation in his voice.

'He's right, Peter,' interjected Amber. 'He'll want minimum publicity to avoid his father and wife finding out. If the cops do get involved he won't cooperate.'

'I'm not as convinced as the rest of you.'

'Once we've got the money, we walk out, leave in the Volvo,' said Dormer, ignoring Chance. 'We'll drive to the farmhouse we've rented near Beaudesert, do the split there, sit tight until we figure it's safe then go our separate ways. Never see each other again.'

'Farmhouse? This is the first I've heard of any farmhouse.' Chance grabbed the road map, located Beaudesert, a town about seventy kilometres inland from the Gold Coast.

Curry sat forward, put a hand on Chance's knee. 'Peter, we're telling you now.'

'If it'll make you feel any better, we can go there after we're finished here, you can check it out for yourself,' said Dormer.

'What about her?' Chance looked at Sophia. 'If the police do get involved, first thing they'll want to know is how the bandits got the pass card.'

She lit a cigarette off the butt of the current one. 'I don't plan on turning up for my next shift at the hotel. I'll join you at the farm. When it's safe, I'm out of here, kiss Surfers Paradise and this whole fucking country goodbye.'

'So if everyone is decided—' Dormer glanced at the people sitting around the coffee table, '—let's go through things again.'

Twelve

The farmhouse was an old weatherboard, peeling paintwork, sagging front porch, freestanding barn that could easily accommodate two vehicles. Most importantly, it was remote, one road in and out, no other dwelling as far as the eye could see.

Curry had approached Chance after the meeting, put an arm around his shoulder. 'It's natural to be edgy before something like this, son. Used to happen to me all the time. Just keep your head down, do the job, make some money.'

Chance had nodded, unsure whether Curry was trying to be fatherly or threatening.

The plan was for Chance to check out of the hotel, leave his car and possessions at the farmhouse, and drive back to Surfers with Dormer. The directions took him through a seemingly endless stretch of new suburbs, rows of semi-identical houses. After three quarters of an hour, the dwellings became more sporadic, the landscape slowly transformed into rolling pastures, green with all the rain.

Dormer was waiting, directed him to drive his car into the barn. Chance did as instructed, rolled a cigarette and watched the cloud of smoke mix with dust motes in the shards of light that came through cracks in the wooden walls. Under other circumstances, he wouldn't have minded spending a few days here. But the prospect of being cooped up with Dormer and Lekakis filled him with dread.

Chance had taken part in around half a dozen jobs like this one. Some, like the one in Port Pirie, had fucked up, but most had gone down okay. All of them had involved a degree of danger and risk. But tonight's enterprise, now little more than a simple smash and grab, had more loose threads than a cheap shirt.

He didn't like the people he was working with or the speed with which events were moving. He was used to nerves, the sharpness in his gut before a job. But what he felt now, more like a dull ache in the pit of his stomach, told him to walk away.

Only problem: where would he go? The Chinaman had taken him back after Port Pirie, thrown him this job, screwed him on his share as punishment for trying to go independent. Even so, Chance needed the money, a stake to take him somewhere far away where he could plan his next move on his own terms.

'What do you think?' Dormer stood in the entrance to the barn, his outline framed against the sunlight.

'It'll do.'

'Rented the house for a song and no questions asked from a bloke whose business was about to go under, needed money fast.'

'Seems to be a lot of that going around.' Chance walked past Dormer, into the daylight.

'Sophia will be around later with supplies.'

Dormer stood, eyes partly closed, a crooked smile on his face, as if savouring something.

'You got that feeling, Jacobi, like someone's tugging at your balls, the dryness in your throat? I used to get it something fierce in Iraq and Afghanistan, the hours leading up to a patrol. Will there be contact? How bad will it get? I've got it now and I love it.'

Chance realised what he disliked so much about the man standing in front of him. Dormer was what was known as a gladiator digger, the kind of soldier who sunbathed in tactical positions, hit golf balls into Taliban territory, posed for photographs next to bloodied, cowering prisoners. They enjoyed the glamour and machismo of war, revelled in the everyday acts of random ugliness and brutality that were part of it.

He'd always avoided them. They were dangerous, the kind of people who could get you killed.

Thirteen

Two in the morning and the street outside Gao's hotel was still busy, young people in various states of intoxication taking advantage of a break in the rain to party. Chance leaned against the Volvo, watched the revellers flow by.

Almost an hour since Gao and Amber had disappeared arm in arm through the double doors. He finished his cigarette, took out his phone.

Dormer answered on the third ring.

'Ready?'

Dormer hung up, materialised on the street next to Chance a couple of minutes later carrying a canvas bag.

'Let's do this.'

Sophia Lekakis was alone at reception. Without shifting her eyes from the screen in front of her, she slid two pieces of white plastic across the counter to Chance and Dormer.

When the elevator doors closed Dormer laid the bag on the floor. Both men put on latex gloves and balaclava hoods. The wool felt prickly on Chance's face. He wriggled his nose and mouth in an attempt to get comfortable.

Dormer reached into the bag, withdrew a pistol, the barrel fitted with a silencer. Chance undid the clasp on his ankle holster, took out the snubnose. The elevator stopped on the fifth floor. Dormer got out to look for Tavener. Chance continued to the next and final level. His job was to deal with Gao's bodyguard, wait for Dormer to bring up the American, so that everyone was in one place.

The elevator door opened onto a red-carpeted hallway, a set of double doors at the end. Chance slid the piece of white plastic into the slot on the double doors. The light flashed green and he turned the handle.

The room had a sunken lounge area, corridors leading to bedrooms on either side. Along one wall, a sliding glass door to a large patio. A flat-screen TV, the volume loud, provided the only light. It was tuned to an all-night news show, images of wild looking men firing guns, bodies in the street, a voice-over with an American accent. Share market information ran along the bottom of the screen.

Nelson slept on a couch facing the TV. A pistol grip protruded from the holster strapped to the bodyguard's broad shoulders. A book lay open on his chest, 'Holy Bible' in embossed gold letters on the cover.

The Filipino opened one eye and was on his feet within seconds. One hand shot out, gripped Chance's neck.

Chance felt Nelson's fingers dig into the soft flesh under his jaw. Tiny dots of light swarmed his vision and he started to feel dizzy. His arms flailed for a moment, before he brought the butt of the snubnose down hard against the side of Nelson's head. Nelson's grip loosened. Chance repeated the action. Nelson let go and fell backward onto the couch.

Chance rolled the balaclava up over his face, gulped air. No sign of movement from the bedroom. The noise from the TV had drowned out the fight.

Nelson was out cold, a bloody gash on one side of his head. Chance tucked the snubnose into the waistband of his pants, withdrew the bodyguard's pistol from its shoulder holster, ejected the clip onto the floor. He secured the bodyguard's hands with plastic cuffs, patted him down, found a handkerchief, wadded it up and stuffed it into the man's mouth.

Chance crept down the corridor on the left. A crack of light was visible from underneath the door.

The balcony was almost as big as the lounge room. The hotel's swimming pool was directly below, a large kidney shape of shimmering aqua. Chance massaged his neck while he watched the white line of surf break in the distance, wanted for a cigarette, knew he didn't have the time.

He heard someone move about in the lounge room. He took out the snubnose, went inside, gun first.

Dormer had an aluminium suitcase open on the couch next to the unconscious bodyguard, was checking the contents. There was no sign of Tavener.

'Where the hell is the American?' hissed Chance.

'He wasn't there but I found this in his room.' Dormer moved aside to allow Chance to see that the suitcase was filled with neat bundles of money. It was the same suitcase Chance had seen on the floor next to Nelson at the side game the previous night.

'We've got the money, why don't we piss off?' said Chance.

'More where that came from.' Dormer looked in the direction of Gao's room, gestured at Nelson with the barrel of his pistol. The bodyguard was now semi-conscious. 'Bring him.'

Chance refitted his balaclava over his face, picked up the bodyguard by the scruff of the neck. The big man teetered for a moment before standing up straight, glared at Chance. Muffled sounds escaped through the fabric stuffed in his mouth.

Chance poked the gun into Nelson's stomach, nudged him toward Gao's bedroom.

Gao lay alone in the tangle of sheets on the bed, stared wide-eyed at the strangers who had suddenly appeared in front of him. On the bedside table sat a silver ice bucket with a bottle of champagne, two half-empty glasses. A sliding glass door, partly open, looked onto another million-dollar view. A white curtain billowed in the breeze. The Bee Gees played from a wall-mounted CD consul.

Chance pushed Nelson onto the bed next to his boss.

Dormer reached over Gao and turned off the music. Gao glanced in the direction of the bathroom. There was a flushing sound and the door opened to reveal Amber in a white terry towelling dressing gown.

'Where's the heroin?' said Dormer.

'The floor to ceiling wardrobe in the other bedroom,' she said, scrambling out of the dressing gown and into her underwear.

Chance looked from Dormer to Amber. 'Heroin?'

Amber looked away, picked her black cocktail dress from where it lay on the floor and slipped it on over her head.

'Shut up, Jacobi, and keep them covered,' Dormer said as he left the room.

An alarm bell went off in the back of Chance's mind. They'd agreed beforehand not to use names in front of Gao. And what heroin was Dormer talking about? Chance didn't fool himself, knew he couldn't do what he did without sometimes bumping up against drugs. But he avoided them whenever he could. They made people greedy and careless.

'What the fuck is going on?' he hissed at Amber.

'Just do what you're told,' she said, still not meeting his eyes.

Gao had regained his composure, sat up in bed. The sheet only covered his lower half, his upper body plump and untoned. 'Hello, Peter,' he said calmly. 'When my father hears what you have done, you are dead. He will hunt you down, every member of your family, kill them all.'

Chance ignored Gao. 'What is Dormer talking about?'

'I told you, don't ask questions,' Amber said. 'Please, just do what Frank says.'

Dormer returned with an aluminium suitcase identical to the one he found in Tavener's room. He lifted it onto the bed, snapped it open. It was full of white bricks wrapped in plastic.

Dormer shut the case, smiled. 'That wasn't so hard, Freddie, was it?'

Gao watched, a mournful look on his face.

'We've got your drugs, can we just get out of here?' said Chance.

'There's one more thing.'

Chance sensed something was wrong, raised his pistol.

Dormer smiled over Chance's shoulder.

Sophia Lekakis stood in the doorway, her face set at a determined angle. Nelson's gun looked large and unwieldy in her hands.

'You said it yourself, Jacobi.' Dormer pocketed his own pistol and took the gun from Chance's hand. 'We can't very well just let Gao walk out of here.'

Amber whimpered. 'This wasn't part of the plan, Frank.'

'Plan's changed,' Dormer said, patting the pockets of Chance's suit coat until he located the keys to the Volvo.

Chance wrenched off his balaclava, ran his free hand through his hair. 'You're going to kill Gao and Nelson?'

'No, Jacobi, you are. The police will find your gun and your body here to prove it.'

'You don't have to do this, Dormer,' said Chance. 'I'll walk away. You can have everything.'

'I'm afraid not. You remember the first time we met, what I said about the sharks? The strong ones eliminate the weak to keep the rest of the school healthy. Gao and Nelson are the weak ones. You just happened to be in the water at the wrong time.'

Dormer swivelled, aimed Chance's gun at Gao. The Filipino snarled, launched himself at his assailant. He knocked Dormer to the ground and fell on top of him.

Lekakis watched the two men wrestle on the floor, unsure what to do. Chance saw his opportunity, charged at the woman, one shoulder forward, knocked her out of the way.

He reached the main room, heard a shot from the bedroom, followed by a woman's scream.

Chance looked around wildly, noticed the sliding door was

open from when he'd gone out on the balcony earlier. He cleared the doorway as another shot, this one suppressed by the silencer, rang out. The floor-to-ceiling glass next to him disintergrated. More shots, something sharp bit into his left shoulder. He ran across the patio, leapt over the railing.

His arms clawed at the darkness and cold air. The ghostly-lit shape came at him with terrifying speed and his world was transformed into a translucent blue.

His body glanced off the bottom of the pool, hard, but not the fatal force had he hit the shallow end. He slowly surfaced, his breath ragged in his ears, his skin tingling from the impact. He made to swim for the side, but a bolt of pain halted him mid-stroke. He noticed a slow motion swirl of red in the blue around him from a wound somewhere near his left shoulder. His chest throbbed as he hauled himself out of the pool. His peripheral vision was a technicolour glaze, like the onset of a migraine. He peeled off his latex gloves, took his phone out of his trouser pocket. Pool water had ruined it. He tossed the device into a nearby clump of ferns.

There was an entrance to the pool area that looked like it would take him through the lobby, the way they'd come in, but Dormer might be waiting for him.

That left the beach-facing wall. He hauled his body over, felt like he was going to pass out with the pain as he landed feet-first on the sand. He stood very still for a few minutes, tried to breathe normally.

He took a tentative step, then another, walked across the sand as fast as his battered body would allow.

Fourteen

A taxi was parked under a light at the end of the street facing onto the beach. A swarthy looking driver stood smoking next to the vehicle.

Chance had found a towel abandoned on the beach, ripped part of it off to use as a makeshift tourniquet for his wounded arm. Dark spots showed through the fabric. The driver didn't bat an eyelid as he approached. Wherever he was from he'd probably seen worse. He agreed to take Chance without putting on the meter for a hundred dollars. Chance climbed into the back. The effort flooded his body with pain.

The radio was tuned to an Arabic station. A male voice chanted a prayer. The melancholy tones soothed Chance.

He stopped the cab opposite a piece of parkland a block away from Curry's house. The reflection of the moonlight on the canal was visible through the low-hanging trees. He leaned forward from the back seat, peeled off a couple of sodden fifty dollar notes, passed them to the driver, paused, peeled off two more to be sure he'd bought the man's silence.

Soft rain started to fall as Chance walked down the incline of the park toward the canal. He felt his shoes sink into the mud at the water's edge. He parted a clump of reeds, kept going until the water was up to his neck. Urban legend had it the waterways around Surfers were populated by Bull sharks that had swum in from the sea. The idea suddenly amused him. He had much bigger predators to worry about.

In all likelihood there were now two bodies lying in the hotel suite back in Surfers. Gao and his bodyguard, both executed with a gun covered with his fingerprints. Chance knew the Chinaman would have put in place enough layers to prevent the gun being traced back to him. The wily old bastard hadn't survived this long without learning how to insulate himself when things went wrong. Chance doubted he'd be so lucky. He had to get as far away from Surfers as possible. But first, he had to find out whether Curry was in on the double-cross, and, if so, whether the Chinaman was involved, too.

He turned on his side, waded through the cold water with his good arm. Vegetation brushed against his feet. He heard a siren in the distance. It was joined by the call of a waterbird somewhere in the blackness.

Chance swam until he reached the back of Curry's residence. The windows of the house and the dwellings adjoining it were dark.

He grunted in pain as he pulled himself onto a concrete ledge running along the back of Curry's property. He manoeuvred around the patio furniture, tested the glass sliding door. It was unlocked. He glimpsed a hammer amid a stack of tools on the table, picked it up, stepped inside.

The familiar contours of Curry's kitchen and dining area came into focus. The only sign of life was a thin line of light from under the door to Curry's study. He pressed his ear against the cool wood, heard nothing, opened the door and stepped in, the hammer held at his side.

Curry lay on the floor, the top half of his body visible in a circle of lamp light. Chance knelt next to the body. The old man had a surprised look on his face, eyes wide, mouth partly open, like he'd been interrupted in the middle of one of his stories. There was a single entry wound on the middle of his forehead. The shag pile around the back of his head was thick with blood, a spray of gore on the nearest wall.

Chance turned his head slightly, found himself staring into the quivering barrel of a sawed-off shotgun. Amber stood at the other end of the weapon, still in her black cocktail dress, barefoot, her large blue eyes bloodshot and lined with streaked mascara.

'Put the hammer down,' she said.

Chance did as he was told.

'Let's get a couple of things straight. I knew about the heroin but I didn't know Dormer was going to kill Gao and the bodyguard, pin it on you.'

He said nothing just looked into her big blue eyes.

'If you don't believe me, just slowly back the fuck out of the room, leave the house and don't let me see you again.'

Chance replayed the scene in Gao's hotel suite, Amber's reaction when Dormer had revealed his true intentions. The look of genuine fear on her face couldn't have been faked.

'I believe you.'

She lowered the sawed-off, glanced at Curry's body on the floor.

Chance jumped up, grabbed the barrel and yanked it from Amber's hands. She stumbled backward onto a black leather couch. He sighted the gun centimetres away from her face.

'How does it fucking feel to have a gun pointed at you?' he wheezed. His body felt on fire and it took all his willpower not to pass out.

'Nothing I haven't experienced before, bastard, believe me.' She didn't flinch, returned his glare, her eyes hard slits, fists balled at her sides.

'Who killed your boyfriend over there?'

'Dennis wasn't my boyfriend.' Amber stifled a sob. 'He and Kerrigan were lovers. Had been for years.'

'So where's Kerrigan?'

'No idea.'

'What happened to you?'

'After you did your high dive act, Dormer came back into the bedroom.' Amber spoke quickly, her breath a series of sharp gasps. 'He just walked right up to Gao and Nelson, shot them with your pistol. Sophia just watched, said nothing. I was scared, all I could do was play along.

'We left the hotel with the heroin and the money, headed for the farm in Beaudesert. Call me a suspicious bitch, but after what happened in the suite, I had the impression I wasn't exactly a key part their plans. When the car stopped at a red light, I got out and made a run for it. When I felt it was safe enough I came here. Didn't know where else to go,' she glanced at the body. 'Dennis was already like this.'

'Dormer tying up loose ends.'

Amber wiped a forearm under her nose, nodded.

'Did Curry know about the heroin?'

'No, he thought we were only after cash. Dennis hated drugs, never touched them after what they did to his son.'

'What are you talking about?'

'His son, Sean, died of a heroin overdose.'

Chance lowered the gun. He remembered the photograph of Curry standing on a beach with a young man. He hadn't noticed a family resemblance. Then again, he hadn't been looking for it.

'But you knew.'

'Yeah, Dormer told me Gao wanted to get into the heroin business. Gao brought the American, Tavener, along to broker the deal. The gear had already been smuggled into the country, Gao took possession, was going to sell it in Sydney. I'd hoped to convince Curry to go along with it, at least take his cut of the cash from it. I owed him that much.'

Sweat dripped from Chance's face and his entire body ached. He slumped on to the couch next to Amber, looked at the sawed-off in his hands. Probably Curry's. Maybe even the gun the old man had used on the Ferret back in Melbourne all those years ago. It was certainly old enough, the barrel scratched, the wooden stock worn and nicked.

He looked at the lifeless old man on the carpet. 'What a

fucking mess.'

'What are we going to do now?'

'What do you mean "we?" By morning I'll be wanted on a double murder charge. You do what you want. I'm getting the hell out.'

His words trailed off, he winced in pain.

'You're not going anywhere in your condition.' Amber leaned over, peeled away the crude tourniquet from the wound on Chance's arm.

He tried to wave her off, was too weak to stop her.

'Nasty.'

'You a doctor now?' He drew a sharp breath as she probed around his ribs.

'Nothing's broken, but something's damaged, you've probably fractured a rib or two. You aren't going anywhere. Not alone, anyway.'

'What are you suggesting?'

'You're not the only one that's been cheated. I don't work for free, either. Besides, when the police discover the bodies in that suite, how long do you think it will take them to make a link to me? The places they'll find my DNA, I don't even want to think about. Whatever, I've got no more interest in hanging around here than you do.'

'How do I know I can trust you?'

'Peter, you've got two choices. You're hurt pretty bad. You can come with me or be a tough guy, stay here on the couch, and let the cops find you in the morning.'

She'd fully regained her composure, her voice calm and clear.

'Okay, help me up,' said Chance.

'Any idea where we go?' she said as she draped his arm over her shoulder and pulled him off the couch.

'Ahh shit, that hurts.' Chance groaned as he stood. 'I know a great Chinese restaurant, about two days drive from here, in a little town near Canberra called Yass.'

'That's a long way to travel to order takeaway.'

66

'Trust me. It's worth the drive.'

'I'm game, Peter, anywhere that's not here.'

'Peter's a false name I used for this job. My real name is Gary. Gary Chance.'

'Nice to meet you, Gary,' she said, smiling. 'Since we're in a sharing mood, my real name is Kate. Kate Norliss.'

Fifteen

Detective Sergeant Elyssa Blake parked on the shoulder of the dirt road, walked the remaining hundred metres to the farmhouse. She hoped the exercise would stave off the headache lurking on the fringes of her skull ever since she'd awakened that morning.

The sky was overcast, grey cloud streaked with black. Rain again last night, more forecast today. The fields on either side of the road were a rich emerald colour from all the moisture. A rainbow was visible above the paddock to her right. She briefly wondered what was at the end. Probably another corpse, if the last couple of days were anything to go by.

She walked over a rusty cattle grid and up the slope toward the house, cursed as mud splashed on her expensive leather shoes.

Next to the house was a ramshackle barn, doors open to reveal the rear of a red Toyota Corolla. Two police vehicles were parked on the lawn under a large tree. A young uniformed officer stood talking to an overweight man who puffed on a cigarette, a criminal investigation branch detective named Gavin Nolte.

The uniform nodded in her direction, Nolte turned, walked down the incline toward her.

'Is it him?' she said.

Nolte exhaled a stream of cigarette smoke and fixed her with the world-weary look. 'Yeah.'

Nolte flicked his cigarette butt into a nearby puddle, hitched up the pants of his turd-coloured suit and indicted for her to follow.

'Who's the uniform?'

'Bloke called Reagan. Don't worry, he's sorted.'

'Who else knows?'

'Only the owner. He's got a couple of priors for holding unlicensed rave parties on the property, just wants the whole thing to go away.'

A tall, skinny detective with a shock of sandy hair named Dundee met them at the front door of the house. He held a plastic evidence bag containing a pistol.

Dundee led them down the dark hallway to a kitchen. A wood stove, an ancient-looking fridge in the corner. The body of a man lay on the floorboards in the centre of the room, next to an overturned chair. Even with half his head missing, Blake recognised him from his mug shot.

'Meet contestant number four,' said Dundee.

Blake flinched, caught herself before either of her male colleagues noticed. Despite nearly a decade in the job, she still found the hardest thing about being a cop was the casual disregard some officers showed to the dead.

'Jesus Christ.' Nolte ran a hand through his almost non-existent hair, lit a cigarette.

Blake went as close to the body as she could without getting blood on her shoes. 'Another execution-style killing?'

Dundee nodded.

She looked at the bag in Dundee's hand. 'The murder weapon?'

'Probably.'

'Where'd you find it?'

'Bushes around the side of the house.'

'Been fired?'

'Five shots.

Gao, his bodyguard Nelson, Curry, and now Malcolm Kerrigan, all killed, execution-style, with a hollow-point round to the head, fired from a .38 snubnose pistol, the same make as the pistol in the bag.

Blake made it a point never to underestimate the stupidity of the average criminal. But whoever had murdered Gao and the others was not an average criminal. They were professionals and professionals didn't accidently leave a weapon in the bushes near a murder scene. Police had also found a vehicle abandoned on the outskirts of Brisbane that was licensed to a long-time Surfers Paradise resident named Dennis Curry. The same Dennis Curry who organised a well-known poker game Gao frequented whenever he was in Surfers. Police had gone to Curry's house to question him, found the old man murdered, same as Gao and the bodyguard. It was as if someone wanted to leave a trail of signposts leading to whomever had committed the crimes.

'I've already phoned in the serial number for the gun,' said Dundee. 'Viljoen is working on it and lifting the prints from the Volvo as we speak.'

'Why Kerrigan?' she said aloud to herself.

'Maybe he pissed someone off,' said Nolte hesitantly.

Blake looked at her colleague, thought of a piece of graffiti she'd once seen on a toilet wall. 'I know a cop that's so dumb the other police have started to notice.'

'Four bodies, Stretch,' she said, using Dundee's nickname, 'a Gold Coast record. What else have you got?'

'Signs at least another two people were staying here, one of them a woman.' Dundee held up another evidence bag. It contained several dozen-cigarette butts, the ends encircled in lipstick.

Blake placed a thumb and forefinger on her head, slowly massaged her temple.

This morning's media reports had described Curry as a colourful local identity, a throwback to the Coast's more free-wheeling past. What they hadn't mentioned was prior to coming to Queensland, he had sported the moniker 'Dennis the Menace.' A former enforcer for a faction of the once notorious Victorian Painters and Dockers Union, he'd fled north after allegedly killing a member of a rival faction in a bar at the tender age of just twenty-two. He'd landed a job on the Brisbane docks and for many years was a key player in the city's flourishing crime scene.

Curry had retired to Surfers a decade ago, made a name for himself as an entrepreneur, philanthropist and regular fixture on the city's social circuit, quick with a risqué joke, full of old-school criminal charm.

Curry had lived with two people.

A woman, first name was Amber, last seen in Gao's company the night the Filipino was murdered.

The second was the man lying on the floor in front of them, Curry's longtime lover, Malcolm Kerrigan, or 'Mad Mal' as he used to be known. Kerrigan's criminal lineage dated back to the Clockwork Orange Gang, a group active in the seventies who wore bowler hats, carried canes, and roared around Brisbane on Harley Davidsons. Say what you want, thought Blake, but at least the crims back then were original.

The Clockwork Orange Gang had kept sweet with the cops by doing the occasional job for them in addition to their other criminal activities. They were also tight with the Brisbane branch of the Painters and Dockers, which is where Kerrigan had met Curry.

'Kerrigan had on occasion acted as an informant for the Queensland police,' said Blake. 'Think that might have anything to do with his killing?'

'Maybe,' said Dundee. 'Live by the sword, die by the sword.'

Nolte snorted. 'Check out Mister fucking Shakespeare.'

'Actually, it's from the Bible, shithead. Gospel of Matthew, verse twenty-six, fifty.'

'Given the shit this has stirred up, divine intervention might be the only thing that saves us,' said Blake.

The three of them stared at Kerrigan's body. Blake used the silence to make a mental checklist of the investigation so far.

Whoever killed the two Filipinos had gained access to their hotel suite with a pass card that was most likely supplied by some-one working for the hotel. That was almost certainly a woman named Sophia Lekakis, the receptionist on duty at the time of the killings. Lekakis, who had disappeared, was probably also responsible for disabling the hotel's internal video surveillance cameras, depriving the investigation of any footage of the murderers entering or leaving the building.

In addition to Lekakis and the woman known as Amber, police were looking for two other people. The first was Gao's chauffeur, a male in his mid-thirties named Peter Jacobi. The second was the American citizen who'd accompanied Gao to Australia.

Blake's mobile rang. She recognised the number on the screen, Viljoen, a ruddy-faced Boer and Costello's main attack dog. A former member of the South African police, Viljoen accumulated excessive force charges like most people collected frequent flier points.

'What?'

'We've got Jacobi's real name,' said Viljoen in a thick accent.

'Well, are you going to give it to me or do you want a drum roll?'

'Gary Chance, former truck driver in the Australian Army. His prints, all over the Volvo, match his ADF file.'

'Anything else?'

'Yes, it gets better.'

'Let me guess, the pistol's registered to the chauffeur?'

'You got it,' said Viljoen, his voice smug. 'The papers are obviously fake, I'm looking into them further.'

'Who else has this information?'

'Just us, for now.'

'Okay, I need to get moving.'

'One other thing,' Viljoen said, before Blake could hang up.

'What?'

'Davros wants to see you.'

Blake pocketed the phone, turned to Nolte and Dundee.

'Clean this place up and get rid of the body. I've got to go and see Costello.'

Sixteen

Blake turned on the car radio, skipped between stations. The airwaves crackled with the killings, their aftermath and associated rumours of police corruption on the Glitter Strip.

She felt cold fury as she listened to the self-righteous shock jocks and their legion of incensed talkback callers, the naivety with which they discussed police corruption.

Tackling corruption involved more than weeding out a few bent cops. Surfers Paradise had forty licensed premises, and fifteen thousand hotel rooms and units in a two-block radius. More went up all the time, the buildings spreading like algae bloom. Add to this the continuous year-round stream of tourists wanting to be fed, fucked, and watered. The idea of clamping down on corruption when there was that much money about was idiocy.

Blake switched off the radio, thought about her son, now living with her ex in Western Australia. Four years of watching the boy grow up via the occasional Facebook update or colour photo included with a birthday card.

The police career that had devoured her marriage now drilled into the core of her being, seeking out the last few drops of anything she had in reserve. She sensed herself losing the ability to feel empathy, to converse with anyone other than cops, to talk about anything other than the job.

She could still recall with razor-sharp clarity the first time she'd seen a cop take a bribe. She and her partner, an older officer near retirement, were on patrol in Fortitude Valley. The owner of a nightclub had slipped him a thick envelope. She'd thought it was strange, an on-duty cop getting a gift from a member of the public, only realised later that night what had actually been going on.

If corruption was a well-oiled machine, Costello was the master mechanic. He only picked cops who had something to lose or hide, was famous for being able to find people's weaknesses, their dark secrets, twist them to his own design.

Years after the nightclub incident, she'd been investigating a suspected rapist stalking Brisbane's southern suburbs. She had a strong suspect, knew he was guilty, but couldn't fit all the pieces together to make it stick.

One night she got drunk, followed the man, confronted him as he was about to get into his car in the empty parking lot of a suburban shopping mall, told him she was going to take him down.

He'd just smiled and said, 'Do your worst, bitch. You've got nothing on me, otherwise you wouldn't be here.'

Something inside her snapped. Blake pulled her service revolver, shot him dead.

She tried to make it look like self-defence, still wasn't sure how the hell Costello had found out. A week later Dundee appeared on the doorstep of her apartment, asked if he could come in. He seemed almost apologetic as he told her she had two choices, work for Costello or her career was over, she'd be disgraced, probably end up in jail.

It was no choice at all. At least that's the way it had seemed back then.

A grey-haired woman answered the front door of the white weatherboard house.

Inside was a slice of bygone Australia: doylies on a polished mahogany dining table, three ascending porcelain ducks on the wall. The bookshelves were lined with thick sporting biographies and framed pictures, a few family shots, but mainly Costello and his fellow officers. Smirks on their faces, all in on 'The Joke,' the nickname for the network of corrupt police that extorted money from illegal gambling and prostitution in Brisbane in the sixties, seventies, and early eighties.

'Would you like a cup of tea, dear?' the lady said as she ushered Blake onto a screened-in balcony, children's laughter audible from the backyard.

'No, thank you.'

Costello sat in a wheelchair in semi-shadow in the far corner of the balcony. Despite the heat, he had an old grey cardigan over his shirt, a tweed cloth cap. A blanket covered his knees. He glared at her, eyes magnified through his coke-bottle glasses, the skin around his face loose, like it no longer fit.

She met the old bastard's stare, shivered. Blake doubted Costello could piss without help but he was still a fearsome presence, last man standing from a generation of bent cops. He'd survived everything thrown at him, even the Fitzgerald inquiry into corruption. Ancient history now, but at the time, Fitzgerald had been like a cluster bomb let off in the middle of a tightly packed formation of infantry. When the smoke cleared bodies were everywhere, but Costello had emerged unscathed.

He was retired now, but still influential, sheer willpower plus several decades of the dirt he reportedly had on politicians, journalists and fellow officers. Not even a bout of throat cancer had killed him.

Blake faced him, hands clasped behind her back, like she was at parade rest. 'You wanted to see me.'

Costello placed a mechanical larynx against his throat.

'Detective Sergeant.' His voice came out a flat mechanical buzz. 'You've just come from the scene of the Kerrigan murder?'

'Yes.' They'd kept Kerrigan's death out of the news, so how did he know? Viljoen had obviously briefed him.

'Knew Kerrigan from the old days. He was a dog, deserved to die like he did.' The old man paused, took a raspy breath, repositioned the mechanical larynx. 'What else you got to report?'

'We think we've got the weapon used in all four murders. It's registered to Gao's chauffeur, an ex-Army man. Hopefully, there'll be prints on it, and they'll match the ones we found in the Volvo that was parked near the hotel.'

She stopped, noticed the look of disinterest on the old man's face.

Costello was just going through the motions, Viljoen would have already told the old man everything they'd found out.

'I don't give a fuck who shot the chink or his bodyguard. Where's my bloody heroin?'

'I don't know.'

The old man's face twitched in disgust or anger, Blake couldn't tell which.

'Do you know how much heroin was stolen from Gao's room the other night?'

'No,' she lied.

'Twenty-four kilos. Pure. That's around ten million dollars. Gao bought it in, was going to sell it to some associates in Sydney who'd already paid a deposit. Now their money and their drugs are gone. The robbery occurred on our patch. That means I'm responsible for their losses.'

It wasn't hard to see how Costello had got the nickname Davros: the metallic drone of the old man's voice, the jerky, mechanical nature of his movements. Blake stared at the old man, her fascination momentarily getting the better of her fear.

'I want my heroin and the thieving bastards that stole it.'

'Do you have any idea how much heat is on this case? It's a bloody miracle we've managed to keep the heroin and mention of you out of the news. The toecutters are already sniffing around. I'm not sure how much longer we'll be able to sit on it.'

Costello's eyes grew large at the implied threat. The mechanical larynx trembled in his hand.

'I'm not the only one hiding things, Detective Sergeant Blake. Don't forget that. If you haven't got the bottle to do what's required, you can fuck off and I'll get someone who has.'

Blake felt the skin on her face burn, forced herself to meet Costello's stare. 'All I'm saying is the best hope of finding the drugs is finding the man who shot Gao.'

'Then find him. I don't care what you have to do, but find him and get my drugs.'

Without another word, Blake turned and left.

She paused by her car and looked back at the Costello's house, rain and the restless ghosts of Queensland's underworld past swirling in the air around her.

BUSH CAPITAL

One

Kate Norliss drove, eyes constantly on the rearview mirror, she wasn't sure for what. Half an hour across the border into New South Wales, the realisation of what she'd done hit her like a punch to the stomach.

She brought the car to a sudden stop at the side of the road, opened her door, vomited into the darkness, kept going until there was nothing but bile and hot breath. A giant semi-trailer illuminated her in its headlights, roared past, momentarily sucking up the air around her as it hurtled into the darkness. She sat up, wiped the tendrils of saliva from her mouth with the sleeve of her denim jacket.

Chance slept undisturbed in the seat beside her, his legs bent under the dash. Kate had changed out of the black cocktail dress into her Rolling Stones T-shirt, sneakers, and black jeans. He was still in the shirt and pants, the fabric next to his wound caked with dried blood. She'd offered to try finding something for him from her housemate's clothes, but he'd waved her off, said they had to make the most of the limited time until the police discovered the bodies of Gao and his bodyguard.

Hank Williams' scratchy twang serenaded her as dawn broke, streaks of pink unfurling across the sky, mixing with the clouds like coloured ink being added to a jar of water.

An hour later she pulled into a rest area, spread the map of New South Wales on the bonnet. Chance had insisted they take the inland highway to Yass, not the coast road, said there were likely to be fewer speed cameras, even if it prolonged the thousand-kilometre journey to Canberra.

Chance hobbled out of the car, stood unsteadily at the edge of the clearing and pissed. The pain on his face and the early morning light made him look old and frail.

Kate smiled to herself, remembered how Chance's jaw had dropped when she'd told him Amber wasn't her real name. As if he were the only one smart enough to try and shield his identity.

'Did you get rid of your mobile phone?' he said, as he walked toward her.

'No, I thought it would come in handy—'

'Give it here,' he said clicking his fingers. 'The police can use it to find the nearest reception points, track us.'

'This part of your tough guy act?' she said as she handed him the phone.

Chance ignored her, concentrated on taking the phone to pieces.

Kate went back to studying the map. She didn't need medical experience to know Chance must have lost a lot of blood and at least one or two of his ribs were cracked. Taking him to a doctor or a hospital was out of the question but she could get him something for the pain, make him more comfortable until they got to Yass. She selected their next stop, folded the map.

'We'll drive another two hours, stop to rest and I'll do what I can for your arm.'

'It looks far worse than it is. It's more important we get to Yass.'

'Suit yourself, tough guy, but I need food and sleep, and the car won't run on air. You can stay in the front seat for all I care, but we're stopping in another two hours. No argument.'

She went to the boot, unzipped the army surplus duffle bag she'd brought from Curry's. It contained three thousand dollars, all the money in the house, clothes, and toiletries. She'd also taken the sawed-off shotgun, a box of shells and, on a last-minute whim, the framed photograph of the old man and Sean at the beach.

She picked up the photograph, admired her former lover, his fierce, lean features, before the smack had ravaged them. Kate could already feel the bond she had had with Dennis Curry, their stunted shared history, start to fade, willed it to disappear completely. The connection to her former lover was not broken so easily.

Two

The motel was an architectural refugee from the seventies, two-dozen rooms in a single-story cream brick U-shape. Faded blue letters, medieval style, spelled out the name 'King's Court' for passing traffic.

Chance crawled onto one of the two single beds, immediately fell asleep.

Kate went into the cramped bathroom, looked at the remains of last night's mascara vying with the dark circles around her eyes. She took a hot shower, dressed, got back into the car, and drove the two kilometres into the town centre.

She found a drug store that was open, bought bandages, syringes, and antiseptic. She picked up water, a bottle of scotch, a fresh pack of tobacco, and a lighter from the supermarket. In a bargain store next to the supermarket, she bought a fresh set of clothes for Chance, and sunglasses and a baseball cap for herself.

She loaded her purchases into the back seat, walked along the main street to scope out the town. Early Sunday afternoon and the place was empty, apart from a few men sitting on benches on the side of the road and the occasional young mother pushing an oversized pram.

There was a used car lot at one end of the street, a banner with the words 'Cash for Cars' strung across the entrance. She'd come back tomorrow morning, trade in her almost new Camry for a black seventies Holden Ute she spied among the vehicles for sale.

The town had two pubs. One was boarded up, a for sale sign bolted to the front. The other was a two-story wooden building, a balcony around the length of the second level. Pinned to a corkboard covered in bank notes from all over the world was a notice advertising tonight's entertainment, an eighties cover band, free admission.

Her reconnoitre finished, Kate felt hungry, realised she hadn't eaten since early the previous evening. The nearest café was empty except for an emaciated old man mopping the floor.

She gazed at the menu in chalk about the counter, ordered two burgers with the lot and chips to take away. She sat in one of the Formica and wood booths while she waited for the food, looked at the framed black and white photographs of old film stars, Bogart, Monroe, Chaplin, that peppered the walls.

On her way back to the car she caught sight of two teenage girls standing at the doorway of a milk bar. The girls reminded her of the long Sunday afternoons in a one-street town not unlike this one, the mixture of boredom and desperate anticipation, waiting for something, anything, to happen.

At twenty-six, Kate didn't have any excuses for where she'd ended up in life, didn't feel the need to make any. She was smart, came from a good enough home. She didn't hate her parents, just didn't want to be like them.

She finished school, got out at the first opportunity, ended up in Brisbane, took a job pulling beers in a pub. A few gigs like this later she ended up tending bar in a strip club. Graduated to stripping. One night Kate went for drinks with a bunch of the women she worked with, listened with interest when they told her of the money that could be made servicing the mining boom. Soon Kate was part of the fly in, fly out workforce of women selling sex in mining towns throughout Queensland.

She remembered her first night on the job. She'd sat on the end of the bed in a motel room, waited for the customer. Her stomach churned as she kept telling herself it was just sex. Part of her hoped he'd never turned up. He did. The world didn't end, just went on from there.

What she did never struck her as sleazy or demeaning. It was just a job, and a well-paying one. All she needed was a hooker name, Amber, an ad in the local paper, a mobile phone full of credit, and she was in business.

The mining boom was in full swing. Sleepy rural towns were suddenly packed with young men with money to burn and a shortage of female company. She was popular. Something about her face, her large eyes, made her look vulnerable. Men thought she needed to be rescued.

She'd been working in Gladstone, Queensland's biggest coal exporting port, when she met Sean. He turned up one night, still in his overalls and steel-capped boots, good looking, blue eyes like hers, shoulder-length dark hair. He told her he worked as a shot firer at one of the mines, looked after explosives and super- vised blasting.

He visited her every night that week she was in town. Against her better judgment, she gave him her address, said to call next time he was in Brisbane.

A month later he did.

Three

Chance was in the shower when she got back to the hotel, his soiled clothes in a pile by the bathroom door. The TV was on, a show about fishing. She turned it off, sat at the table against the wall, poured a finger of whisky into one of the hotel glasses, topped it up with water, and downed it in a single gulp. She bit into her burger. It tasted good despite being lukewarm.

The bathroom door opened. Chance emerged, a towel around his waist, a trail of vapour following behind him.

He sniffed the air. 'Smells great.'

'Burger and chips,' she said, chewing her food. 'There's one on the table for you.'

She could tell Chance was making an effort to appear normal as he walked across the room, but the tension in his body, how he slowly lowered himself into the chair, gave away the pain he was in. There were dark bruises around his chest. The wound on his left shoulder where a chunk of skin had been taken out looked bloody and raw; the entire arm was stiff and held close to his body.

Chance reached forward with his good arm, undid the wrapping on his food, picked up a chip.

'Any sauce?'

'Afraid not.'

'Things are grim.' He put the chip in his mouth. 'Any hope of a whisky?'

She made him a drink. He knocked it back, held out his glass for more.

When they'd finished eating, she sat him on the bed, rolled him a cigarette, and got to work on his shoulder.

'They've found Gao and Nelson,' he said, blowing smoke toward the ceiling. 'There was a female cop, talking about it on the news. She looked like a real hard case. No word yet about Curry.'

The way he said it, the casual tone, alarmed Kate. She wondered if he was testing her, what her reaction would be.

'Doesn't change anything.' She dabbed his wound with antiseptic, put a large square bandage over the wound. 'Tonight you rest. Tomorrow we swap cars and drive to Yass, do it in one trip.'

When she'd finished Chance lay back against the bed head, the towel still around his waist. Conscious of him watching, she stripped down to her bra and panties, drew the heavy curtains, set the alarm, threw off the quilt cover on her bed and climbed in. She lay there in the semi-darkness, listened to the noise of vehicles and people moving about outside.

'Not that I'm ungrateful, but you'd stand a much better chance on your own,' said Chance.

'Don't think the thought hasn't crossed my mind,' she said. 'Truth is, right now I don't know what else to do. Three thousand dollars isn't going to get me far. At least you have a plan, someone who will help you when we get to Yass.'

'Don't get your hopes up,' the voice came back in the darkness. 'We've still got to get past the police. Not to mention whoever else might be looking for us.'

Kate rolled over. Chance's outline on the other bed reminded her of Sean.

She'd been seeing him on and off for several months when he suggested she move to Gladstone, live with him. She bought a plane ticket, moved in to his motel, a single room that cost the same as a flat in Brisbane.

In the following weeks she discovered he had two jobs. The day job he'd told her about, another dealing drugs.

Those few months with Sean, before everything blew up, Kate learned a lot about the drug trade.

It involved a lot of money. It required a machine, a seller wanting to be paid, a buyer expecting delivery, a hierarchy of management, fixers, enforcers, dealers and mules. Most of the time the machine was invisible. That was a good thing. The only time you ever saw it was when something went wrong.

Four

Kate switched off the alarm. The light through the crack in the curtains was faint. Disorientated, she recognised Chance's shape in the next bed, remembered where she was.

Kate forced herself up, went into the bathroom, splashed cold water on her face, thought about putting on make-up, settled for red lipstick. She climbed into the clothes she'd worn earlier, picked up her car keys, the roll of cash.

The dusk sky bathed the town in soft golden light. The streets were quiet. The only sign of life was the pub, customers spilled onto its front porch. She drove past, parked around the corner.

Inside was packed. People lined the bar, sat at tables. A small group danced in front of the band, four middle-aged men in acid-washed jeans and T-shirts. The drummer wore a red bandana.

Kate pushed her way to the bar, leaned over the counter, shouted at the man behind it for a whisky on the rocks. When her drink appeared, she downed half, turned around, scanned the crowd.

She drained her glass, ordered another. She had to attach herself to a local, someone who knew the place. She scanned the room again, focused on a woman standing by herself in the far corner. She wore jeans and a faded black T-shirt with a car logo on it, tapped her feet and moved her shoulder-length hair from side to side slightly in time to the music. Kate picked her as the

kind of woman determined to have a good time whenever she
went out, edged across the room toward her.

'Local boys?' Kate said, leaning in close to the woman.

'Yeah.'

'They're good.' Kate sipped her drink.

'You're not from around here,' the woman said in a mock
southern drawl.

'That obvious, is it?'

'Yeah.'

'Just passing through. Staying at one of the hotels, wanted a
drink, a bit of fun. Looks like I've found the right place.'

'Honey, you've found the only place.'

'I'm Amber.'

The woman put her hand out. 'Denise.'

'Nice to meet you, Denise.' As they shook hands the lead
singer announced the band was taking a break.

'So what do you do in town, Denise?'

'I run the local hairdressing salon.' She ran a hand through
Kate's hair. 'Actually, your hair feels like it could do with some
TLC. Stop by tomorrow, I'll help you out.'

'Love to, Denise, but I've got to make tracks early in the
morning.'

'Then at least let me buy you a drink.'

Kate drained her glass, placed it on the nearest surface. 'Sure.
Scotch rocks.'

Denise returned five minutes later carrying a glass of red
wine and another whisky.

'Cheers,' Denise said and downed a generous slug of her red.

Kate bit her lower lip. 'Between us girls, I wonder if you
could help me out with something.'

'What's that?' said Denise.

'I'm not travelling alone—' Kate stumbled, unsure how much
to say. Denise reminded her of some of the older fly in, fly out
sex workers she'd met, women who'd had tough lives but never
came off as spent and bitter. Her instincts said she could trust

Denise. She didn't have time to be sure.

'Do you know anyone in this pub that can sell me some smack?' Kate heard a pleading tone in her voice, tried to modify it. 'It's not for me. I promise.'

Denise put up a hand to silence her.

'Honey, you do what you need to do, you'll get no judgment from me.' She drank half the red. 'Bloke over there, he's your man.'

Kate followed her gaze to a thin man standing on the opposite side of the room. He wore a Jim Beam T-shirt, jeans, sunglasses.

'Mister shades over there?'

'That's the one.'

'Thanks, Denise.'

Before Kate moved, the woman grabbed her by the wrist. 'Be careful, honey.'

'I can take care of myself.'

'I don't doubt it for a second.' She feigned a smile. 'Just don't go back to his house.'

Kate went to the bar, ordered another whisky. She watched the dealer over the rim of her glass, waited until the band started playing again to make her approach.

Kate had agreed to meet the dealer around the corner in fifteen minutes. The night was warm. She listened to the band inside, aware of the irony of her situation. Less than forty-eight hours ago she'd been standing next to a suitcase full of heroin. Now, here she was trying to buy two grams.

Kate remembered the shotgun in the boot. She popped the trunk, moved the weapon to within easy reach, just in case the dealer tried anything funny, covered it with an old blanket.

Just as she started to wonder whether the dealer would show, he turned the corner and walked toward her.

The dealer held out a small plastic bag of white powder.

She gave him the money, reached for the bag. He pulled it away just as she was about to take it.

'You want somewhere nice to take this?' The dealer smiled, revealed a mouth of tiny crooked teeth. 'My place ain't far. You could follow in your car.'

'Thanks, but no thanks.'

'Your loss.'

Kate snatched the bag.

'Somehow I don't think so.'

Five

Chance didn't move when Kate opened the door to their motel room. The air inside smelled stale, fast food, body odour, and cigarette smoke.

She kicked off her boots, turned on the bedside light. Chance moaned, spots of blood visible on the bandage she'd applied earlier.

Kate sat on the edge of his bed, took hold of his uninjured arm, inspected it. Spoiled for choice in terms of healthy veins. Her fingers paused on the stub of his little finger, taken clean off at the lower joint. Must have hurt like hell.

'Kate?' said Chance weakly, eyes half open.

'Shut up and lie still.'

She used Chance's belt as a tourniquet, cooked a little of the white powder on a metal teaspoon from the tray of complimentary tea and coffee, watched it boil and dissolve, sucked it up with the needle, got ready to shoot him up.

Chance's eyes focused on the needle, became alert. He grabbed her wrist, held tight.

'What the fuck,' he hissed. For a moment she thought he was going to snap her wrist.

'It'll help with the pain,' she said. The needle hovered mid-air above his skin. 'You've got nothing to worry about, Gary, I promise.'

She watched him deliberate what to do, the pain making

even simple thoughts difficult. His grip slackened. He let go, allowed her to shoot him up. His body stiffened slightly, his eyelids fluttered, his mouth drooped and he went limp.

Kate rolled herself a cigarette, poured a generous shot of whisky, channel surfed, the volume low.

She glanced at Chance every now and again, thought of the nights spent watching Sean on the nod, the state junkies got into when their eyes are closed and they look asleep, but they're actually awake, going with the pleasure.

Kate knew drugs were a part of life for many of the workers in the mining industry. There was so much money around and so little to do. On their first real date Sean had turned up in a hire car with an ounce of coke in the glove box. He had access to cash, far more than his mining salary, thought nothing of dropping two, three hundred dollars on dinner. Once, he flew them both to Bali for a long weekend, picked up the tab.

Sean was different from other men she'd dated. He talked about the share market and the importance of China to the Australian economy. He told her, now the mining boom was starting to cool, that they had to have other options. He wanted to go back to Brisbane, start a family. He and Kate would buy old houses, do them up and sell them for a profit. In retrospect, that was the problem. People made a little money, started talking and acting like they were economic experts, whereas, in reality, they knew jack shit.

They'd been living in Gladstone six months. She worked whatever jobs she could find. He had his mining job, dealt drugs on the side. Recently, he'd branched out into steroids, performance enhancing drugs, stuff with names he couldn't even pronounce. He told her it sold like a bomb to image-conscious young men in the industry.

He used a little, coke, a bit of heroin every now and again, nothing major, and his rapid-fire metabolism seemed to purge them from his system almost as quickly as he took them.

Kate rarely touched drugs, didn't know where Sean sourced

his product. She never asked and he never volunteered the information. Every few weeks, he'd drive off around sunset, return several hours later with a new supply.

One evening, out of the blue, he said he needed her to drive him to a pickup.

'My usual guy can't make it,' was his only explanation. The word 'drugs' was never used, almost like he was embarrassed to say it out loud.

It struck her as strange, but given that she had been living off the proceeds from his trade, it was only fair she help out.

After two hours of driving, they came to a fork, a crumbling stretch of bitumen running off the main road. Sean told her to take the turnoff. She drove until they arrived at an abandoned service station. The headlights illuminated the decayed façade, window smashed in, walls covered in graffiti, nothing else but flat earth dotted with scrub in every direction.

A four-wheel drive ute was parked in front of the building, the heads of its two occupants silhouetted in the rear windscreen.

'Who are they?' she asked.

'Always the same two guys, don't know their names.'

He leaned forward to pick up a small blue backpack on the floor between his legs. As his T-shirt rode up, she saw something metallic. It had never occurred to her he'd be carrying a gun. She didn't know he owned one.

'I give these guys money,' he said when he noticed the look of concern on her face. 'They give me something back. Simple. You just stay here, it'll only take a minute.'

She started to speak, stopped herself, nodded.

'Everything's going to be cool, okay?' His face looked pallid in the ghostly light from the consul, sweat beaded on his forehead and upper lip, despite the air conditioning.

Kate peered at the section of disused building illuminated in the two circles of light, tried to make sense of the graffiti, turned her attention to Sean. He walked toward the waiting vehicle, the backpack over his shoulder.

Sean placed one hand on the roof on the driver's side of the vehicle, knocked on the window. She watched him step away as the car door opened and a large, bald man stepped out. He wore heavy work boots, a reflective orange safety jacket over grease stained overalls. The man held a blunt shape in one hand, pointed it at Sean's face. It took her a moment to realise it was a gun. She watched Sean's mouth move rapidly, panic on his face.

She sat, stunned, as a thin, pinch-faced man emerged from the other side of the car. His long hair poked out from under a blue woolen beanie, but otherwise he was dressed like his partner. He also had a gun.

Pinch-Faced Man looked directly at Kate, started to walk toward her with long, deliberate strides. He raised his gun, fired several times. The shots illuminated the night like a strobe light.

Kate heard the bullets hit the radiator, the front tires. The car wheezed and hissed. A spiderweb of cracked glass appeared on the car's windscreen. She ducked below the windscreen cavity, her head in her hands, eyes screwed shut. She realised how stupid it was for her to be here, all the bad things that could happen.

The door opened. Pinch-Faced Man wrenched her from the car, patted her down as she struggled on the ground, found her mobile phone, pocketed it, dragged her along cracked concrete toward the sound of Sean's voice. He was begging his captor to leave them alone, not to hurt her, pleading that he hadn't done anything wrong, that he wouldn't do it again. Sweet Christ, he would never do anything wrong again.

Pinch-Faced Man let go. Kate opened her eyes, saw two enormous steel-capped work boots in front of her, the dusty leather worn and nicked. She sat up, looked at Sean. He'd stopped speaking, knelt on the ground, weeping. Bald Man stood next to him, hands by his sides, relaxed.

She reached out for him, felt a burst of pain as Pinch-Faced Man kicked her arm away.

Bald Man shot Sean in one kneecap. Sean screamed, a high

pitched animal sound that reminded Kate of the time she'd ran over one of the dogs with her father's tractor.

She sat very still. The echo of the shot in her ears vied with the sound of her lover's pain. Bald Man stepped forward, put his boot against her temple, pushed her cheek-first onto the concrete.

'You tell that old queer his son's a fuckup,' he said, not taking his boot away. 'Tell him, it ever happens again, it'll be him lying on the ground with a shattered kneecap, or worse.'

Bald Man took his boot away. Kate didn't dare move, just lay there, stones and grit biting into the side of her face, listened to the two men get into the car and drive away.

Sean eventually stopped screaming, the pain and blood loss lulled him into a state of semi-consciousness. She dragged him under what was left of the service station's awning, covered him with an old blanket from the boot of their car and started to walk the way they'd come.

She eventually hit the highway, walked another hour until a set of headlights appeared in the distance. Kate stuck her thumb out. A light blue seventies-era VW Combi Van, the side speckled with rust, slowed, stopped. The driver, a young man in his twenties, agreed to help her. Sean was nearly dead by the time they got to him. He lived but lost the leg.

Sean didn't talk much about what had happened that night. She pieced it together from scraps of conversation. He'd gotten greedy, stiffed someone for money they were owed, something like that.

They moved to Brisbane, he started using heavily. She wasn't sure whether it was a response to losing the leg, the humiliation or the guilt at nearly getting both of them killed. When she found his bluish-tinged body on the floor of their bathroom, she was relieved. The police ruled it an overdose.

Sean's father, Dennis, came down for the funeral. He asked if she wanted to move into their place in Surfers Paradise, just until she got her life sorted out. She started an arts degree at university, got bored, dropped out, tended bar at some of Curry's side games, eventually went back to work at the strip club.

She was working a slow night, got talking to one of her co-workers, just back from a stint in Gladstone. The coworker said a group of local kids had discovered the bodies of two men in a gutted vehicle in the clearing of a cypress forest on the outskirts of town. The joke doing the rounds was they must have got caught in a lightning storm.

She knew enough about Curry's past not to mention the deaths. Truth was, if it was him who'd had them killed, she was grateful.

So, when Curry mentioned a Filipino high roller stopping off in Surfers Paradise, asked if she'd like to keep him company while he was in town, she said yes.

Six

The second-hand car dealer reminded Kate of Curry, the way he called her 'love,' his rough, old-school charm. As expected, he jumped at the opportunity to swap the ute she'd eyed the previous day for her almost-new vehicle, no questions asked.

The transaction completed, Kate went back to the motel, dressed her semi-conscious traveling companion in the clothes she'd bought for him, blue jeans and black windcheater, white sneakers. She helped him into the car, gave him a small shot of heroin.

She bagged the drug detritus, other rubbish that lay around their hotel room, threw it into a dumpster at the rear of the motel, added the framed photograph of Sean and Dennis Curry.

She'd always relied on people to do the right thing without knowing the whole picture. It was time she woke up. She no longer owed the father or his son anything.

Kate drove for eleven hours, stopped only to get petrol and give Chance more heroin. She grabbed whatever food was on sale at service station counters, ate behind the steering wheel or stood outside in the dust and glare, watched the passing traffic.

The forests of northern New South Wales slowly transformed into rolling paddocks dotted with clumps of gum trees, the occasional barn or homestead. The terrain became drier, more monochromatic, washed out browns and yellows, the closer they got to Canberra. Fast moving clouds cast the landscape in alternating pools of light and shadow, the postcard scenery broken only by road kill, bloated bodies of kangaroos and wombats, more frequent the closer they got to the capital.

She interrupted her three-disc play list to catch a mid-day news bulletin. The police had found Curry's body. She listened to the report, more concerned there was no mention of Mal Kerrigan's whereabouts than about Curry's death. Kate was no fool, she knew about Mal's past, the things he'd done. But that was a long time ago. Unlike Curry, he was well out of the life, a harmless old man who had treated her well.

She put the music back on. At one point, a police car passed in the opposite direction. She gripped the steering wheel, kept her eyes front, turned up the music, Gran Parsons singing Las Vegas.

'Better get used to feeling paranoid, Kate,' she said to herself.

Just after nine, the ute's headlights briefly illuminated a sign, 'Yass 50 km.' As if on cue, Chance stirred. He opened his eyes, sat up in his seat, yawned, and scratched the dark stubble around his jaw.

'We there yet?'

'Not long now.'

He groaned, rubbed his forehead. 'Anything to drink?'

Without taking her eyes off the road she passed a half full bottle of water.

'What did you give me?' He raised the bottle to his lips, gulped the liquid down.

'Heroin.'

'My mother told me to stay away from hard drugs, said they were no good.'

'Your mother obviously never used H. All that stuff about one shot and your hooked is a load of crap. You've got to be pretty determined for that to happen.'

'You obviously knew what you were doing. Apart from a bit

of a hangover, I feel okay.'

Chance smoked in silence until they hit the outskirts of Yass. Halfway down the largely empty main street he told her to take a right turn and stop outside a Chinese takeaway.

She peered across him at the shop front. The words 'Jade Dragon Restaurant' were written in large, orientalised green letters on the front window, the dimly lit interior visible behind them.

She looked at him questioningly. He pretended not to notice. 'Just go inside, get a table. I'll join you after I finish my cigarette.'

A bell tinkled as she pushed open the door and stepped inside. The decor was basic, tables covered in white tablecloths, white plaster walls. The lights were filtered through Chinese lanterns hanging from the ceiling. Classical Chinese music, plucked string instruments, played in the background. She was the only customer.

As she hesitated in the doorway an elderly Chinese man emerged from the kitchen, stepped out from behind the counter. 'Come in, come in,' he said, and gestured toward the empty tables. 'You want to eat, yes?'

Kate took a seat as the old man placed a laminated menu in front of her, hovered like a large skinny bird.

'What would you recommend?'

'All is good, best Chinese food in Yass.' He beamed at her expectantly.

The bell tinkled, Kate looked up, saw Chance in the doorway.

'Try the Chinese money bags, Kate, they're particularly good.'

At the sound of Chance's voice the old man wheeled around. The village idiot routine drained from his face like dirty water down a plughole.

Chance winced slightly as he sat at the table next to her, his pain returning as the heroin wore off.

The old man inclined his head toward the kitchen, yelled in

Chinese. A young woman materialised in the doorway, her face alert to the tension in the room.

If Kate had to guess, she would put the young woman in her late teens. But despite the knee-length hemline on her school dress, the simple bob hairstyle, she projected an air of worldliness.

The young woman's look transformed from concern to anger as she registered Chance's presence. 'Do you know how much danger you have put us in by coming here?'

Chance said nothing, pretended to study a menu.

The young woman went to the front door, turned the sign hanging on a chain from 'open' to 'closed.' She approached their table, a determined look on her young face, stood next to the old man.

'You need to leave now,' she said.

Kate looked expectantly between their two hosts. 'Does this mean we're going to have to get takeaway?'

'I should have warned you, Kate,' said Chance, his eyes still on the menu. 'The old man hardly speaks English and his daughter has no sense of humour.'

'Are you deaf, Mister Chance?' the young woman said. 'You need to leave now.'

Chance breathed out slowly, put the menu down and looked around the room. 'I see you've redecorated since the last time I was here.'

'Competition from the Vietnamese restaurant around the corner,' the young woman replied. 'My father thought it would bring in customers if we had a more modern look.'

The old man said something in Chinese. The girl hesitated before translating. The old man spoke again. She interrupted and the two engaged in a rapid-fire exchange in Chinese. She turned to Chance and translated only after her father overruled her with a wave of his bony hand.

'My father says to follow him.'

The old man led them through the kitchen, down a corridor

lined with shelves heaving with cans of cooking oil and sacks of rice, into a small backyard surrounded by a high wooden fence. Kate saw an old-fashioned out-house, piles of oil tins and plastic containers stacked against one side. On the far side of the yard was the rear of a red brick house.

The old man strode purposefully across the yard, opened a screen door. He motioned them into a lounge room, went in after them, sat in a recliner chair, took a cigarette from a pack on a side table next to his chair, lit up, and looked to the ceiling. Kate presumed he was waiting for his translator to join them. A large white cat appeared from behind the recliner, jumped onto the old man's lap. The old man stroked under the cat's chin as he smoked.

Kate joined Chance on a brown corduroy couch facing the old man, surveyed the room. Threadbare carpet, mismatched pieces of furniture, wallpaper with a faded bamboo pattern. Stacks of yellowing Chinese language newspapers on the floor.

'Who are these people?' Kate whispered to Chance as she brushed what looked like white cat hairs from her black jeans.

'My employers.'

'What do you mean?'

'They recruited me for the job Curry was planning.'

'For the representatives of a criminal organisation, they live in a fucking dump.'

'Looks can be deceiving,' said Chance, using his normal voice. 'And you don't have to whisper. I've told you, our host doesn't speak English.'

'And that little attack dog is his daughter?' said Kate, still whispering.

'Dao Ming, she's something, isn't she? Her name means 'shining path' in Mandarin. If ever there was a more misnamed child...Have you got the rolling tobacco on you?'

Kate fished the tobacco from the pocket of her denim jacket. She looked at Long in his recliner, saw another corrupt old man, was seized by a feeling of revulsion, scratched the nape of her neck, as if trying to tear the sensation away.

Dao Ming entered the room, stood at her father's side, one hand protectively on his shoulder. 'The police are looking everywhere for you. What if they trace you to here?'

'Where else was I supposed to go?'

The old man's eyes narrowed as the girl translated.

'My father says that is not our problem.'

'Not your problem?' Chance nodded slowly to himself as he lit his cigarette, the smoke wafting from his mouth and nostrils. 'Let me tell you something, it is very much your problem. I'm a fugitive now. If you don't help me, I'll get caught. If I get caught, I'll spill about everything, including how I got this job, you, your father, his whole shitty criminal empire.'

The old man looked at Chance as Dao Ming translated, his face betraying no emotion. When she finished he spoke softly.

'My father wants to know, did you really kill those two Filipino men and Curry, like the police said?'

'No. It was a man called Frank Dormer and a woman called Sophia Lekakis.'

'My father doesn't know them.'

Chance reached across, mashed out his rollie in a large ceramic ashtray with flowers painted on it. 'Curry sourced them from his end of the operation.'

'What went wrong?'

'They got greedy, decided they wanted all the money. They killed Gao, his bodyguard, Curry as well. Framed me for the murders.'

'How does my father know you are telling the truth?'

'How do I know your father didn't double-cross me?' spat Chance.

Dao Ming looked genuinely shocked. 'My father would never do such a thing,' she said, without bothering to translate for her father what Chance had said. 'My father and Mister Curry were business associates for a long time, he—'

'Spare me the family history lesson,' said Chance, pulling at the stump of his missing finger. 'Let's just say I believe you because this fuckup has cost your father money. And if there is one thing I know your father hates, it's losing money.'

A faint smile flickered across Long's face as his daughter translated. Father and daughter conversed for a few more moments. The young woman turned and looked at Chance, a steely expression on her young face.

'Who is this woman?'

Chance hesitated before answering. 'Her name is Amber. She helped me.'

'The police say she was the woman with Gao.' Dao Ming indicated to Kate with a nod of her head as she spoke, but otherwise ignored her.

'Yes,'

'Can you trust her?'

Kate felt her face flush with anger, moved to the edge of the couch. 'Hey,' she said to Dao Ming. 'I'm not with anyone, and I don't appreciate being spoken about as if I'm not here.'

'If it wasn't for her, the police would already have me,' said Chance. 'Right now I trust her more than I trust you.'

'Hey, did you hear me?' Kate stood up, took a step toward Dao Ming. 'I said I don't like being talked about as if I'm not here. Keep doing it and you'll be in line for a slap across the chops.'

Dao Ming flinched but did not back away. Kate felt a hand on her shoulder, looked around, saw Chance standing next to her. 'Kate, come on, she didn't mean anything by it, relax.'

'I've just driven for eleven hours to get to this dump and what do I get when I arrive, the fucking third degree.'

'Kate, sit down.'

'Seriously, who does this whiney little bitch think she is?'

Chance's hand tightened on Kate's shoulder. 'Shut up and sit down.' He pronounced each word louder than the last.

Kate sat back on the couch, folded her arms across her chest and glared at Dao Ming. Chance sat next to her, grunted. Kate looked around, saw him clutch his side with one hand.

'What is the matter with him?' Dao Ming noticed the look on Chance's face.

'Cracked ribs, maybe broken, a gunshot wound. He needs medical attention.'

The old man barked something at his daughter.

Dao Ming produced an iPhone from the pocket of her school uniform, keyed a number, put it to her ear, turned her back on them and moved to the corner of the lounge room. After a brief, inaudible conversation, she faced them.

'That was someone who will come and tend to your injuries. Now we need to get you accommodation,' she said as she scrolled through the contacts on her phone. 'You cannot stay here.'

Kate looked at the young woman as she spoke into the iPhone, hard guttural sounds. Dao Ming met her gaze as she talked. What did Kate see in her eyes—fear, greed, ambition, or a mixture of all three? She realised this schoolgirl was not just her father's translator. She was his protégé.

Seven

Chance lay on the single bed, naked except for his underpants, rubbed the sleep from his eyes. Weak light seeped through the thin fabric over the window. He registered the room's minimal furnishings, lightbulb on a cord from the ceiling, cheap-looking pine wardrobe, open to reveal a line of wire hangers, a plastic accordion door to the living area and the other bedroom.

He propped himself up on an elbow, inspected the fresh bandage on his shoulder. There was no longer any pain around his rib cage when he moved.

Chance wheeled his legs over the side of the bed, sat on the edge, the soles of his feet resting on the cheap polyester carpet. He heard music from the next room, thought he must be imagining it, recognised the hoots and applause as Johnny Cash serenaded Folsom Prison.

He fished out a pair of shorts and a grey T-shirt from the clothes scattered on the floor, put the shirt on over his head as he slid the accordion door open. Kate sat on a faded floral-patterned couch next to the kitchenette, read from a thick paperback. At the foot of the couch sat a portable CD player and a stack of disks.

Chance felt a swirl in his chest, couldn't put a name to the sensation. He concentrated, identified a trace of desire. Another sign he was better.

'Where'd the CD player come from?'

She looked at him sheepishly.

'I went into town and got it while you were asleep this morning.'

Chance made a tutting noise.

'I know, I know, we're not supposed to leave here, but I missed music. I swear, I just went in to buy the CD player, a few discs, came straight back.'

Chance pushed open the front screen door, stepped into late afternoon sun. He heard shouting, the clink of metal being driven into the ground in the paddock opposite.

A travelling circus had appeared the previous day, started setting up camp. Chance had been awakened by the noise, found Kate and a collection of the caravan park's residents watching the new arrivals. The circus folk had made a lot of progress since then, the twin spires of a large red tent visible above a line of caravans and vehicles.

He sat in an old deck chair by the door to their cabin, tried to figure out what day it was, decided it must be Friday, nearly two weeks since they'd arrived in Yass.

They'd left Long's house, driven through the darkness to a caravan park on the outskirts of town. They were met at the entrance by a skinny red-haired youth who guided them to one of a row of timber cabins at the rear.

A dishevelled middle-aged woman arrived early the next morning toting a large leather medical bag. She reeked of nicotine and an odour that reminded Chance of wet dogs. Her thick glasses were held together with duct tape.

'Are you a doctor?' he heard Kate ask as the woman poked and prodded him.

'Close enough,' she'd replied out of the corner of her mouth.

'What do you mean, 'close enough?'' said Chance.

'I'm a vet.'

'You telling me the best Long could do is a bloody veterinarian?' said Chance.

'Man or beast, we're all God's creatures,' she replied absentmindedly. 'You've cracked a couple of ribs and that shoulder wound will need stitches.

She gave him a local anaesthetic, stitched up his arm. A smouldering fag dangled from her lip as she worked.

She left Kate with a supply of dressings, antiseptic, syringes for the heroin, which she told her to keep administering in small quantities until it ran out. They never saw her again.

What had started out as an enforced living arrangement gradually morphed into a comfortable co-existence. Chance spent most of the first week sleeping or dozing under the effects of the heroin. When he felt well enough, he canvassed the surroundings. The caravan park was bordered on three sides by dry-looking paddock. The rear, behind their cabin, backed onto a patch of forest.

While he'd been recovering, Kate slept and read paperbacks sourced from another of Long's cut-price minions, a teenage Emo girl who delivered leftover Chinese food and other supplies every second day. They didn't have much to do with the park's other inhabitants, mainly grey nomads and a few long-stay residents. The exception was the red-haired youth, Fergus, their guide on the first night, who managed the park. Sometimes Kate visited his office, a portable cabin near the entrance, to partake in a joint from his abundant stash.

After dinner Kate and Chance watched TV, went for walks around the park, or sat in front of the cabin, enjoyed the late summer evenings, the balmy air, alive with insects. One night, they broke Dao Ming's strict instructions, drove an hour to Canberra, Australia's 'Bush Capital,' ate overpriced restaurant food and drank beer in a student bar that smelled like a toilet.

Neither of them had talked much about what had happened in Surfers, what would happen next, but a vague awareness that their time here was coming to an end had taken root in his mind the previous night. They'd been watching TV after dinner when a segment came on recapping the events in Surfers Paradise. Stock footage of the officious female cop in charge of the investigation, Gao's hotel, a cop lifting blue- and white-chequered crime scene tape to allow a body to be wheeled out on a gurney from Curry's house. It cut to a female reporter talking to the camera about the lack of progress, pressure on the Surfers Paradise police to come up with answers, questions of their competence, thinly veiled innuendo about their possible involvement.

He and Kate watched in silence, unsure of what to say. He'd gone to bed half expecting the police to come crashing through the door at any moment, weapons drawn, slam him to the floor while they cuffed him.

Chance watched a flock of white cockatoos explode from a nearby gum, screech across the sky.

The lack of progress in the investigation made no sense. The female cop in charge of the case was no mug, he could tell that much from the footage of her press conference. The police would almost certainly have the gun, his prints all over it. From there, it should not have taken much to crack his false identity. His face should be all over the media, but there was nothing.

He was roused from these thoughts by the creak of the front screen door. He saw the curve of Kate's outline against the sun.

'Hey,' she said.

'Hey yourself.'

'How are you feeling?' She passed him a mug, steam rising from it, perched herself on the front step.

'Better each day.'

Chance lit a rollie, dropped the match into the tin can they used as an ashtray, offered the tobacco pouch to Kate.

'Who would have thought we'd have a circus on our doorstep,' she said as she took the pack.

Chance sipped the coffee, dragged on his cigarette to remove the bitter taste. They only had instant, which Kate always made too strong for his liking.

She looked up from rolling her cigarette. 'How's the coffee?'

'Is that what you call it?' Chance made an exaggerated grimace. 'For a second I thought I was back in Afghanistan, captured by the Taliban, and they were forcing me to drink this as some sort of torture.'

'Very funny.' Kate lit the smoke. 'So, you're not going to report me to Dao Ming for heading into town to get the CD player?'

'No.'

'Thanks, she scares me.'

'She's a piece of work, that's for sure.'

Kate picked a strand of tobacco off her lip. 'How'd you hook up with her and her old man, anyway?'

'By accident, like most things in my life.'

Chance spared her the details, another job that had gone sour, bullshit over money and personalities.

'How much longer do you figure we'll be able to stay here?' Kate looked away as she spoke, tried to feign disinterest. Chance felt apprehension nibble at the edge of her voice.

'The police, Gao's people, they'll be looking for us. We'll need to move soon.'

'Will Long help us? Can you trust him?'

'He'll help as long as it suits him, which it does at the moment because he knows if we get caught, we'll lead the police to him. But there's a limit to his generosity.'

'What are you going to do when you leave? I mean, don't get me wrong, I'm not trying to ride on your coattails,' she added when he didn't answer immediately. 'I'm just being nosy.'

'I don't know yet.'

'Strange, I thought someone in your line of business would always have a contingency plan in place for when things go wrong.'

'My line of business?'

'Come on, you know what I mean.'

'You're wrong about me, I'm not the world's biggest planner.' Chance pulled at the stub of the missing finger.

'Does that make you angry?'

'You going to psychoanalyse me now?'

'I don't have to. Playing with your missing finger, I've figured out it's your tell, what you do when you're angry.'

'Do I? I never thought about it like that.' Chance looked at
the missing digit. 'Maybe I'll try my luck in the opal fields to the
northwest. Supposed to be the real outback. You?'

'I've always wanted to spend more time in Asia. Maybe I'll
take that fake ID your mate Long is fixing for me, head to
Korea or Japan. I've heard there's good money working as a
hostess.'

They were both silent, aware the conversation was edging
them into unfamiliar territory.

'Listen to me. I've slept with men for money, lived with a
drug dealer, then a couple of retired gangsters. Now I'm looking
at a lifetime of running because of what happened a couple of
weeks ago. Do you honestly think I give a shit what's happened
in your past?'

'I suppose not,' said Chance.

A lot of people spent their lives navigating the line between
right and wrong, the life they lived and the life they wanted to
live. Chance just accepted things, seldom questioned where they
led him. This life, being paid to steal, sometimes to drive people
who stole, it was just something he'd drifted into, like joining
the army. His whole life had been a series of decisions made
without regard for what came next and where it landed him.

Chance had left the army after Afghanistan, drifted. There
was nothing fucked up or post-traumatic about it. His old life
was just a skin he'd shed. When he tried to put it back on after
returning, it wouldn't fit.

'I tried to go back to the way things were after the army, but
they just didn't work out,' said Chance slowly. 'I was working
in a nightclub when I made a decision to get involved in something, a robbery. It ended very badly.' Chance held the stump of
the missing finger up for effect.

Her eyes on his, she reached out, wrapped her big fingers

around it. Chance was taken aback by the gesture.

'Tell me the story,' she said.

'I busted a guy called Noonan for selling speed to a couple of underage girls in a club I was bouncing. I was about to throw him out when he started going on about a sweet little score he was hatching to knock over an ecstacy lab that was cooking a batch to sell at a dance party in the city the coming weekend.

'I needed the money, a circuit breaker to get me out of Melbourne and started somewhere else. Noonan needed backup. 'A piece of piss,' he told me. 'Just stand there and look scary; I'll do the rest."

Eight

Chance and Noonan entered the drug lab through the back. The two cooks inside made no effort to resist, just looked up from their chemistry equipment and smiled.

'Old man Aydin is going to be mighty pissed at you two,' the taller of them said.

Chance recognised the name from stories in the city's tabloid newspaper. Aydin, Turkish for 'enlightened,' not a term anyone would have ever used to describe one of Melbourne's most feared drug dealers and his extended family of pit-bull sons.

Chance shot Noonan a *what the fuck* look.

'Don't tell me you two brain surgeons don't even know whose lab you're ripping off?' the tall one added with a laugh, at which point Noonan shot him twice in the chest. He would have shot the other man had Chance not restrained him.

After that their only option was to grab the drugs and get as far away as possible.

Noonan had been driving. He'd taken one hand off the steering wheel to reach for the mobile phone, ringing in his jeans pocket, took his eyes off the road just as they were about to take a corner, lost control, and their car swerved and shot over the side into a ravine.

When Chance opened his eyes the world was upside down

and Noonan headfirst through the windscreen. He felt like he was floating but there was no water, only a blast of cold wind from the hole in the windscreen.

Chance released his seat belt, opened the passenger's door and crawled into the freezing embrace of the snow. He pulled Noonan's body from the overturned vehicle, laid it on the snow, grimaced as he felt for a pulse and found nothing.

He stood and took in his surroundings. At least half an hour had elapsed since they passed the last green pre-fab buildings in Marysville, erected to replace those devastated by the bush fire that had ripped through the town several years earlier. A blanket of snow covered the slope on either side. Blackened tree trunks protruded like gnarled hands trying to claw their way out from underneath.

It would be dark soon. He was dressed in jeans, sneakers, and a hoodie. Good clothes for knocking off an ecstasy lab, not for spending a night in freezing weather. The deceptively deep snow had already soaked through his sneakers. Chance felt a slight numbness he knew would eventually lead to hypothermia.

He removed Noonan's boots. Size ten, at a guess, one size smaller than Chance wore, but they'd do.

'Sorry, mate, I need these more than you,' he said as he unthreaded the laces. He eased the polar fleece jacket from the corpse, wiping it against the snow to remove the worst of the blood, found a thick roll of money in one of the pockets. Noonan must have swiped it during the robbery when Chance wasn't looking. The drugs had been in the back seat of the car. He went back to look for them, saw the plastic bag had come undone, tiny multi coloured pellets spread all over the inside roof of the upturned car.

It was almost dark by the time Chance reached the road. He walked down the middle of the two lanes, unsure which direction he was headed, hoping to Christ to see headlights in the distance.

The cold was becoming unbearable, and Chance was on the

verge of surrendering to the urge to lie down, give up, when out of the corner of his eye he caught a pinprick of yellow several hundred metres to his right. He ran toward it, almost colliding with an iron gate. It was padlocked. He clambered over it and walked briskly down a track recently cleared of snow.

The house was old, a bushfire survivor. Soft light glowed in the windows, smoke curled from the chimney. Chance crouched next to a woodpile and scoped the area. There was no sign of any dog and the carport was empty. He fingered the 9mm Beretta in his belt, thought better of it. He put the gun under the domed lid of a nearby barbecue half submerged in snow, stepped onto the porch and knocked.

He was about to knock again, when the door swung open to reveal a woman. She gazed at him impassively.

'Please, I don't mean you any harm,' Chance stammered. 'I've been in an accident. I just need something to eat and a place to stay tonight. I promise I won't be any trouble and I'll be gone in the morning,' he continued in the face of her silence. 'I have money.' He fumbled for the cash. 'I can pay you.'

She stepped aside, nodded to him to enter. Chance walked past her to the far end of the room where a large open fire crackled. He sank to his knees in front of it and stretched his hands toward the flames until the heat started to hurt.

He showered and changed into fresh clothes the woman had placed on the bathroom floor for him, grey tracksuit pants and a faded Harley Davidson T-shirt.

Chance stood in the kitchen doorway, drying his short black hair with a towel slung around his neck, and watched the woman stir something on the stove, her back to him. She was as tall as Chance, with a slim, almost boyish figure under her tight blue jeans and black turtleneck sweater.

'Thanks.' Chance kept rubbing his hair with the towel.
'For what?'
'For letting me stay.'
'It is not a problem.'

Her accent sounded Eastern European, exactly where Chance couldn't tell and didn't suppose it mattered.

Chance leaned against a bench, looked sideways at her. The woman had a narrow face and large brown eyes accentuated by the whiteness of her skin. She had a crooked mouth that sat in a slight pout when closed. Her shoulder-length, jet-black hair was unkempt, the fringe falling over her eyebrows. There was a small tattoo of a black star on her neck.

'If you're not going to tell me where you're from, at least tell me your name,'

'Irina.'

'Irina, I'm Gary. Do you live here by yourself?'

'No.' Her attention remained focused on a saucepan of food on the stove. 'With my husband, Rocky.'

Chance hadn't noticed any sign of a male presence in the bathroom or the rest of the house. Come to think of it, the place was empty of the usual tell-tale signs of co-habitation; no photos on the wall, none of the shit couples amassed in the course of their lives. It suddenly occurred to him he'd seen no telephone or computer, either.

'Where's your husband?'

'Rocky works as a security guard in the city during the week, comes home on weekends.'

'You must get lonely during the week,' said Chance.

She shrugged, her gaze fixed on the pot on the stove.

'Do you have friends, people who visit?'

'Rocky doesn't like visitors.'

'People you go and see?'

'Rocky doesn't like me leaving the house.'

'I see. What else doesn't Rocky like?'

'People who ask too many questions.' She inclined her head in his direction and gave him a thin smile to take the edge of her statement. 'Now go and sit in front of the fire. The food will be ready soon.'

* * *

They ate in silence. After she'd cleared the dishes, she led him to a single mattress in an empty room at the back of the house. He fell asleep as soon as his head touched the pillow.

Chance was awakened by a hard poke in his side. Irina stood in the corner, a pink terry cloth dressing gown wrapped around her, a look of panic on her face. A narrow-faced slim woman in a tight blue uniform stood above him, nudged his stomach with her booted foot.

Chance saw the small truncheon she held in one hand. With a fluid movement she raised it and brought it down, sent him crashing back into darkness.

He came to facedown on cold, hard tiles. The bathroom. His head throbbed. He attempted to get up but one of his ankles was cuffed to the metal pipe connected to the old-fashioned cistern.

The slim woman sat on the edge of the bath, smoking. Irina sat at her feet, a purple bruise on the right side of her face, a dark ring around one of her eyes.

The woman dropped what was left of the cigarette on the floor and ground it under her boot as she looked at Chance.

'Where'd you put the ecstacy?'

The woman's gaze remained fixed on Chance as she produced an asthma inhaler and sucked deeply.

'What ecstacy?'

'Don't bullshit me.' She ran a hand across her short brown hair. 'I hate people lying to me. Makes me very cranky. Irina tells me you turned up covered in blood, said something about being in an accident. Meanwhile, I hear on my scanner the cops found a wrecked car several kilometres down the road from here. Said vehicle matches the description of one last seen leaving the scene of a drug heist in the outer eastern suburbs of Melbourne yesterday afternoon. Two people were seen driving away in the car, but the cops only found one body.'

'Honestly, I don't know what you're talking about,' said Chance.

'Okay, okay, have it your way.' She shook her head, stood up and left the room.

'What the fuck is happening?' whispered Chance.

'Rocky came home early in the morning, saying something about having a fight with the people she usually stays with in Melbourne,' Irina said moving closer to him.

'That's Rocky? How the fuck did you get mixed up with her?'

'I am illegal in your country. Rocky says she will report me to immigration if I try and escape. I am a prisoner in this house.'

'I don't have the drugs. It's the truth, I left them back at the car.'

Irina shook her head. 'It doesn't matter, she will kill you anyway.'

Chance thought for a moment. 'My gun. It's underneath the barbecue out front. You have to go and get it.'

Before she could answer, Rocky returned, carrying a heavy gunmetal toolbox, and placed it on the floor in front of Chance. She clattered around in the box for a moment, held up a large pair of wire cutters for him to see. Then, with surprising strength, she grabbed Chance's hand, splayed his fingers out and rested a little finger between the cutter's blades.

'This is how it's going to work. I'll ask you nicely once more, and if you don't answer, I'll cut this little finger off. Then I'll start on the others, working all the way down to your dick, comprehendo?'

Irina spoke rapidly, English interspersed with a language Chance couldn't understand. 'Rochelle, dorogay—darling, please he never did anything, I swear it.'

'Shut up with the mongrel yapping of yours, woman,' Rocky responded, still holding Chance's finger in the cutters. 'Go and get something to clean the bathroom. This is going to get messy. Okay, hot shot.' Rocky looked at Chance, the cutters poised. 'Where are the drugs?'

'Rocky, please, come on, mate, there's no need for this. Surely we can negotiate something—'

Chance screamed, nearly passing out as he watched his blood gush from the severed joint of his little finger.

Rocky took a hit on her inhaler.

'I'm afraid the time for negotiating is over, sunshine,' she said, moving the blades to the next finger.

Irina reappeared behind Rocky, raised the Beretta in both hands and aimed it at the back of Rocky's head.

Rocky turned around and said something but the words were drowned out by the gunshot. Irina kept firing, Rocky's body jumping at the impact. The smoke burned Chance's nostrils.

Glassy eyed, she swivelled slightly and aimed the gun at Chance.

'Irina, what are you doing?' Chance could hear the panic in his voice.

She squeezed the trigger. Chance raised his arms in a futile gesture to shield his face, but the hammer clicked on an empty chamber. Chance heard the hollow metallic click several times until Irina slowly lowered the pistol and dropped it on the floor.

She bent down, took a key from Rocky's trouser pocket, and unlocked the handcuff on Chance's ankle.

'There's bandages in the cabinet,' said Irina, looking almost absentmindedly around the blood-spattered bathroom. 'I have to clean up this mess.'

She was dousing the kitchen with petrol from a can when Chance emerged from the bathroom, his hand wrapped in bandages. He'd also swallowed several prescription painkillers he'd found in a bottle.

He'd just finished dressing when he heard the sound of a revving engine. Irina sat in the front seat of a large four-wheel-drive ute, still in her pink dressing gown, eyes straight ahead. Chance climbed in next to her. She took off without a word, the first tongues of flame rising from the house, visible in the rearview mirror.

Nine

Chance was almost asleep when he heard noise outside his window. He rolled out of bed, reached for his jeans and T-shirt. He slid his feet into his runners, didn't bother with the laces, went to the kitchen, retrieved the shotgun from the cupboard above the sink. He cracked the breach, checked it was loaded, slowly snapped it shut.

A single cotton sheet covered Kate's sleeping body. Her chest rose and fell in time with her breath. Chance set the shotgun on the floor next to her, leaned in close, put a hand over her mouth.

She woke with a start, eyes wide in the darkness. He held her down, hot breath on the palm of his hand.

'Shush, it's only me.'

She recognised him, relaxed. He took his hand away.

'Listen to me very carefully. Someone's moving around outside the cabin. It might be one of the residents, but I don't think so. Get out of bed, put your clothes on, the rest in a bag along with whatever money is left. Stay here. Do not come out of the room until I say. Understood?'

She gave him a precise nod.

Chance went back into his room, tore away the thin material covering his window, removed the screen, and climbed out. He crept around the side of the cabin, looked around the corner. A figure stood next to the chair he had been sitting in that afternoon.

Chance peered hard into the darkness around the cabin, expected to see other shapes moving about, saw no one. The police or Gao's people would have come in greater numbers. Chance stepped out, the shotgun held waist level. 'Put your hands above your head, lace your fingers together, don't move.'

The man did as he was told. He was tall, his face hidden in the shadow cast by a hat on his head.

'Front door's open.' Chance gestured at the front screen door with his weapon. 'Go inside, stand in the middle of the room. Don't try anything. I'll be right behind you.'

Chance stood in the doorway. He held the gun in one hand, felt for the light switch on the wall with the other. The exposed fluorescent tube flickered, came to life.

Chance tightened his grip on the shotgun, tried not to show his surprise. 'What happened? You get lost?'

'I could say the same about you, son,' Tavener replied in a relaxed drawl.

'You can come out, Kate,' said Chance. 'Or maybe I should say Amber.'

The plastic accordion door to Kate's bedroom slid open and she stepped out, dressed in the clothes she'd had on earlier, leaned against the door frame.

'Evening, miss,' Tavener said without looking around.

Kate walked across the room, stood next to Chance. Her mouth formed into a silent 'O' as she recognised the man in front of them, his hands still laced on his head. Tavener wore a grubby white polo shirt under a sleeveless vest jacket, baggy khaki pants, a beige canvas fishing cap on his head.

'I hate to disappoint you, but if you've come for the drugs or the money, we don't have either,' said Chance.

'I know, son.'

'You know? Is this some sort of game?'

Tavener unlaced his fingers, raised his hands above his head. 'Okay if I put my hands down?'

Chance kept the shotgun levelled on Tavener's midsection, nodded.

Tavener rubbed his wrists as he spoke. 'Listen to me, this is a real nice little get together, but unless you want to continue our discussion in police custody, I'd suggest we get moving.'

Chance and Kate exchanged glances.

'I can understand you have a lot of questions.' Irritation crept into the American's voice. 'You're thinking, what's he want, who's he working for, is it a trap, that kind of thing. If I wanted you both dead, you'd be dead. Believe me. Ain't working for Gao's old man or your former partners, either.'

'How do we know you're telling the truth?' said Kate.

'You're just going to have to trust me.'

'Trust's one thing I'm running pretty low on at the moment.'

'Be that as it may, for now it'll have to do.'

'We've got this far,' said Chance. 'Why shouldn't we just kill you now and keep going?'

'You haven't done too bad a job hiding your tracks, but the police have found you. You wouldn't get more than a few kilometres before you got caught.'

'What are you proposing?'

'I've got a car waiting on a track on the other side of the forest. Let's take a drive, visit the Asian fella who's helping you out, see if we can't discuss ourselves all a new arrangement.'

'How long until the police arrive?

Tavener smiled as all three of them heard the noise, the slow crunch of car tires on gravel, far away, but getting closer.

'About sixty seconds.'

Chance tried to read Tavener's face, got nothing.

'Okay, but remember, I've got the shotgun.'

'That antique? You'll be doing well if you don't trip and blow your head off.' Tavener unzipped the nylon money pouch strapped around his waist, took out a blunt-looking black pistol with a square barrel. 'This place got a rear exit?'

The sound of cars grew louder.

Chance bundled the two of them ahead of him into his bedroom, pointed at the open window. Kate was first out, followed by Chance. Tavener landed on the grass next to them, headed for the cyclone wire separating the caravan park from the forest, waved at them to follow.

When Tavener reached the fence, he turned, ran alongside it for a hundred metres, stopped. A square hole had been cut in the wire, big enough for an adult to climb through.

Chance heard a vehicle come to a stop, car doors slam, people move about inside the cabin, swearing. Tavener stood next to the hole, his pistol aimed in the direction of the noise, as Chance and Kate climbed through.

Almost immediately they were engulfed in thick under-growth. They waited for Tavener, followed him as he ducked and weaved around the crooked trees.

Chance heard a grunt behind him, turned, saw Kate had fallen. He doubled back, reached out. Her strong fingers en-twined in his and he pulled her up. They stood still for a mo-ment, faces inches away from each other, as shafts of torchlight appeared in the forest behind them. Chance counted three, maybe four.

He ran, pulled Kate after him. He tried to locate Tavener in the shadows as they moved. They reached an incline that started gentle, became steep. They paused halfway up, panting for breath. Chance swivelled his head from side to side, still no sign of Tavener. Torch beams probed the forest at the base of the incline. Above them a line of trees was silhouetted against the night sky.

Chance tried to steady himself on the angle, leaned against an overhanging branch. The dry wood snapped, broke off. Kate gripped his shoulder to stop him tumbling after it, the shotgun fell to the ground, went off. The boom reverberated through the trees like a canon.

'Over there,' yelled a male voice. More shouts. The torch beams changed direction, came toward them.

Chance and Kate raced the remaining distance up the hill, half ran, half stumbled down into a shallow valley, ignoring the branches that scraped and tore at their clothes and exposed skin. The torch beams kept up their pursuit.

'Where the hell is Tavener?' hissed Chance.

'Maybe it's a trap.'

Chance had been thinking the same thing. The lights reached the top of the valley, moved down, gaining on them.

Nearby lay the outline of the trunk of a large fallen tree. They wedged themselves under it. Kate nuzzled against his shoulder, her hair smelled of strawberries amid the dirt and moss. They watched two pairs of men's legs come into view and stop, followed by a slimmer pair in calf-high boots, a woman's.

'I swear they were over here,' said a rough-sounding male voice. The other man laughed.

'Shut up and just keep looking,' snapped the woman.

'It's not just Chance and the woman we've lost, where's Viljoen?' said the other man.

Chance and Kate lay completely still.

'Probably trying out some of those famous Boer tracking skills he's always boasting about,' replied the rough voice.

'Jesus Christ, will both of you just shut up. They've got to be close by.' The woman moved away from the log. The men followed.

Chance and Kate exhaled, waited for a few more minutes until they were sure it was safe to get up.

'Over here.' The heavily accented voice came from behind them. They turned, immediately found themselves looking into strong torchlight. 'Both of you, don't move—'

Chance heard a thud. The torchlight fell from their faces, rolled on the ground, illuminating a thin slither of forest floor.

Tavener appeared over the crumpled figure, bent over, grunted as he scooped up the unconscious form, threw him over his shoulder. 'This way,' he wheezed.

They climbed up the side of the valley, edged down sideways, crab-like. The incline straightened out several metres from the dirt track. Chance saw the outline of a vehicle, ran toward it. Tavener opened the boot, heaved the body over his shoulder into it. He leaned in, delivered two solid blows to make sure the man stayed unconscious, closed the boot.

Tavener pushed Chance and Kate into the car ahead of him, climbed into the driver's side, started the engine and released the brake. He slammed his foot on the accelerator and the car took off.

Ten

Chance turned the old-fashioned twist bell several times, heard a faint ringing on the other side. A soft light illuminated the pane of frosted glass, the door opened.

Dao Ming stood in the entrance in a blue dressing gown, regarded Chance and Kate with a mixture of anger and suspicion. She inclined her head to their car parked in the street in front of the house, where a man she didn't know was retrieving something from the boot.

'I need to talk to your father.' Chance pushed past the young woman, headed down the hallway.

'You were told not to come here under any circumstances,' she said after him.

The old man stood in the middle of the lounge room. He wore a chequered wool dressing gown over striped pyjamas, slippers. He reached into one of the pockets of the gown, produced a packet of cigarettes and a lighter.

'Sorry for the intrusion,' Chance said. 'Tell your father we need to renegotiate the terms of our agreement.'

The old man nodded as his daughter translated, said something back.

'He wants to know what you mean.'

Tavener entered the room, the unconscious man over his shoulder, poured him onto one of the armchairs.

'This is what I mean,' said Chance.

Dao Ming gasped at the sight of the wounded man. The hardness fled from her face, left it childlike and frightened. She put her hand over her mouth and reached for her father.

Chance studied the unconscious man. He was medium-sized, well built, not unlike himself, clad in hiking boots, jeans and blue T-shirt under a black zip-up jacket. Blood oozed from a gash on the side of his head, and there was a large purple bruise on his face where Tavener had punched him in the boot of the car.

'Any chance I could get a cup of Good Morning America?' Tavener looked around expectantly.

'Who are these men?' Dao Ming said in an effort to regain control of the proceedings.

'Guess not.' Tavener threw a set of car keys to Kate. 'Miss, if you'd be so kind as to move my car so it's off the street.'

Without waiting for a reply, he frisked the unconscious man. He pulled a phone from one of the man's pockets, removed the SIM card and threw the phone against the wall. It shattered and fell in pieces to the floor. Dao Ming jumped at the sound, tightened the grip on her father. Tavener twisted the man's body, removed a wallet from his back pocket. He withdrew a wad of money, slipped the notes into one of his own pockets.

Long lit a cigarette, nodded, as if he'd reached a decision, spoke softly to his daughter. She started to argue but the old man silenced her with a single word. 'It seems that things have indeed changed,' said Long in English.

Chance did a double take. 'I thought you didn't speak English.'

'I never said I couldn't speak your language. I just choose not to. This is a small town and I am a foreigner. It seemed easier if people thought I could not understand them.' He stroked Dao Ming's hair. 'This is not something my daughter needs to see. Dao Ming, go to the kitchen.'

'You can introduce me to your American friend later.' Long cocked an eyebrow at the unconscious man. 'For now, I'm more interested to know who he is.'

'Say hello to Matthias Viljoen, homicide detective with the Queensland police.' Tavener slid something out of one of the folds of the Viljoen's wallet, handed them to Chance. 'No prizes for guessing who he was looking for.'

The photograph must have been from his army file. Chance, ten years younger, the blank stare and crew cut. There was a second photograph, a barely recognisable security camera image of Kate.

Viljoen groaned, moved his head slightly.

'Shall we see what our police friend knows?' Tavener grabbed a white Chinese teapot from a side table, poured the contents on the unconscious man's face. 'Wakey, wakey, Matthias.'

Viljoen coughed, his eyelids fluttered, opened. He glanced around the unfamiliar surroundings, his eyes narrowing as he registered Chance's presence.

Tavener waved the man's police ID card in the air in front of his face. 'Bit out of your jurisdiction, aren't you, Matthias?'

'Fuck you,' spat Viljoen in a thick South African accent.

Tavener smiled, slapped him across the face. Viljoen flinched. Tavener slapped him again.

'I know you. You're the American Gao bought with him.'

Tavener nodded grimly, slapped the South African several more times. 'Why have you come all this way, why didn't you use the local boys?'

Viljoen's wiped wet tea leafs from his face, said nothing

Tavener pursed his lips, like he was dealing with a recalcitrant child. Without warning he grabbed the man by the hair, pulled his head back and punched him. The South African's head bounced off the lounge chair's headrest and back up again. He dabbed at his split lip, saw blood on his fingers, flashed Tavener a venomous look.

'Costello told us to locate them and the heroin before anyone else did.'

'Costello?' Chance looked from Tavener to Long.

Tavener raised a hand to silence Chance. 'Costello thinks this man here has his drugs?'

Viljoen nodded quickly.

'How did he find us?' said Chance.

Tavener nudged the South African with the toe of his sand shoe. 'Don't be rude, answer the man.'

'We divided up a few days ago to cover more territory. I was checking Yass, saw Gao's whore in town this morning.' Viljoen spat a ball of bloody saliva out of the side of his mouth. 'I followed her to the caravan park, called the others, waited until they arrived.'

Chance cursed under his breath. 'Who's Costello and what the hell's going on?'

'I was going to ask the same thing.' Kate stood in the doorway, twirled the car keys off a finger, her face set at a determined angle.

'How long have you been standing there?' said Chance.

'Long enough.' She threw the keys to Tavener. 'Car's parked in an alley a block away.'

'Miss, this could get ugly,' said Tavener. 'You might want to go, wait in the kitchen with the old man's daughter.'

'Newsflash,' Kate snarled. 'It already is ugly.'

Chance took a step toward her. 'Kate, come on—'

'No, I'm sick of being treated like some fucking extra in a boy's only adventure. So I fucked up going into town to get the CD player. But if it wasn't for me you'd probably be dead or in custody, you said so yourself.'

'I don't want you to get involved any more...' Chance realised how stupid the words sounded, stopped himself.

'Than what, I already am?' Her large blue eyes bored into him. 'I was part of that cluster fuck in Surfers Paradise, drove you all the way here. I bought you heroin for your pain, been hanging out with you in that shithole caravan park while you get your health together. Yeah, I'd say I'm pretty fucking involved. I want to know what's going on. Everything.'

Chance nodded wearily.

'So who's going to be kind enough to fill me in?' Her eyes swept the room. 'Tavener, the old man who is not supposed to speak English but does, the guy in the seat? I don't care who talks as long as someone does.'

'Okay,' said Tavener. 'Your friend Gao had ambitions to get started in the drug trade. Surfers was supposed to be his first deal; he brought me in to help get him started.'

'Why you?' said Chance.

'Let's just say I have industry experience. Gao had the drugs shipped in a couple of weeks before his arrival and we took possession of them when he got to Surfers.'

Chance remembered tailing Tavener to Coolangatta, the meeting in the restaurant, following him and the other men to the block of flats.

'He was going to offload the drugs in Sydney,' Tavener said.

'Then we showed up,' said Kate.

'Yeah, you showed up.'

'Is Costello the buyer?'

'No, ma'am, but he's associated with them. They paid a deposit and since the drugs disappeared on Costello's patch, his business partners are holding him responsible for their losses.'

'Is he some sort of criminal?'

'Of the worst kind,' said Tavener. 'Used to be very corrupt cop. Retired now, but still has his fingers in a lot of illegal pies. Our friend Matthias here works for him.'

'And this man, Costello,' Kate said, 'he thinks Chance and I have the heroin?'

'Yep.'

'Are you saying this man doesn't have the drugs?' Viljoen looked around, his bruised face screwed up in confusion.

'Give the man a prize,' said Tavener.

'Then who does?' said the South African.

'That'd be a fella by the name of Frank Dormer and his accomplice, Sophia Lekakis, right, Gary?'

'And a man named Kerrigan,' added Chance.

'No, he's dead,' interrupted Viljoen. 'We found his body in an old farmhouse on the outskirts of Brisbane.'

Chance felt Kate flinch. Her lip trembled. She tried to control it before it was too noticeable.

'Didn't hear about that in the media,' said Tavener. 'Cover it up, did you?'

The South African nodded, happy to be of use.

''There's one thing I don't understand,' said Chance.

'What you don't understand, be a long list, son, but go on.'

'Where were you the night of the robbery?'

'I was lucky enough to be out sampling some of the extra-curricula delights of Surfers Paradise.'

'What?'

'I was getting laid,' Tavener pronounced each word slowly, as if speaking to a child. 'What? I'm not a fucking monk. I came back a few hours later, found someone had turned Gao's suite into a slaughterhouse, and the money and drugs were gone. Didn't fancy hanging around, having to explain myself to the local law enforcement, so I split.'

'How did you find us?'

'It's a talent I have. Look, we don't have time for any more of this.' Tavener turned back to Viljoen. 'Aside from you, how many cops has Costello got looking for these two?'

'Three.'

'Which means we need to think fast.'

'What's the fucking point, like you say, they've framed me tighter than a fish's arse.' Chance felt a wave of exhaustion course through him. 'We can't go to the police, all we can do is get as far away as possible.'

Tavener smirked. 'And how far do you think you'll get with Costello after you?'

'What are my alternatives? Trust you? I don't even know who the fuck you are.'

'Costello won't give up.'

'We can do a deal,' blurted out Viljoen. 'I'll tell Costello you don't have the drugs, that you'll help us find them. I swear I can protect you.'

Tavener gave the South African a withering look, unzipped his money pouch, whipped out the pistol, bought the butt of the grip down hard on the side of Viljoen's head. The South African went out like a light being switched off.

'If you'll allow me to speak,' said Long. 'I have an idea.'

All eyes focused on the old man. He studied the twist of smoke from his cigarette.

'As your friend Mister Tavener here says, Costello's people won't give up.'

'It gets worse,' interjected Tavener. 'Word is a couple of guys flew into Brisbane from Manila a week ago. They're not as good as me, still looking for Chance on the Gold Coast, or at least they were according to the last information I received.'

Long and Tavener exchanged a furtive look.

'And exactly when were you planning on telling me this information?' said Chance. 'Dormer's got the money and the drugs, not me.'

Tavener shrugged, scratched his nose with the muzzle of his pistol.

'According to my sources, Dormer's gone back to Afghanistan, along with the Lekakis woman, will most likely stay there until the heat dies down.'

Long pretended to concentrate on butting out his smoke, his brow furrowed. But Chance could tell the old man was sniffing the wind, thinking through all the options. He glanced at Kate. She sat on the couch, momentarily lost in grief over Kerrigan, oblivious to how close both of them were to joining him. He had to make himself relevant, quickly, before Long and Tavener cut a deal that didn't involve him.

'This idea of yours, Long, what is it?'

The old man gazed at Chance, his eyes hard little slabs of obsidian in the brittle light.

'The police, Gao's people, they can't find you if they don't know what you look like.'

'What the hell are you talking about?'

'Surgery, to change your face, make you a better hunter.'

'Are you serious?'

'Plastic surgery is a very easy procedure. I have contacts in Thailand who can arrange it for you.'

'Why go to all this trouble,' said Chance. 'What's in it for you?'

'Let's just say I'm protecting my investment,' Long's thin lips formed a knowing smile as he spoke. 'I'll get you out of the country, put up the costs of the surgery, any other expenses. In return, once it's done, you retrieve the drugs and money.'

'Plus with me out of the country there's less possibility I'll fall into the hands of the police and lead them to you?'

Long acknowledged the point with a slight tip of his head. 'All things considered, the most convenient solution for everybody.'

Chance noted the implied threat, felt like a dog that would do anything to avoid its master giving it another kick.

'Guess I don't have much choice.'

'Not unless you want to keep walking around with a target on the middle of your head,' said Tavener, placing the pistol back in his money pouch. 'Mister Long, exactly how many ways would you be prepared to split up the proceeds from the Surfers' job?'

'I would be satisfied with a three-way split. Consider your end payment for accompanying Gary to Thailand, making sure he comes to no harm while he's there.'

'Sounds good to me.' Tavener rubbed his hands together. 'I've always wanted to see Thailand.'

'What about me?' Kate looked up from where she sat on the couch.

Long and Tavener didn't respond, but Chance could see them deliberating Kate's fate, weighing up the pros and cons of adding another body to the pile.

'She's no threat,' said Chance. 'The police don't even know her real name, she'll just disappear, right, Kate?'

'I haven't come this far to be left on the side of the road,' said Kate.

Buried by the side of the road if you're not careful, thought Chance. 'We're talking about going to Thailand, who knows for how long. Your anonymity is your disguise here. There's no need for you to come.'

Kate sat there, stone-cold determination on her face.

'I have no objection to her accompanying you to Thailand, but her expenses will come out of your end,' said Long. 'Understood?'

Chance nodded.

Long's thin lips formed a knowing smile. 'We can talk about the details later, right now we have more pressing matters to discuss.'

'What's that?' said Chance.

'Our South African friend, we have to get rid of him.'

Kate looked up, alarmed. 'What, you're going to kill him?'

'I'm afraid he's right,' said Tavener. 'Viljoen's not a fish, we can't just throw him back.'

Kate stared at Chance, as if expecting him to support her.

Chance shrugged. 'You wanted to know everything.'

Eleven

Elyssa Blake watched with mounting frustration as the two police detectives worked over the young redhead. The light from the single fluorescent tube cast the pre-fab cabin's interior in a sickly lemon hue. Blake looked around, dirty clothes on the floor, unwashed dishes in the sink, a stack of porn magazines on a kitchenette table, something about naughty matures peeked out at her from under an overflowing ashtray. Heavy metal blared from a CD player, the perfect soundtrack to cover the smack of fists on flesh and the young man's grunts of pain.

The caravan park manager, Fergus, had received a late night call a couple of weeks ago, was told to expect two new tenants. It wasn't the first time. All expenses would be covered, the caller had told him, plus extra for his silence.

Two people arrived half an hour later, the woman and a man who never left the car. Fergus put them in a cabin at the rear of the park. The new arrivals kept to themselves, although sometimes the woman, Amber she called herself, visited Fergus to share a joint. She didn't talk much about herself or why they were there.

Blake yanked the power cord out of the wall. The CD player went silent, Dundee and Nolte paused mid-blows.

'That's enough,' she barked. 'He's told us everything he's going to.'

Nolte was sweating from the exertion of the beating he'd

helped administer. He wiped his forehead on the sleeve of his jacket, put a hand against the small of his back, pushed his gut forward. Dundee stood, head slightly stooped to avoid hitting the low roof. Fergus sat between them, his face a mass of cuts and contusions.

'What now?' asked Dundee.

'Leave him here, it's not as though he'll go to the police.'

A traffic camera had caught a car registered to the late Dennis Curry crossing the New South Wales border the same night Gao and his bodyguard were murdered. Blake and her squad checked all the larger towns heading south from Surfers Paradise. A used car dealer in a one-horse town called Tenterfield reported he'd traded a black ute for Curry's, the same ute that now sat abandoned outside the empty cabin at the rear of the caravan park. The customer matched the description of a woman last seen in Gao's company on the night of his death. The dealer remembered her saying something about going to Canberra.

When Canberra had drawn a blank, they'd split up, cased the surrounding satellite towns. Viljoen had taken Yass, got lucky, spotted the woman on the main street and followed her here, called Blake and the others.

One minute, Blake and the others had been chasing them through the bush, the next they'd vanished. Worse, it looked like they'd taken Viljoen as a hostage. But how the hell had Chance and the woman found out they were coming? Someone must have tipped them off. She was pretty sure it wasn't Fergus. So who?

Blake stepped outside into a pool of burnt-orange cast by the hooded light above the door. Insects swarmed around her.

She noticed a tear in her cotton pullover, cursed. Blake was a city girl, Sydney, then Brisbane, regarded the bush as enemy territory. The prospect of spending any more time in it than absolutely necessary was hell.

Forensics had found traces of blood around the pool at the hotel in Surfers Paradise and matched it to the blood type in

Chance's military file. It meant Chance was wounded. Blake and her team had tossed the cabin used by Chance and the woman, found a stash of medical supplies, bandages, needles, a blackened T-spoon, and a small plastic bag with traces of fine white powder. Heroin, the pain relief of kings.

The reception door slammed behind her, Nolte emerged, a cigarette dangling from his thick lips.

'What do you think?'

'I should have done that hairdressing course after school instead of joining the police.'

Nolte looked at her blankly.

'I mean about Viljoen?'

'What do you suggest, Gavin?'

Nolte kicked a loose rock with the toe of his boot. 'We can't just leave him here.'

She'd lost count of the number of times the Boer had talked about his time as a scout in the South African defence force. The story he always repeated, chasing an African National Congress guerrilla three days through the bush, shooting him just as he was about to reach the border between Namibia and Angola. Viljoen had inspected the body and found the man had been running barefoot the entire time.

'Good riddance to the prick,' Blake muttered under her breath.

The rest of the investigation had ground to a halt. No sign of the others involved in the robbery, the woman on hotel reception, Sophia Lekakis, and the other man seen leaving the hotel with her. Like Chance and the woman called Amber, they'd vanished into thin air.

You don't steal ten million in heroin, thought Blake, hole up in some shit hole caravan park, barely one step ahead of the law and whoever else is after you. Money like that at your disposal you disappear without a trace just like the others involved in the robbery.

The nagging voice in the back of Blake's head became deafening. She was chasing the wrong people.

Twelve

Blake stood in front of the old man, in a neutral voice recited the facts of what had happened. At several points during her monologue, Costello raised the mechanical larynx to interrupt, only to lower it, unable to comprehend what he was hearing.

Blake had left Nolte and Dundee to clean up the loose ends in Yass, driven straight through what was left of the night to Canberra airport, waited for the first plane to Brisbane. She glanced at a magazine but took in nothing, poked at her in-flight meal, on emotional autopilot. Two weeks tracking Chance and the woman, only to have them slip away. It took all her strength to keep on top of the fear and apprehension at having to confront the old man, the consequences of what she would tell him.

Costello sat in his wheelchair in the same corner of the balcony. The backyard was still, stripes of brilliant green visible through the slats in the wooden porch screen. No grandkids today. The only sound was the drone of a solitary lawn mower in the distance.

'What about Viljoen?'

'I don't know where he is.'

'What do you mean?' His face contorted as he spat out words. 'Are you playing a fucking game with me, Detective Sergeant?'

'No.'

'Because if you are—'

'It's no game,' she repeated firmly. 'Chance and the woman were in their cabin in the caravan park until the moment we arrived. They fled into a patch of forest behind the park. We followed them. One minute I thought we had them the next they'd disappeared and so had Detective Viljoen.'

'What about my drugs?'

'No sign of them, either.'

'How can that happen?' came the old man's metallic reply.

'Someone obviously tipped them off.'

'Who?'

'Your guess is as good as mine. For all I know it was your boy, Viljoen.' Blake saw the look of horror on the old man's face, like she'd slapped him. 'How do you know he wasn't working with them? Ten million in heroin beats the hell out of a police pension.'

'That's not possible, this man Chance, and the woman, they must have taken the drugs when they fled.'

'I can't see how they would've been able to flee so quickly through thick bush, hauling twenty-four kilos of heroin—'

'Fucking useless as tits on a bull,' interrupted Costello. 'Doubted you had the metal for the job, and I was right. I'll get someone more suitable, maybe Dundee, to take over, go after Chance and the woman.'

'Don't you understand? I don't think they had the drugs, never did. The people who do have your heroin are far away by now. The last two weeks have been a complete waste of time.'

'The premier, the media, they've wanted someone to blame for the lack of progress on the Gao case,' Costello continued as if she hadn't spoken. 'They bloody can have you. I throw you to them and they can tear you to pieces for all I care—'

Costello paused mid-sentence. She noticed his bloodshot eyes start to wander, followed the direction of his gaze to nowhere in particular. His skin was pale, his mouth drooped slightly, like plastic left too close to an open fire. The rest of his body had gone rigid, as if he'd been given an electric shock. He dropped the mechanical larynx. It fell to the floor, rolled under the wheel-chair.

The old bastard was having a heart attack. Blake reached for her phone, started to dial zero-zero-zero, paused, slipped the phone back into her pocket.

Costello stared at her, glasses askew, his eyes wide. His fingers clutched at his chest. The wheelchair wobbled from side to side and backward and forward, looked like it was going to topple over.

Blake took a deep breath, leaned forward and gripped the worn vinyl armrests to prevent the wheelchair from falling over. It felt like bearing down on a frightened child but for the smell—stale breath, decaying flesh and menthol rub. She made herself look directly at the old man's eyes, bear witness to the last moments of his life.

It was several minutes before she dared let go of the wheel-chair. She placed two fingers on the clammy skin on the side of his neck, got no pulse, drew herself up slowly, as if worried any sudden movement might break the spell, bring Costello back to life.

Blake heard an angry whistling sound somewhere in the house behind her. A kettle. It became high pitched, stayed like that for what seemed like an eternity until someone killed the flame underneath.

She willed herself to think straight, not to give in to the urge to flee. She manipulated the old man's body into a normal posi-tion, his hands resting in his lap, brushed his eyes closed, rear-ranged his glasses so they sat straight on his nose. She reached under the wheelchair, picked up his mechanical larynx and placed it amid the jumble of used tissues and plastic pill bottles on a rattan table next to him.

She retraced her route through the house. Costello's wife appeared in the doorway to the lounge room. 'Going already, dear,' she said wiping her hands on a tea towel. 'I was going to ask if you wanted tea.'

'No, thanks.'

Costello's wife smiled, made to go in the direction of the back porch.

'I think your husband will be okay for now. He's sleeping.'

'Right then, I won't disturb him. You okay to let yourself out?'

'Absolutely.'

Thirteen

Tavener sat in the back with the unconscious cop and two shovels, while Chance drove. They hadn't exchanged a word since leaving Long's house an hour earlier. Chance hoped it was a test, that at some point Tavener would tell him to pull over, open the door, throw the South African onto the side of the road, laugh as they drove off. Instead, the American sat calmly, gazed at his own reflection in the darkened window.

'Why do I get the feeling you've done this before?' Chance tried to make eye contact in the rearview mirror, but the American's face was in shadow.

'In my previous line of work, I'd sometimes get a phone call in the middle of the night, a guy sounds like he's gargled Drano, tells you there's a problem. Occasionally it'd end in a bit of spade work.'

'And what exactly was your previous line of work?'

'This and that.'

'How'd you come to work with Gao?'

'I've got two ex-wives, three college-age children, a mother-load of bills to pay and my finances were shot to shit during the global financial crisis. I'll work for anyone.'

Chance realised now wasn't the time to push for more information, kept his eyes on the road.

'That Dormer fella you pulled the job with back in Surfers, he sure did stitch you up good, didn't he?'

Chance sensed the American smiling in the darkness.

'Don't take it personally, he knew what he was doing.' Tavener leaned forward in his seat. 'That's the turn-off the old man suggested.'

Long had given them detailed directions, obviously knew the area well. Chance speculated it was not the first time a body had been buried out here.

Chance pulled into a picnic spot screened off from the road by a row of gum trees. He killed the engine, sat in the car.

'Don't just sit there,' growled Tavener as he walked to the rear of the car. He opened the boot, emerged holding a halogen lantern. A soft circle of light illuminated the area around the car.

Chance got out, saw a treated pine picnic table and bench, the long dead remains of a campfire, scorched and twisted beer cans in the ashes.

Tavener placed the lantern on the car's roof, reached into the back seat, handed Chance the shovels, one at a time. He helped Viljoen out. The South African stood uncertainly, still groggy from being pistol-whipped. Tavener picked up the lantern, withdraw the gun from his nylon money pouch, jabbed the barrel into the small of Viljoen's back and pushed him forward

They walked into a thick glade of trees. Viljoen led the way, followed by Tavener; Chance brought up the rear. The night sky was cloudy and the only light came from the lantern. Chance could smell eucalyptus. The noise of cicadas surrounded them, like the roar of a restless crowd.

As if coming out a trance, Viljoen started begging, half in English, half whatever language he spoke back in South Africa.

'This is as good as any place,' said Tavener. 'Stop here.' Viljoen halted, turned to face them. The South African blinked, struggled to focus. Tears ran down his cheeks, a dark stain appeared around his crotch, spread down his trouser leg.

Tavener took one step forward, raised his pistol, shot Viljoen in the forehead mid-plea.

'Let's get digging,' he said.

When Tavener said 'Deep enough,' Chance was smeared in dirt, slicked with sweat and the area where he'd fractured his ribs throbbed. He climbed out of the hole, picked up Viljoen by the arms. Tavener took the legs. Holding the body, they waddled to the side of the hole, slung it in.

Viljoen gazed lifelessly up at them. Chance started shovelling dirt onto the body, face first, covering it as quickly as his aching arms would allow.

'Powerful feeling, killing a man. Watching him die.' Tavener leaned on his shovel and gazed at something in the dark only he could see. 'You feel horror but also a sense of relief it's over and there's no going back.'

Tavener took his fishing hat off, ran a hand through his snow-white hair. 'Thing like that makes a man put a name to his fear, come out the other side stronger.'

Chance stared at the American, unsure what to say, realised Tavener didn't expect a reply, resumed shovelling dirt onto the corpse.

When they'd filled in the grave, Chance levelled it off as best he could, covered it with leaves and brush.

'That'll do.' Tavener slung the shovel over his shoulder and without another word started to walk back in the direction of the car.

LAND OF SMILES

One

Chance sipped his soda water, glanced around the nightclub, the cheap chrome finishing, grimy black and white floor tiles, an assortment of leather couches and armchairs, ripped and scarred by countless fumbled cigarettes.

On a small stage to his right, an overweight man in a tight-fitting T-shirt crooned a Thai pop song. Eyes closed, microphone clasped in both hands, the singer ignored the reverb and distortion from the old speakers. 'Happy New Year' in gold tinsel letters was strung on a piece of string across the wall behind him.

A revolving glitter ball in the middle of the ceiling sent shards of light marching languidly around the room. Chance looked at the way the shapes played on the soft brown skin of the woman next to him, the reflection on the sequins of her polyester halter-top. She had a lean, hard body, probably gained from a previous life working in a rice paddy or hauling nets on a trawler on the Gulf of Thailand. She gave him the occasional bored grin, her slightly crooked teeth a white slash across her dark features, otherwise stared into the space in front of her.

Tavener sat opposite, dressed in a black polo shirt, baggy shorts with a floral pattern, the fishing cap he'd worn the night he'd first appeared back in Yass. Three women sat around him, topped up his whisky, fussed and pawed as they vied for his attention.

Chance played in the circles of moisture on the glass-topped table, tried to quell the urge for alcohol and cigarettes. Both were on Doctor Wirapol's long list of no-nos that could hamper the healing process for his face, lead to infection.

Not that Chance could see how the result could be anything worse than it was.

After touching down at Bangkok's Suvarnabhumi International Airport, Chance, Tavener and Kate were whisked away in a waiting mini-bus. The three-hour trip south to Pattaya was one continuous stretch of concrete and brick, houses, machine shops and factories, interspersed with only the occasional patch of green, as though Bangkok never ended.

The mini-bus dropped his companions at a hotel, drove Chance another half hour to a large white building on the edge of Pattaya with gleaming windows and manicured lawns. A Thai nurse in a spotless white uniform met him at the entrance, led him to a waiting area.

'What are you in for?'

Chance looked around, saw the question came from a fifty-something Caucasian male in a stylish white linen suit, sitting in a seat opposite him.

'Sorry?'

'What are you here to have done? Hold on, let me guess, your nose is too big, yeah?'

'You got it,' Chance replied hesitantly. He'd never thought of his nose as particularly excessive. 'Yourself?'

'A nip and a tuck, mainly reducing the bags under my eyes.' The man looked proud. 'Whatever gives you an edge, know what I mean?'

The nurse re-appeared, told Chance that Doctor Wirapol would see him.

Wirapol was a thin, nervous man with a head of sharply parted black hair and wire-framed glasses. 'I believe you want more than aesthetic plastic surgery,' he said without introducing himself. His English had no hint of an accent. 'You're after full facial reconstruction.

'Let's see, nose, chin, eyelid correction, rhinoplasty, some of the bones on your face will need to be cut and moved.' The nurse briskly jotted down notes on a clipboard as he spoke. 'As for the missing stub of your little finger.' He lifted up the digit in question, 'we should be able to fix that by grafting part of the toe on it.'

'Whose toe?'

'Yours.' The doctor looked at him, deadpan. 'We'll harvest part of one of your toes, graft it onto your damaged finger. Take off your shoes, please.'

'You're bullshitting me?'

'Let me assure you, Mister Chance, toe-to-hand surgery is very much a reality,' said Wirapol, his professional ability impugned. 'It's been a routine procedure for dealing with severe hand injuries for some years now.'

Chance unlaced his runners as the doctor talked.

'The surgery is lengthy and complicated, and the results are not always perfect.' The doctor leaned down, inspected Chance's naked feet. 'Yes, we'll take a bit from the long toe, second from your big one.'

Wirapol went over to a basin, washed his hands. 'The first two weeks after surgery will be difficult,' he said over his shoulder. 'Once the pain medication wears off the nerves start to wake up. You should make a full recovery in about twelve to fourteen weeks.'

Chance was operated on the next day.

He remembered when the bandages came off. Wirapol hovered over him. Kate and Tavener had come along for moral support.

Kate gasped, realised her reaction and assumed a neutral expression.

A crooked smile spread across Tavener's face. 'Suits you, son.'

Chance had peered hard at the mirror, tried to make out the contours of his new face under the spiderweb of scar tissue and swelling. The features were fine individually but combined made him look like one of those identikit composites he'd seen on the front page of his hometown tabloid. His jaw was hardened, mouth larger, nose flatter. His eyes looked expressionless and slightly askew. Chance had gone from being an anonymous everyman to having a face people would cross the road to avoid.

He turned to the doctor. 'What did you do the surgery with, a hammer?'

The doctor uttered a high-pitched, nervous laugh.

'As the body recovers there will be lumps, bumps, unevenness, bruises and ooze.' The doctor avoided Chance's gaze, looked instead at Tavener and Kate. 'There may also be—' the doctor searched for the right words, '—a brief period of postoperative depression.'

Wirapol pointed to the bandage around Chance's new finger. 'We shall have to wait a little longer before we can see how the new finger is coming along.'

When his condition was deemed good enough to leave the hospital, the minibus re-appeared, took him and his companions to a hotel in Sri Racha, a small fishing town two hundred kilometres south of Bangkok.

His skin too tender to shave at first, he decided to let the hair keep growing. The mass of wiry dark strands offered a partial disguise for his new features. As Wirapol had promised, the toe-to-hand surgery had been successful. His new digit looked somewhat bent and stunted compared to his other fingers, but nothing that wouldn't pass casual inspection.

Chance hardly left the hotel room for the first week. Even after his face had healed up, he could only bring himself to lurk around the environs of the hotel and relented to Tavener's repeated requests to accompany him on his nightly soirees when it was clear the American wouldn't take no for an answer.

While Chance had spent the better part of two months cooling his heels as his face mended, his companions acclimatised to Thailand in their own ways.

Tavener had spent his time drinking and whoring, most of it in the establishment they were in tonight. The dwarf doorman greeted the American like a long lost brother, the octogenarian mamasan cackled at his jokes in bad Thai. All the women who worked there knew him by name and responded to his antics with a mixture of steely business sense and fascination, like children relieved by the presence of an eccentric uncle at a boring family gathering.

As if in a direct inverse response, Kate adopted an air of cultural inquisitiveness. She'd hung around the hotel staff, got a Thai teacher. From what Chance could tell, her attempts to learn the language progressed quickly. She'd also taken to exploring the area around Sri Racha by herself on a rented motorcycle.

Chance was pulled from his reverie by the shrieks of the three Thai women on the other side of the couch. The overweight man had finished his song, bowed slightly, hands held together in front of his face.

The women egged Tavener on to sing. After feigning reluctance, Tavener drained his whisky, put both hands up in mock surrender, shimmied across the floor, and mounted the stage. The room erupted in applause at the opening chords of the song, an old stadium rock number Chance could remember dancing to when he was younger.

As the audience hooted and clapped, Chance felt a presence next to him, smelled a metallic tang of aftershave. He looked up. Milo's face leered down at him.

'Alright, mate?' he said in his cockney drawl. Without waiting for a response, Milo sat down on an unoccupied section of the leather couch, barked in Thai at the woman next to Chance. She hastily mixed a highball from the bottle of whisky on the table, passed it to Milo without meeting his eyes.

'Nice to see you sampling the delights of Sri Racha's night life, Gary.' Milo crossed one leg over his other and took a long pull of his drink, smacked his lips. 'You know what they say, all work and no play. Not exactly Soho, but a tart's a tart, no matter where you are.'

Milo had appeared on Chance's doorstep his second day in Sri Racha, introduced himself as a representative of Khun Issarapong Boonchu, 'under whose personal protection you and your friends are during your stay in the Kingdom of Thailand.'

'You don't mind if I have a butcher's hook at your digs?' Chance had stepped aside to let the man enter his hotel room. Milo noted the cheap furnishings, shrugged. 'Well, at least you've got your privacy and fresh sea air will do wonders for your Chevy Chase.'

The son of an English merchant seaman and a Thai woman, Milo was brought up and educated in London, where he worked as an investment banker. By his own account, he'd had the makings of a promising career until the global financial crisis resulted in his retrenching and having to resort to alternative means to make a living—drug dealing.

Things had gone well until an episode involving a shipment of party drugs, a luxury flat belonging to a couple of criminally inclined web designers and a concierge who'd become suspicious of the comings and goings at all hours. Milo had fled London, berthed for a while in Cambodia, where he engaged in various schemes, including trying to buy and sell an island off the southern coast. When that went bad, he headed to Thailand.

'Let's just say I got into a spot of bother with Issarapong's old man,' Milo had said with a wink and a sly smile. 'He wanted to kill me, but lucky for my scrawny hide, his son had slightly more vision, saw my skills could be useful in his quest to diversify the family business.'

Chance didn't trust Milo any further than he could comfortably spit out a house brick. It also struck him as weird that anyone, let alone a powerful Thai businessman, would employ a Cockney spiv as a public face.

'How's the Chevy Chase coming along?' Milo leaned in close, his voice loud, to make himself heard above Tavener's singing. 'Looks almost completely healed to me.'

'I'd say so,' said Chance.

'That's the Dunkirk spirit. Now you're all better, maybe you'd like a little trip.' The mock playfulness faded from his face. 'Khun Issarapong requests the pleasure of your company at his residence tomorrow. He'd like to meet the person who has been under his care all this time.'

Chance's eyes narrowed. The only reason he could think of that Milo's boss wanted to see him was there'd been word from Long in Australia.

'Be outside your hotel at ten tomorrow morning. I'll arrange for a motor to come and get you.' Milo eyed Tavener finishing up his karaoke number. 'And leave your China plate up there behind, okay?'

Without another word, he stood up, left.

Chance was vaguely aware of cheers and clapping as Tavener finished his song. The American sat in the spot Milo had occupied, eyes clear and sober. He smiled at Chance, as if already privy to the previous conversation, sipped his drink. 'What did our little friend want?' he asked.

When Kate had questioned Chance about why he'd agreed to let Tavener accompany them to Thailand, Chance had recited an Arab proverb he'd heard from an Australian soldier who'd served in Iraq: "In the desert of life the wise person travels by caravan, while the fool prefers to travel alone."

'What does that even mean?'

'Long didn't give me much choice in the matter. Plus, it's better to have him working with us than against us.'

Despite having spent the better part of two months in Thailand with Tavener, Chance knew almost nothing of substance about the American, except that he had an unnerving ability to switch personas, as if moving in and out of character. One minute he was gregarious, the life of the party, the next, sober, calculating the angles.

'He wants me to meet his boss tomorrow.'

Tavener raised his eyebrows.

'He said I was to come alone.'

'What do you reckon Issarapong Boonchu wants to talk to you about?'

'Long has been in contact with him. He's found Dormer and it's time to call in my debt. It's the only reason I can think of.'

'Well you can be damn sure it's not a social call.'

'Maybe you should come with me, rattle Milo's cage a little?'

'Son, Milo may come across as a fool, but I can assure you the person he works for is not.' Tavener swirled the remaining golden liquid around in his glass, peered into it as if examining the fluid for some portent.

'Something tells me you know more than you're letting on,' said Chance.

'Issarapong is what is colloquially known in these parts as 'a person of influence.' My Thai is shit, but I believe the exact term the locals use is jao pho, or godfather, a particularly aggressive species of local entrepreneur, major police and military connections, operates totally above the law.

'Issarapong's had the business handed to him by his father, Kriansak Boonchu. Kriansak got his start in the late sixties working as an enforcer for the local jao pho at the time, a guy called Dang. Story goes, Dang passed him over for promotion in favour of someone else, so Kriansak took matters into his own hands, killed Dang, took out his car with a rocket-propelled grenade as it was travelling down a rural road, assumed control of the entire operation. Prostitution, narcotics, illegal timber, you name it, he was involved. Kriansak owned this town. Shit, he owned most of Chonburi province. Now it all belongs to his only son, Issarapong.

'That's a long-winded way of saying Issarapong is not a dude whose cage you want to rattle. He wants you to go alone, go alone. He ain't going to hurt you. He's had plenty of opportunities to do that already, if he wanted to. Believe me, no one around here would've stood in his way.

'Eat, drink and be merry, son, for tomorrow we die.' Tavener patted Chance on the shoulder, drained his glass and motioned to one of the women opposite him for a refill. 'I got to take a leak.'

The woman sitting next to Chance made to top off his soda water.

Chance put his hand over the top of the glass, left it there. 'No.' He shook his head. 'Whisky.'

She paused, soda bottle mid-air, smiled with renewed interest.

Two

The woman lying on the mattress next to him was older than she'd appeared last night. Faint lines emanated from the corners of her eyes, stretch marks, and a pink Caesarean scar ran across her lower belly.

Chance sat on the edge of the bed, his feet splayed on the worn wooden floorboards, stared at his shortened mutilated toe, one deformity swapped for another.

His room was one of a warren of ramshackle wooden apartments, the timber faded by years of sun, that sat on barnacle-encrusted wooden pylons over the mop-water-coloured ocean. Chance had spent weeks in the two rooms, knew every inch of the layout, every item it contained.

When he wasn't in his room, he spent most of his time sitting on a large expanse of wooden decking at the end of the hotel complex. At night he watched the lights of passing freighters, the sea breeze cool on his boiling face, and tried to push away the memory of the South African pleading for his life in the soft lamplight, the crack from the single pistol shot.

Apart from his two companions, Thais occupied all the other apartments. Pot plants and rows of laundry screened off the tiny balconies in front of the rooms for privacy.

Chance listened to the lapping of the sea underneath the floorboards, the uneven whirr of the ceiling fan, the two-note solo of a gecko chasing an insect across the plywood ceiling.

Kate had been his most frequent visitor, brought him food and water, sometimes sat with him and read as he stared at the sea. Tavener dropped in occasionally, drank beer and imparted snippets from his life in his monotone drawl.

Doctor Wirapol had appeared a couple of times at the beginning of Chance's stay. He was soon replaced by one of the Thai nurses from the hospital. When she stopped coming, Chance figured he had a clean bill of health.

He reached down, picked a plastic bottle of lukewarm water, guzzled. His throat felt dry, his head throbbed. He'd been careful not to drink too much last night, aware of his meeting with Issarapong, but after so long off alcohol and cigarettes, it hadn't taken much to give him a powerful hangover.

He heard a soft knock. He grabbed a sarong draped across the edge of the bed, wrapped it around his waist, opened the door.

Kate stood framed in the morning light. She'd dyed her hair black since arriving in Thailand, let it grow long. Two plastic bags of iced white coffee dangled from rubber bands around one of her fingers.

Chance scratched at his chest. The fresh air accentuated the stale atmosphere in the room, a mixture of sweat, perfume and sex.

Kate sucked from the straw in one of the bags, looked over Chance's shoulder to the woman lying on the bed, a neutral expression on her face. 'I see you have company.'

He avoided her eyes, embarrassed.

The Thai woman stirred, threw an arm over her face to block out the light from the open doorway.

'I bought you a coffee.'

Kate handed him one of the bags, walked past him and sat at the Formica table.

Chance drained half of the sweet, nutty-flavoured brew. The Thai woman sat up on the bed, hair askew, looked around the room. She registered no alarm at Kate's presence.

'Aren't you going to introduce me to your friend?' Kate sipped from her drink. Her large blue eyes peered at him expectantly.

Chance fumbled for the words, realised he didn't know the woman's name.

Satisfied she made her point, Kate said something in Thai. The woman replied. Chance stood in the centre of the room, drank his coffee, watched the two females talk.

After several minutes, the Thai woman stood up, stretched, collected her clothes from the back of a chair by the table. Her naked body, which he'd had no inhibitions about mauling the night before, now made him feel awkward. The woman walked into the bathroom without acknowledging his presence, shut the door behind her.

'For your information, her name is Kamala,' Kate said dryly.

'I bet it is,' said Chance, finishing off his ice coffee. 'Just like yours is Amber,'

Kate smiled. 'Bit old for you, isn't she?'

'What's the matter with older women?'

Kate shrugged, kicked at an empty beer bottle lying on the floor. 'Didn't the doctor say no cigarettes or alcohol?'

'Maybe you haven't noticed, but he hasn't exactly left me looking like Brad Pitt. Can't see how a little drink is going to make a difference.'

'Your new face is not all that bad. I think it's got character.'

'Yeah, like Frankenstein.'

Chance picked up his jeans from the floor where he'd thrown them the night before, sat on the bed, pulled the legs the right side out. He heard water being splashed about in the bathroom.

'Don't get me wrong, I think it's good you went out.' She sipped her coffee. 'Anything's better than moping around in this room forever. What'd you do?'

'I accompanied Tavener on one of his nightly outings.'

'That sleazy karaoke bar he hangs out in?'

'It wasn't so bad.' Chance took his wristwatch from the table, looked at the time. 'Milo dropped by.'

'Ugh, he is such a toolbag.'

'Hang around, he'll be here in half an hour and you can say that to his face. He's taking me to see his boss, the man who's been looking after us in Thailand.'

Her face became fragile. 'So this is it?'

'What do you mean?'

'This man wanting to see you can only mean one thing. Mister Long has located Dormer, wants you to go back to Australia.'

'Let's hope so.'

'I know it's been tough on you, the surgery and all, but I love it here. Even in this shithole hotel. I don't want to go back.'

'Don't fool yourself, this was always going to happen.'

The bathroom door opened, Kamala emerged, stood awkwardly in front of Kate and Chance. Her wet was combed straight, last night's clothes ill-fitting and out of place in the light of day.

'See you 'round,' muttered Chance, only half meeting her eyes.

Kamala started to say something to Chance, changed her mind, spoke to Kate instead.

'She wants to be paid,' said Kate absentmindedly.

'What?'

'Money. For last night.'

Chance felt his face flush. He fumbled for the roll of Thai Baht in the pocket of his jeans.

Kate watched the money change hands with disinterest.

She turned to Chance after Kamala had let herself out. 'Looks like I'm not the only one fooling myself.'

Three

It was only mid-morning but already the heat was intense. Chance sheltered from the sun under the corrugated tin awning at the hotel's entrance, watched the laneway for his ride.

He'd decided to shave for the meeting, the first time since his surgery. He had peered into the round bathroom mirror with grim fascination as the disposable razor sheared away the whiskers. The smooth, clean-shaven skin only seemed to exaggerate the hard angles and asymmetry of his new face.

A white Hilux pickup appeared at the mouth of the laneway. Chance climbed into the back seat next to Milo. The Cockney gave him a quick once-over, grunted, leaned forward and spoke to the driver, a stocky dark-skinned man who glared at Chance in the rearview mirror.

The traffic was light and they cleared Sri Racha quickly. The terrain became more rural as they headed inland, snatches of emerald rice paddies and stunted, dust-covered foliage interspersed with roadside cafés, grease-spattered garages, and businesses selling agricultural equipment.

At one point, a section of the roadside gave way to a long line of billboards advertising a new housing estate: sleek modern apartment buildings, an azure-blue swimming pool, fashionable white people strolling around a mall and sipping coffee. The images flashed past the tinted windows, a glimpse of a parallel reality, before the scenery reverted back to rural Thailand.

The truck eventually turned off the road, made its way along a pot-holed dirt track, stopped in a clearing crowded with similar vehicles. A carbon copy of their driver stepped out from behind a large tree, directed them to a parking spot.

Milo got out of the truck, walked toward an open, thatched-roofed compound. Chance followed, the driver a few steps behind him. Chance noted the chunky Buddhist amulets on a chain around Milo's neck, the buffalo head belt buckle, and the bulge on one side of his untucked flannel shirt.

Inside the building, about fifty men were seated on circular metal benches descending toward a circle of dirt about a metre deep. The makeshift arena was splattered with patches of dark liquid and lined along the side with blue plastic sheeting. Two men squatted at opposite ends of the ring. One held a rooster by the neck, poured water onto the creature, massaged the moisture into its oily feathers. The other nestled a similar-looking bird against his huge stomach as he attached curved metal blades to its ankles with masking tape.

Milo left Chance in the crowd, worked his way around the ring toward a youngish man flanked by what were obviously two bodyguards. The young man's clothes mimicked the aesthetic of the spectators, blue jeans, faded work shirt, baseball cap, but he lacked their rough, weather-beaten look and manner. Chance guessed he was Issarapong.

The bodyguards eyed Milo suspiciously as he approached. The nearest grudgingly allowed him to slip past, sit next to his boss. Milo talked nervously into Issarapong's ear. The jao pho had a downturned mouth, sharp eyes that locked on Chance, coolly appraised him as Milo spoke.

Chance switched his gaze to the ring. The handlers gripped their birds firmly by the neck with one hand, caressed and stroked them with the other. A man in a white shirt and black jeans stepped between them, a microphone in his hand. As he addressed the crowd, the handlers moved closer together, sat on their haunches and angled their birds so they faced each other.

The referee placed a piece of Perspex between the two birds, signalled the handlers to let them go. The fowls sized each other up through the plastic for a moment and the referee lifted the screen.

The birds went for each other, pecking, biting, scraping. The crowd cheered and gesticulated wildly but all Chance could see was a blur of coloured feathers. Bored, he glanced at Issarapong. The jao pho continued to stare in his direction.

The birds clinched again. One got the other's neck in a solid grip with its beak. They remained like that for a moment, moved as if in some bizarre sideways dance. There was a small spray of blood and it was over. The spectators exploded in a frenzy of cheers. Issarapong nodded to Milo and his two bodyguards, and the four men stood up. The crowd parted to let them out.

The victorious fowl gave the limp bird a desultory peck and strutted around the ring.

They tailed the vehicle bearing Issarapong for an hour before both cars halted in front of a double-fronted wrought iron gate covered in gold metal scrolling and surrounded by a high, cream brick wall. A camera mounted next to the gate watched their every move. A man in jeans and a Bob Marley T-shirt, a machine gun slung casually over his shoulder, opened the gate from the other side.

Chance was transported into a faux European terrain of lush, well-maintained lawns, hedges and sculpted topiaries. A lagoon with an ornate fountain lay in the middle of the grounds, flamingos and peacocks on the grass around it. Such a display of wealth served only one purpose: to demonstrate the power of its owner.

The driveway terminated in front of a two-story house, bay windows, six white columns across the front. Chance's vehicle kept its distance, engine idling, while Issarapong stepped out of the lead car and disappeared through the front door.

Chance's vehicle pulled up to the entrance a few minutes later and he and Milo went inside. The first room was a massive entrance hall, polished marble floor and walls of inlaid wood. A curved wooden staircase led to the upper floor. A large crystal chandelier hung from the domed ceiling.

Milo led Chance up the stairs, down a lengthy hallway, stopped outside a wooden door. He opened the door without knocking, ushered Chance inside.

Eighteenth-century Europe transformed into the set of a B-grade science fiction movie. The large room was crowded with computer equipment, monitors, hard drives, and modems. More lined the shelves around the walls. Tiny lights flashed, data scrolled down screens, machinery hummed, and cables ran in all directions.

The only respite from the high tech avalanche was a large oil portrait of a hawk-faced old man in a well-cut blue suit next to a floor-to-ceiling window. Chance stood at the window, watched two armed men stroll around the lagoon, nearby, a male peacock spread its tail feathers out in a fan of colour.

Issarapong entered through a doorway on the far side. He'd traded his rural Thai fashion for chinos, a powder-blue polo top, clothes that made him look like he'd dressed for casual Friday at the office. His hair was wet and he rubbed at it with a towel slung over his shoulder.

Issarapong seated himself in a black padded office chair behind the desk, motioned to Chance to take one of the two stiff-backed wooden seats facing him. Without being asked, Milo seated himself in the second.

'You look surprised, Mister Chance. What were you expecting? An overweight country bumpkin on a wooden throne with buffalo horns, smelling of rice whisky?'

His English had an American accent. Old man Boonchu had no doubt packed his son off to university in the States. Given the profusion of computer equipment, there were no prizes for guessing his major.

'How do you like your new face, Mister Chance?'

'It'll do.'

Satisfied with the answer, Issarapong turned to Milo, spoke in Thai. Milo replied and the two men fell into a conversation, the purpose of which was to put Chance in his place, reinforce his status as an outsider.

'That was an interesting little show back there,' Chance interrupted.

Issarapong looked at him coldly. 'Aow jai puak chao ban. Or as you farangs call it, 'bread and circuses.' One must keep up appearances, especially in this period of transition following my father's death.'

Issarapong typed something on the keyboard of a laptop on the desk in front of him. 'Do you know why I have summoned you here?' he said without looking up.

'I can only guess you've heard from Mister Long in Australia?'

'My father and Long were associates in the old days, back when they were both starting out in their respective businesses.'

'Let me guess: they were apprentices in the same Triad together,' said Chance, annoyed at the Thai's games. He noticed Issarapong's face stiffen at the insult, felt satisfaction at his unease.

'Something like that.' Issarapong returned his attention to the laptop. 'Yes, I have had a message of sorts from Long.' Issarapong swivelled the laptop around so the screen was facing the two men sitting in front of him, hit a tab. 'Why don't you watch it for yourself.'

A grainy flesh-coloured blur appeared on the screen, accompanied by a soundtrack of laboured breathing. The camera panned back to reveal a man, his head slouched forward, chin touching his chest, framed in a circle of light, an anonymous red brick wall in the background.

A gloved hand reached into the frame, grabbed the man's hair, forced his face to look into the camera. It was Long, his features distorted by a mass of purple bruises and deep cuts, his upper lip swollen to almost comic-book proportions. One eye

166

was a black welt. The other gazed into the lens, unseeing.

Despite the arctic chill from the air conditioning, a blast furnace opened up in Chance's chest. A drop of sweat travelled down his spine to the small of his back. Aware Issarapong was measuring his reaction Chance relaxed his hands, sat very still. He swallowed, his throat dry.

A shrill mechanical whine started. The source of the noise came into view, a handheld circular saw, like the ones he'd seen advertised on shopping channels back in Australia, the blade a blur of steel.

The camera panned away, focused on the texture of the red brick wall. An animal scream echoed in what sounded like a large, empty space. The hair on the back of Chance's neck stood up. The taste of bile crept up the back of his throat. He forced it back down.

'Stop,' said Chance, his voice hoarse.

Issarapong tapped a key. The film stopped. He snapped the computer shut.

Chance breathed deeply for several moments. He had no love for the old man, but no one deserved to die like that.

'I've only shown you the final moments of the film. Long was a tough old man. He withstood a lot of punishment. A fitting tribute to his strength of character.'

'What about his daughter?'

'I don't know. She's not in the movie.'

Chance felt a rush of relief. 'Who would do that?'

Issarapong said nothing.

'Gao's people,' Chance answered his own question.

'The obvious choice.'

'How much do you know?'

'About what, that unpleasant business you and your friends were involved in in Surfers Paradise? Everything.'

Chance tried not to let the surprise show on his face.

'Do you really think I would have agreed to look after you without knowing the circumstances of how you came to be in my country? This equipment is not just for show. I know every-thing on the public record about you and your friends.' Issara-pong smiled, patted his laptop. 'And some that isn't.'

'How did you get the film?'

'It arrived a few days ago. I don't know where it was sent from, but I'll find out.'

Issarapong leaned forward, rested his chin on his hands.

'What is important is the sender knows you are here under my protection. My father made the agreement with Long to protect you. I honoured the deal because my father and Long were friends. Now that Long is dead, I consider the arrange-ment void.'

Chance started to speak, but Issarapong talked over him. 'Any other course of action in the current circumstances would be poor business sense. If I continue to harbour you, I will make an enemy of a powerful person, perhaps more powerful than me. I have little choice but to turn you and your friends over to Gao's people.'

Chance had no comeback, no choice but to wait until the Thai revealed what he wanted.

'My father stayed in control of this organisation for nearly forty years by killing anyone who stood in his way. He sent me to study in the U.S. because he wanted something different for his only son. Unfortunately, his illness ended those plans. Now I am in charge, I have to do exactly as he did, just as ruthlessly.' Issarapong paused to let his point sink in. 'That is, unless you can do something for me, something that might make it worth it to me to prolong our business arrangement.'

'Such as?'

Issarapong opened the laptop, typed something on the keypad. The screen sprang into life, an image of a tall man dressed in a jacket and open-necked shirt. He had short hair, an unusually angular face for a Thai.

'I want you to kill this man.'

'Why don't you get one of your own men to do it? Maybe

Milo here? He fancies himself as a gangsta,' Chance mimicked Milo's Cockney drawl. Milo looked straight ahead, did not meet his eyes.

'Milo's talents lie in other areas.'

'Then get someone else.'

'My father sold the American alcohol and women during the Vietnam War. He always said farangs were such blunt instruments. No subtlety. There are certain rules that need to be respected, especially in the delicate time following my father's death. It would not be good for me to be seen to have a hand in the killing of one of my senior subordinates, a rival for my position, even one that has been so disloyal.'

'Bad for morale?'

'Exactly.'

'Perform this task for me and I'll allow you to go your own way, no questions asked. I'll even provide new identities for you and your two friends. I'm not just talking about passports. I have the resources to create new data shadows for all of you, histories that won't raise a red flag to more high tech forms of police and security surveillance.'

'You must want this guy dead very badly.'

'I do.'

'What happens if I say no?'

'You will not leave this compound alive and I'll turn your friends over to Gao's people, or our police.'

'Then what other choice do I have?'

Issarapong smiled. 'None.'

Four

This is bad,' said Kate, her voice hollow.

An understatement, thought Chance. Things were so much worse than bad. He sipped his beer to hide his irritation.

Chance, Kate and Tavener sat at a table in Sri Racha's evening market, two dozen stalls under a corrugated tin roof, fluorescent tubes for lighting, a battery of ceiling fans that did nothing to relieve the stifling heat but a good job of evenly distributing the aroma of ginger, garlic and chillies from the surrounding kitchens.

Chance had just finished a heavily edited version of his conversation with Issarapong. Kate, eyes wide, her upper lip curled in horror, chain smoked as he spoke. Tavener lounged in his plastic chair, drank his beer. Chance could tell by the absence of his usual wisecracks and asides, the American was every bit as alarmed by what he had heard as Kate.

'Who does Issarapong want dead?' said Tavener.

'His name is Saradet. One of his senior lieutenants.'

'What did you tell Issarapong?' said Kate as she signalled for another round of beers.

'What the fuck do you think?' Chance said with a pained expression. 'Yes.'

'Can you imagine how much bad karma we're all going to amass from this?'

A vein on Chance's temple throbbed. 'For Christ's sake, spare me the cheap Land of Smiles tourist spirituality? In case

170

you hadn't noticed, there aren't a lot of options on the table.'

'It was a bad joke, I'm sorry.' Kate placed her hand on Chance's forearm.

Chance shook it off, suddenly angry she'd followed him here, that he felt responsible for her safety.

'We don't do this job, Issarapong will turn us over to Gao's people. That happens, we'll be starring in our own home movie.'

'There must be other options.'

'Such as?'

'We could run?'

'In case you hadn't noticed, we're already running.'

Kate glanced at Tavener, got no reaction.

'Listen,' said Chance. 'I don't like this any more than you. It's totally out of my league. I'm a thief. I steal things, usually for someone else. I've thought about the situation all afternoon. There's no other option.'

Chance flinched at the loud hiss of food hitting hot oil in the nearest stall.

'Want to know something else? It's a relief, because at least it's some movement. I've been asleep for the last couple of months, ever since we arrived in Thailand. Now I'm awake and it feels good.'

'That operation didn't just change your face, it changed your personality, as well,' said Kate coldly.

'Don't pretend you ever knew me,' said Chance. 'You don't like the way things are going, be my guest and fuck off.'

'And where exactly would you like me to fuck off to?'

'Wherever. I don't care. I didn't have a choice about coming here. You did. The police back in Australia didn't have much of a line on you. They don't even seem to know your real name. You didn't need to leave. Why the hell are you in Thailand anyway?

The question hung unanswered in the humid night air, as a young woman cleared away their empty beer cans, replaced them with new ones.

'If you two have quite finished.' Tavener picked up his fresh beer, opened it and drank. 'You realise it's probably a set-up?'

'Of course,' said Chance. 'I help Issarapong eliminate a business rival or whatever the guy is, after which he'll frame me for the killing, hand me to the Thai police or shop me to Gao's people. But at least, this way gives us some breathing space, a chance to try and turn this thing around.'

'So, how are we going to go about it?' said Kate.

'Did you say 'we?'' said Chance. 'I didn't say anything about Tavener being involved and I thought you found the whole thing morally beneath you.'

'Let's just say you've convinced me we don't have much choice in the matter. I'm in. What about you, Tavener?'

'Why not? Besides, left to his own devices, Gary would probably just fuck it up, land us all deeper in the shit than we already are. Did Issarapong say where you're supposed to do this?'

'Bangkok.'

'Any other details?'

'No. Milo's our liaison. We're to meet him in Bangkok tomorrow night, he'll run through all the details then.'

'Milo?' Tavener snorted. 'Jesus, that's like crawling into a sleeping bag with a rattlesnake.'

The young woman arrived with their order, several seafood dishes on iron plates that sizzled and hissed in the middle of their table.

'I'm not hungry,' said Kate, taking another cigarette from a pack on the table next to her.

'Well, I'm not going to let it go to waste.' Tavener reached over and helped himself to the nearest dish, a whole fried fish smothered in chilli sauce.

Chance reluctantly spooned some rice onto his plate, picked at it with his fork. He knew he should eat, but images from the movie, the sound of Long's screams on continuous loop in his head, had left him with little appetite.

'Okay, we've got to think carefully about this,' Tavener said as he chewed his food. 'Bangkok is good. It gets us out of this shithole into a bigger playpen. I've also got a contact there that might be able to help us, someone my daddy knew in Vietnam.'

'Tavener has a mother and a father?' Kate's mouth twisted into a wry smile. 'Who would have imagined.'

Five

Chance leaned against his motorbike, watched a group of young construction workers dig away at the earth next to the footpath.

The downpour had subsided. Water dripped from signs and awnings, collected in brown puddles along the gutters. The scent of rain on hot asphalt lasted an instant before being doused by dust and the stench of exhaust fumes from the endless traffic.

A large billboard with a smiling nuclear family, well-groomed and pale-skinned, looked down on the dark-skinned workers. The father held a credit card next to his face. The text was in Thai. Chance couldn't tell what it said but assumed the message and the associated image of affluence wasn't lost on the men digging the hole.

Bangkok was a city where power and wealth dwelt in the sky, trickled down like rain to the streets below. The rich lived in tall, gleaming condominium complexes and luxury hotels like the one where Chance was waiting outside. The poor, the men digging up the road, lived with their families in portable dormitories on the outskirts of town, or corrugated iron and wood shacks in the shadows and crevices of motorways and skyscrapers.

Chance refocused his mind on the task at hand, the few details Milo had revealed when they'd met two nights ago.

The target's name was Saradet Kriansak.

He lived in an upscale condo in Bangkok's northern suburbs with his wife and two children.

Milo would supply money, transport, whatever they needed to get the job done.

They had two weeks.

Issarapong wanted the job done as cleanly as possible.

'This is not fucking Iraq,' quipped Milo. 'The boss wants everything kept low key and don't hurt his family. Everything else is on a need-to-know basis and, for now, you don't need to know anything else.'

Milo was staying at the same hotel as Chance and his companions, a large, featureless building among the architectural and neon chaos of Bangkok's Chinatown. The man who'd driven Chance to see Issarapong—his name was Nareth—had accompanied Milo, sat in the corner of the room, said nothing.

'How am I supposed to kill him?' Chance had asked. 'With my bare hands?'

'You'll get a weapon, whatever else you need, after you come up with a plan,' Milo said. 'Until then, there's too much risk of your being picked up by the local Plod carrying a gun.'

It also made it easier for Milo to control things, thought Chance.

'This setup's got more holes than a hunk of Swiss cheese,' said Tavener after the two Thais had left. 'We need more information.'

He proposed a rolling stakeout to gather intelligence on Saradet's movements, potential weaknesses, whatever additional information would help them pick the best time to move. They agreed to take it in turns, shifts of two days each. Any longer risked becoming too obvious. Chance got the first shift.

'This isn't a movie. How does a foreigner my size tail a Thai gangster around Bangkok without being noticed?'

The solution, Kate's idea, was for him to dress like one of the ubiquitous motorcycle taxi drivers that collected in gangs all over Bangkok: sneakers, blue jeans, long-sleeved top, fluoro vest, gloves, balaclava, helmet.

Chance sweltered under the layers, the helmet and gloves,

but, so far, it had worked. No one bothered him, although Chance had to be constantly alert to ensure the real, and notoriously competitive, motorcycle taxi drivers didn't get suspicious. Aside from that, his main problem had been finding places to piss without losing his target.

Chance spent the first day following Saradet to a series of meetings. The Thai travelled in style, a silver Mercedes Benz, two bodyguards who alternated driving duties. He looked like a typical fortysomething Thai businessman, smart suit, good haircut, latest model iPhone, constantly pressed to his ear, with one difference: his skin was a rich mahogany, like the men who toiled in the muddy hole outside the hotel.

Chance had speculated about the man's origins. Perhaps a farm boy turned enforcer, risen up through the old man Boonchu's organisation. What had Saradet done to earn such a prominent place on his boss's shit list?

The only break in the monotony occurred when they were caught up in some sort of political rally, hundreds of people camped on the sidewalk outside what looked like a government building, wearing identical yellow shirts. They waved Thai flags and held portraits of the country's King. Police watched from the sidelines.

Day two and it didn't look like things were going to get any more exciting. Saradet left his condo early, spent the better part of the morning at Klong Thoey market, a sprawling old-fashioned wet market now surrounded by skyscrapers, then continued on to what Chance assumed was a lunch meeting at this hotel.

Chance's Bangkok geography had come back to him over the last day and a half, and he recognised the hotel's location, a stone's throw from Khao San Road, Bangkok's main backpacker strip. He popped a lozenge in his mouth to soothe his throat, raw from the pollution. It was a part of town he remembered well from a previous visit to Bangkok.

Chance had been in his early twenties, already planning to join the army, but wanted to put off the decision, and travel seemed the best way. He'd backpacked up through Indonesia, Malaysia and southern Thailand, ended up low on cash, marking time in Bangkok.

Mel had been from Sydney, older than Chance by a decade. She was on the run from a marriage she'd got into too young and a small child back in Australia she didn't know what to do with.

She'd been sitting in a cloud of marihuana smoke in the café attached to his backpacker hotel, drinking beer and watching a Sylvester Stallone movie on a TV attached to the wall above the bar. Next to her was a dreadlocked Thai man called Eddie, who Chance had seen lurking around the popular bars on the strip.

Chance and Mel had got to talking. Mel had some money, but more importantly, Chance thought, she could teach him things. They became lovers, sunk into a daily routine of drinking, fucking and dope-smoking, punctuated by the occasional half-hearted trip to a temple or some other tourist site.

They were sitting in the café with Eddie when the Thai suggested the three of them visit a place that sold cheap gems. No pressure, but if they wanted they could buy some, take them back to Australia to sell, make good money.

They went, patiently sat through the owner's spiel about how to recognise fake stones from real, but didn't buy anything. It was so obviously a setup that Chance and Mel wondered whether it was some kind of test. Their suspicions were confirmed a couple of nights later when Eddie made them another offer. How would they like to make ten thousand dollars each? All they had to do was each take a package back to Sydney with them, deliver it to a flat in Bondi.

'What's in the packages?' Chance had asked cautiously.

'What do you think, man?' said Eddie. 'Heroin.'

'What happens if we get caught?'

The Thai had exhaled a lungful of marihuana smoke, smiled. 'You'll go to jail.'

He declined. Mel said yes. She wanted money to start a new

life with her daughter, flew out two days later, the smack taped against the contours of her belly.

The night she'd left Chance got drunk, brought a bar girl back to his hotel room. He woke the next morning, found she'd cleaned him out—passport, what little money he had left, a watch his late father had given him, even Mel's leftover toiletries.

When Chance told Eddie what had happened, the Thai gave him a stoned grin, said he might be able to find a way for Chance to make some money.

He went to work for Eddie, spotting Australian tourists who might be interested in transporting packages back home. Chance was good at it, quickly learned how to pick up the signs of desperation or recklessness that were the prerequisite signs for a possible mule, while his casual, everyman air put people at their ease. When he'd flown home several weeks later, he had money in his pocket and a crash course in human weakness under his belt.

Chance was wondering for the hundredth time whether Mel had got through airport security okay, what had become of her, when he saw the bodyguards exit the hotel, followed by Saradet.

The three men stood on the front steps, waited for a valet to bring the car around. Chance flipped down the visor of his helmet, gunned the bike into life and edged several cars behind them as they turned into the traffic.

Six

Chance parked the motorbike at the entrance to a long strip of go-go bars and pubs, slipped off his vest, helmet and balaclava, carried them under his arm as he waded into the sea of people.

Tavener had called his mobile phone earlier, said to meet him at Soi Cowboy, a notorious strip of go-go bars catering to foreigners.

'I just want to go back to the hotel and have a hot shower,' replied Chance.

'Just be there,' Tavener concluded and the line went dead.

The last daylight had melted into the horizon, replaced with a forest of pulsating neon that bathed everything in a ghostly pink hue.

Chance spotted the meeting place, a Wild West-themed bar, spied Tavener at the table nearest the entrance, resplendent in a blue shirt with bright red flowers, his ubiquitous fishing cap. Kate and another much older man Chance didn't recognise sat with him. Several Thai women dressed in knee-length boots, white miniskirts, bikini tops, and cowboy hats stood nearby, called out to the passing trade.

'How did it go today?' Kate said as Chance sat down.

'A fucking waste of time.' A small bottle of beer appeared in front of Chance. He drained half, looked at the stranger over the top of the bottle, unsure how much else to say in front of him. The old man didn't register his arrival, gazed into the crowd with practiced disinterest.

Tavener cleared his throat, tipped his beer bottle in the direction of the old man. 'Gary, this is Huey.'

'Huey?'

The old man shifted on his stool to face Chance. 'Yeah, like the helicopter.' Huey's face had a gaunt, sallow appearance, accentuated by his grey crew cut and a slight underbite where his lower lip jutted out.

'You don't have to be shy about what you say around Huey, he was an old pal of my dad's,' said Tavener. 'They served in Vietnam together.'

Chance watched the pudgy doorman lift the curtain to the entrance for a customer, caught sight of a slither of blue neon, a mass of serpentine legs shuffling on a stage.

'And what exactly did you and his dad do in 'Nam?' Chance emphasised the last word.

'This and that,' said Huey, his eyes following two passing bar girls.

Chance nodded unenthusiastically. 'Just what we need, another barfly who speaks in code.'

'I've already appraised Huey of our situation.' Tavener smiled. 'He assures me he can provide us with a little off-the-books technical support.'

'Lias here tells me you've got yourself a shitstorm of trouble, boy.'

'Lias?' said Chance, eyebrows raised. Tavener ignored him. 'Old Huey here looks like he has his work cut out staying upright. So unless by *help* you mean buying cheap Viagra, I'm not sure what use he can be.'

Huey turned to Tavener. 'Boy's got a nasty streak to match his ugly face.'

'Things will get off to a much better start if you don't call me boy,' Chance said.

'Believe me, boy, there's still enough strength left in these bones to give you a hiding.'

'Try it, I'm not above hitting an old man.'

'For God's sake, both of you, enough.' Kate slammed an open palm on the table, bottles shook, a couple of nearby cowgirls looked in their direction.

Chance and the old man glared at each other.

'Let's go for a walk.' Tavener stood, threw a couple of purple-coloured Thai bank notes on the table. 'After you, Huey.'

Huey led them away from the brightly lit strip with surprising speed, down several dark winding side streets. He stopped outside a restaurant, waved to a young man stacking plastic chairs inside, disappeared down a narrow alleyway along the side of the building.

By the time Chance and the others caught up, Huey was half-way up a set of dimly lit stairs. He unlocked a metal-reinforced door. A single bulb flickered to life, revealed a large room with dusty, covered tables and chairs stacked against one side, crates and beer kegs against another. In the middle sat an old pool table, half covered by a white sheet. A wooden counter took up most of the far side of the room, along with a set of stairs and a doorway, both leading to darkness.

Chance walked over to a barred window, looked over the alley along the side of the building. 'What is this place?'

'A little social club I used to run,' said Huey. 'Lias told me you needed some place off the grid. Reckon this'll fit the bill.'

'More rooms through the doorway behind the bar,' said Tavener. 'Sleeping quarters, a functioning bathroom. We need a place away from Milo's prying eyes. Somewhere we can talk, put plan B into action.'

'Plan B?' said Chance.

'Figuring out how to whack this guy Issarapong wants dead without winding up in the hands of Gao's people or the Thai police.'

'Use this place whenever you want.' Huey handed Tavener a key. 'Some Thai folks run a soup kitchen downstairs during the day, but they won't bother you none.'

'What's upstairs?' said Chance.

'Take a look for yourself.'

The stairs emerged onto a roofed terrace furnished with a selection of long-dead potted plants and a few mismatched pieces of furniture.

Huey sat in a derelict-looking cane chair, fumbled in the pocket of his shirt, produced something he stuck in his mouth and lit. A swirl of pungent marijuana smoke twisted in the air around him.

'Strictly medicinal purposes, son, if you were figuring on asking.'

'I wasn't,' said Chance.

'Most of the crew I used to run with are gone—' Huey dragged on the joint, exhaled, emitted a moist cough, ' —but I still know one or two folks around town, might be useful. You want anything, just ask.'

'Thanks,' said Chance.

'Not doing it for you. Couldn't care less if they use you for target practice.' The American passed the joint to Kate, who accepted it enthusiastically. 'Doing it for Lias here. Weren't for his daddy, I wouldn't be alive.'

'Huey's already helped me circumvent Milo's restriction on firearms.' Tavener hitched up the front of his tropical shirt.

Chance saw the butt of a small pistol tucked in his pants, the wooden grip dark against Tavener's pale stomach.

'When do I get one of those?' said Chance.

Huey flashed a crooked smile, looked like an old buzzard. 'When you're old enough to use it.'

Huey and Tavener broke into laughter.

Seven

Tavener drained the dregs of beer from the plastic cup, dropped it on the ground. He inhaled the dense, mentholated air pushed around by the stadium's ceiling fans, his eyes moving between Saradet and the two Muay Thai boxers in their respective corners.

Gangsters could always be relied upon to like the fights, he mused as he signalled for another drink. Not that the desire to watch two men beat the shit out of each other was restricted to males, if the number of Thai and foreign women in the crowd was any indication.

Saradet sat ringside, one of the few Thais in an area apparently reserved for foreigners. He used the break between rounds to engage in an animated conversation on his mobile phone. Seated on either side of him were two granite-faced bodyguards who looked as though they might have done a bit of time in the ring themselves.

You sure have landed yourself in it this time, Lias was how Huey had summed up his predicament when they met up the previous night.

It hadn't been the first time in his career Tavener stumbled across dead bodies in a hotel suite. Not running, going after Chance and the Norliss woman, thinking they had the heroin or would take him to the person who did, was a mistake. A far more serious error had been getting involved with an amateur like Gao.

In his experience, survival was twenty percent luck and wits, eighty percent the ability to compartmentalise. You had to focus, not take shit personally, stay uninvolved. He'd broken all three rules big time. All he could do now was try to get out of the situation alive. His Australian friends wouldn't be much help. Kate had spirit. She reminded him of his first wife, a red-haired Texan with a mouth like a sailor. But she wasn't much use in their current situation. As for Chance, he had potential but was still learning, a blunt knife when the situation called for a scalpel.

Thank Christ for Huey. He spoke fluent Thai, knew people and his old bar would prove a useful bolthole. So would the Saturday night special 'belly gun' Huey had sourced for Tavener. Back in the States people would have called it a woman's gun, but it was perfect for Bangkok. Fuck Milo and his no-weapons-until-they-have-a-plan shit. Tavener didn't trust anything that antsy, half-breed scumbag said, felt safer with the chunk of black metal nestled against his skin.

Saradet was off the phone now, his attention on the two fighters in the ring. After spending the first few rounds probing each other for weaknesses, the boxers were becoming aggressive, unleashing a barrage of jabs and solid kicks on each other. Both men had finely chiselled, muscular bodies, looked evenly matched as far as Tavener could tell. Indeed, were it not for their different-coloured shorts, one in blue, the other red, he'd have difficulty telling them apart.

Blue seemed to favour the clinch, holding his opponent close so he could knee him in the kidneys. Red kept trying to break away, get some distance so he could put all his weight into a combination of left-right hooks.

Many of the foreigners and all of the Thai spectators back in the stadium's bleachers were on their feet now, their yelling more frenzied with each blow. Saradet sat back, appraised the action. Not given to impetuous actions, the kind of man used to analysing a situation before acting, the perfect personality for a senior enforcer.

Tavener had followed Saradet around Bangkok all day, hoping to find a chink in his armour, a weakness, something that would suggest the right place and time to do the hit.

Saradet always had two bodyguards with him, travelled nearly everywhere by car, minimised time spent on the street. The only exception had been when Saradet visited a section of the city known as Little Arabia, the streets too narrow and crowded to take the Benz.

Tavener had followed Saradet through a warren of laneways lined with beauty parlours, souvenir shops and restaurants selling Middle Eastern food, jammed with families on vacation, overweight men and women in full burqa, to a hotel where he met several men in traditional Arab dress.

He counted at least half a dozen times he could have just walked up to Saradet, shot him with his Saturday night special. But it would have been a suicide mission. Tavener didn't believe in suicide missions, had spent his whole career avoiding them.

A Thai woman appeared with a tray of beers. Her face broke into a wide smile as Tavener gave her a note, waved away the change. He loved the way Thai women smiled. It was like being hit with a concentrated beam of warmth. One of the many things he loved about the place. The climate was good, the people friendly. Under different circumstances he'd move here in a flash, find a nice bar stool, affix himself to it, grow old like Huey.

He laughed to himself. Stake-out dreams, the term he gave to how the mind wandered when you were tailing a target. A lot of stakeouts since he'd joined the Drug Enforcement Agency at the age of twenty-four. All those years he'd spent fighting the so-called war on drugs until he'd finally left the Agency, gone to work for himself.

Tavener felt the roar of the crowd, looked up. The boxer in the blue shorts lay unconscious on the canvas, his opponent bowing to the crowd, both hands held in front of his face like he was praying.

A moment later, he noticed the young woman who had suddenly materialised in the seat next to Saradet. She had long dark hair and pale skin. Her face was a little pouty for his tastes but the woman's figure looked like it had been poured into her black jeans and halter top.

Most interestingly, she wasn't Saradet's wife.

The American smiled.

'Bingo,' he whispered.

Eight

Third morning in a row, Kate waited in the café at the intersection of Sukhumvit Road—Bangkok's main drag—and the street where the woman's luxury condo was situated.

Kate banked on the woman being a creature of habit, breathed a sigh of relief when she appeared, turned onto Sukhumvit and headed for the nearest Skytrain station.

Kate stood at the opposite end of the Skytrain carriage, waited two stops until the woman got off, followed her through the crowded platform, down the stairs to the street below.

Kate guessed her target was a similar age to herself, mid-twenties. The woman walked a block, stopped at the first of a row of vendors, bought a garland of jasmine, a small orange candle, several sticks of incense, entered the courtyard of the Ewaran Shrine. Kate had looked up the shrine on the internet after following the woman here the last two mornings. One of the most popular in Bangkok, not strictly Buddhist, the golden statue a Thai representation of the four-faced Brahma God, Than Tao Mahaprom, a god of mercy, kindness, sympathy and impartiality, one face representing each trait.

The woman lit her incense from one of several oil lamps positioned around the courtyard, joined a long line of people, waited patiently with her offerings. The statue sat in a hut inlaid with coloured glass and surrounded by railing covered in garlands and narrow concrete troughs filled with sand containing a forest of smouldering incense sticks.

When her turn came, she draped the jasmine over the railing, lit the candle with a lighter from her tote bag and placed it and the incense sticks in the sand. She stood for a moment, head bowed, hands held together in front of her face, moved to make way for the next person.

Hedging her bets, thought Kate, cheeky bitch. Praying to Buddha for good fortune, on the one hand. Fucking Saradet, living in the apartment he probably paid for, on the other.

Chance and Tavener referred to her as Saradet's girlfriend but Kate understood the correct term was mia noi, or 'minor wife.' She wasn't sure what Saradet's actual wife would have made of the arrangement, but Kate could see the advantages from the girlfriend's point of view. Money, a nice apartment, the advantages of a male without the bullshit—no nagging, no sullen guy flaked in front of the TV every night, getting shitty as the years passed him by.

As she watched the woman leave the shrine compound and walk back toward the stairway to the Skytrain, Kate couldn't help but feel strangely envious. If nothing else, the woman knew what she wanted, looked after herself. Kate could take a lesson or two from her.

She was still pissed off at Chance. His words—Why the hell are you in Thailand anyway?—burnt every time she thought of them. Arrogant bastard obviously thought he was the reason she'd followed him to Thailand. She did like him. He had a simplicity she found attractive. There was no guile in him. What you see is what you get. At least that's what she used to think. Whatever slender thread of mutual attraction that might have been developing between them had disappeared along with his old face.

Tavener had suggested putting a tail on the woman. He had followed her and Saradet after the Thai boxing, as they'd driven, sans bodyguards, to a run-down hotel complex, rooms available by the night or the hour, minimal staff.

'It's the perfect set-up,' Tavener told them. 'Out of the way, easy to get into and, most of all, he doesn't take his bodyguards to bed with him when they fuck.'

'Makes perfect sense to me,' Kate had quipped. 'He's a man and men follow their dicks.'

The comment garnered a sly guffaw from Milo, who leaned against the wall, a glass of scotch in his hand. The Cockney was half cut every time she saw him now.

Chance, who looked like he'd been falling asleep when Tavener began his spiel, sat up, his eyes suddenly alive with the possibilities. 'I like it. We follow the girlfriend, hope she hooks up with Saradet and they go back to that hotel.'

'You lads have been following Saradet around Bangkok for the better part of a week, trying to find a chink in his armour, and got nothing.' Milo gulped his drink. 'Don't see what we've got to lose.'

The four of them had agreed Kate was the obvious candidate to tail the woman. It was a relief to be useful and have an excuse to get out of their hotel and away from a sullen Chance and a sleazy Milo. The latter had taken increased interest in Kate since they'd been in Bangkok, constantly hanging around her, even offering to act as a tour guide to the sights.

Kate, who had never followed anyone before, attempted to act inconspicuous, kept her distance while not losing sight of the woman. Not that any of her precautions seemed to matter. This part of Bangkok, Sukhumvit Road leading to the retail area of Siam Square, was farang central. A foreigner, wandering aimlessly, let alone a foreign woman, attracted zero attention. On top of that, apart from her brief interludes at the shrine, her target was almost permanently plugged into her smart phone, gazing at the screen or, earplugs attached, listening to music or talking, oblivious to the world around her.

Kate shadowed her target along an elevated walkway,

watched her turn off at the entrance to one of several large, modern shopping malls at Siam Square. The place was cool and quiet, not yet crowded with shoppers. Kate pretended to be interested in various window displays as she tailed the woman to a chic-looking café, exposed wood, generous booths separated by smoked glass covered with intricate patterns, experimental art on the walls.

Kate took the booth adjoining the one occupied by the woman, sat with her back to the smoked glass partition, listened to the Thai's meandering one-way conversation on the mobile.

Kate had started learning Thai to relieve the boredom of her time in Sri Racha. She'd never tried to learn a language before, found it hard at first, trying to make herself understood in mangled, half-formed sentences, correctly pronounce the tones. But the hotel staff were patient, welcomed the diversion. She'd gradually improved and, to her surprise, found she had a talent for it. She wasn't fluent by any means, but she could listen in to conversations like the one happening over her shoulder, pick up the gist of what was said.

Kate heard the phrase maaw duu or fortune teller. The woman gave a rundown of her most recent session, the fortune teller's advice about an overseas trip she was planning.

Three slim, pale-skinned Thai women appeared and climbed into the woman's booth. As they greeted one another, Kate got the woman's name. Nattiya.

Kate zoned in and out of their conversation, became alert when the subject of boyfriends came up. Nattiya didn't mention Saradet by name, but it was obvious whom she was talking about. Nattiya had met up with him a couple of nights ago at the boxing, gone to what she referred to as a rongram man ruud, a love hotel. The place Tavener had described.

They talked too fast, used too much slang for her to understand the entire conversation. The upshot was Saradet was a tiger in the sack. Goosebumps formed on Kate's skin as Nattiya told her friends they had plans tonight, a nightclub, and then back to the same hotel.

Kate remained in the booth, very still, for several minutes after the women left. She got out her mobile phone, stared at the blank screen, thrilled and scared and sickened by the information she had, what it meant.

She dialled Chance's number.

Nine

Kate glanced around the hotel room, a group of people planning a crime, got a rush of Surfers Paradise, déjà vu.

She would be inside the club, call Tavener when Saradet and Nattiya left, then phone Chance to give him the heads-up.

Tavener would be outside, follow the two Thais, let Chance know when they were coming, advise him of any change of plans.

Chance would be waiting at a bar around the corner from the love hotel. When he got the call from Tavener, he'd go to the hotel, wait for Saradet.

Milo nodded between sips of his drink as they went over their roles. Nareth sat silently in a corner, tried unsuccessfully to fade into the shadows. Kate noticed how the big Thai watched Milo as closely as the others.

When Milo was satisfied everyone knew their part, he stood, produced a gun from his jacket pocket. A masculine smell wafted off the well-oiled piece of metal, cut through the stale air in the enclosed space. Milo slid back the mechanism in an exaggerated gesture, aimed the gun at Chance's face, leered.

Kate felt the room tense. Chance didn't flinch.

Milo pulled the trigger. 'Bang,' he said. Karen jumped at the sound, a dull metal click.

Milo flipped the gun over, handed it grip-first to Chance, laughed. 'It's short barrelled so you'll need to get in close.' The Cockney felt around his jacket pocket, pulled out a clip of ammunition. 'You won't need a spare. Saradet didn't get where he was in Issarapong's organisation by being good at paperwork. You don't get him first shot, you won't get another.'

'What happens then?' said Chance.

'Chocolates, flowers, and a happy ending,' said Milo. 'What the fuck do you think happens? You and the rest of your merry band get to live, isn't that enough?'

Kate met Chance's eyes, looked away. What about the woman? Chance was only supposed to kill Saradet, but Kate knew Nattiya couldn't be allowed to live. She almost said something, stopped herself. There was no point.

Kate paused at the door to her room, took her swipe card from her jeans pocket. She heard movement behind her, turned, found herself inches away from Milo's face. His eyes were bloodshot, his breath rank with alcohol. He was alone.

Milo snickered. 'Men follow their dicks.'

'What?' She pressed herself against the door to her room, tried to put some space between her and the Cockney.

'You said it yourself, the other night about Saradet and his woman going to the love hotel. 'Men follow their dicks.' Clever and true.'

He took a step forward to make up the ground between them.

'Mind you, reckon that's something a bird like you would know from experience.'

Kate ignored the innuendo. 'What do you want?'

'Thought you might fancy a nightcap.' Milo's face twisted around the words, was aiming for suave but it came off a threat.

'No, thanks.'

'Come on. Big day tomorrow, everyone's tense, couple of kitchen sinks, a spot of charlie, take the edge off.'

'You ask me, Milo, you've already had enough.'

Milo put one hand over her shoulder, rested it against the door behind her. 'Don't faff around, love, you're pulled.'

'By you? You must be high as well as pissed.'

Milo's eyebrows narrowed, he withdrew his hand. 'What, saving yourself for Mister Identikit?'

Kate said nothing.

'Suit yourself.' Milo held her stare for a few moments more, walked away.

When he'd disappeared around the corner, Kate stepped into her room, closed the door behind her and pressed her back against it. She realised she was holding her breath, exhaled deeply.

'Jesus Christ, what a complete sleaze.'

She didn't move for several minutes, half expecting Milo to return. When she was certain he wasn't coming back, she kicked off her sandals, did a hundred-and-eighty-degree sweep of the sterile surrounds. Her possessions filled one bag, everything else in the space was ordered, cheap and disposable.

She found a half-empty pack of cigarettes, took a saucer to the window, parted the heavy curtains, gazed down at Chinatown as she lit up. Bumper to bumper traffic, crowded footpaths, everything bathed in multi-coloured neon. She felt totally cut off from the sea of humanity ten stories below. A few muted sounds penetrated the thick glass. Otherwise all she heard was the crackle of tobacco from the tip of her smoke. Kate noticed a dull ache deep in her chest, thought it might be the rough Thai cigarette, realised it was loneliness.

She finished her cigarette and lay down on the bed. Nicotine and adrenaline coursed through her. She knew sleep wouldn't come.

Kate walked barefoot down the hallway, knocked hard on Chance's door.

He peered at her, poked his head out, looked in both directions down the empty hallway.

'Only me,' she said.

He was naked except for a pair of boxer shorts. She remembered him lying on a bed in the cheap motel in northern New South Wales, in a town whose name she had forgotten. His body bruised and battered then, now looked strong and clean, a thin pink scar on his shoulder the only reminder of the time.

'What is it, Kate?'

'I've had enough.'

'Enough what?'

'Don't play fucking innocent. I'm sick of it.' She took a step forward, conscious she was mimicking the behaviour toward her only moments earlier, shrugged the feeling off. 'I can't do anything about what happens tomorrow night, Saradet, Issarapong, Milo, but I can do something about you and me.'

'Why?'

'Sometimes you've got to dance with the one that brought you.'

She pulled his face onto hers, kissed him, broke away. He tasted earthy, the unshaved bristles rough against her skin.

He broke away, looked directly into her eyes. 'This is not the time.'

Kate placed a hand on his hard stomach, moved down, felt his semi-erect penis through the thin fabric of the boxers.

'Your head may think that—' she smiled up at his crooked face, strangely tender in the dim light, '—but the rest of your body disagrees.'

He reached under her T-shirt. She felt a flood of warmth as he cupped one of her breasts. 'It's going to get complicated.'

'It already is.'

She kissed him again, pushed him inside, kicked the door closed behind her.

Ten

Chance picked up the cigarette from where it sat on the edge of the metal ashtray, drew on it hard as he looked at the empty mobile phone screen.

Nearly midnight and the bar still swirled with activity. Dozens of foreign men, twice as many women. People shouted above the blare from a large flat-screen TV showing a soccer match. The men were drunk, the women increasingly aggressive as closing time loomed, and with it the prospect of being left without a customer for the night, their smiles as genuine as the Viagra and designer T-shirts for sale at stalls along Sukhumvit Road.

Fresh meat when he'd first arrived three hours ago, Chance had battered away advances from several Thai women who'd wanted a drink, to sit with him. Now the working girls left him alone, hunted for better prospects.

The bar was the last in a long line of watering holes on both sides of the street. Further on the street curved left, became quieter, small businesses, all closed for the night, guesthouses and hotels, including the one used by Saradet and his girlfriend.

The love hotel was two stories tall, a car park underneath the building, individual parking spaces, each with a curtain that could be drawn to prevent prying eyes scoping out the number plates and make of customers' cars. The only security was an old guy in a wood-panelled office in the entrance foyer next to vending machines selling condoms.

It had been more than an hour since Kate had called to tell him Saradet had left the club with his girlfriend. It was the first time they'd spoken since she'd left his bed that morning. Chance could sense she wanted to say something else, ended the call before she could, told himself he needed to keep the line free.

The televised crowd roared as a player scored, the noise echoed by the men in the bar. Chance picked up his cigarette just as his phone rang and the screen lit up with a single word: Tavener.

'They stopped for a bite but they're moving again,' said Tavener. 'Estimated time of arrival is five, ten minutes tops.'

Chance mashed out his cigarette, threw a wad of crumpled Thai baht notes on the table. He paused at the entrance to the bar, stuck another note in a plastic cup held by a beggar who sat cross-legged on the narrow footpath, a filthy infant asleep in her lap. She grinned; the grime and poverty etched on her face made her appear much older than she probably was.

A travel agency sat opposite the hotel's entrance, faded posters in the window. Chance leaned into the shadows under its awning to avoid being seen by a passing foreign couple, checked out the price of cheap tickets to Europe and the United States.

Headlights appeared in the distance. As the vehicle edged closer, he recognised the familiar shape of Saradet's Benz. Chance withdrew the pistol from the pocket of his denim jacket, checked the safety was off. He jogged after the vehicle as it slowly turned into the hotel parking lot, went down the incline into one of the parking spots under the building.

The curtains were already drawn across the parking spot by the time Chance arrived. He ducked in between the heavy pieces of fabric, crouched at the rear of the car. Heat emanated from metal and a heavy smell of exhaust hung in the enclosed concrete space. Saradet stood by the front passenger's door, faintly illuminated by the overhead light inside the car.

Chance walked around the car, placed the pistol against the

side of Saradet's head. Chance allowed Saradet to swivel his head slightly, his dark eyes moving between Chance and the barrel of the pistol. Chance slowly squeezed the trigger.

'Wait,' said the woman, half out of the passenger's seat.

Kate had said nothing about her speaking English.

He kept the pistol trained on Saradet. The woman slid the rest of her body out of car, stood in front of him in a black cocktail dress with generous cleavage. Ice-blue contact lenses gave her eyes an animal-like appearance. Chance searched his memory for her name. Nattiya.

'Whoever is paying, we'll give you more,' said Nattiya. 'You'll be rich and we can be out of Thailand in twelve hours, disappear.'

Saradet said something in Thai.

'Issarapong sent you,' she translated. It wasn't a question.

Chance knew his hesitation answered the question. Saradet smiled.

'Tell your boyfriend to put both hands on the car roof,' said Chance.

Chance patted Saradet down with one hand, held the gun in the other. When he was satisfied the Thai was unarmed, he prodded him in the direction of his girlfriend. The two Thais stood with their backs against the concrete wall, looked at him expectantly.

Chance smiled. 'Let's go somewhere we can talk.'

Eleven

They cut a deal in the Muay Thai-themed room Saradet had booked for his tryst with Nattiya. It had a round bed, blue-tinted lights inlaid into the floor around the base, a replica of a boxing ring, a bar with several stools, mirrored walls and ceiling. The lighting made the three of them look ghostly, but it was the mirrors that particularly unnerved Chance. His new face stared back at him, strange and unfamiliar, like a fourth person in the room only he could see.

The old receptionist hadn't batted an eyelid at two well-dressed Thais sharing a room with a rough looking farang, passed Saradet the key, told Chance in laboured English to be careful, several guests had broken a leg showing off their kickboxing skills in the ring, returned to his newspaper.

Chance told the two Thais to sit in the middle of the ring. He sat on the bed, the pistol on his knee, while they talked.

Issarapong had two reasons for wanting Saradet dead.

He'd discovered Saradet had been skimming from his operations, the money stashed in a bank account in Dubai, ready for him and his mistress to relocate to the Middle East.

Saradet's face became visibly angry as he spoke and Nattiya struggled to translate the flow of words. It was a familiar underworld story. Faithful lieutenant sheds considerable sweat and other people's blood in the course of years of service on behalf of his boss, only to be passed over, in this case in favour of the boss's spoiled, foreign-educated son. Worse, the son puts his trust in an untrustworthy farang drug dealer to help him.

'You mean Milo?'

Saradet launched into a stream of Thai invective at the mention of the name. Nattiya didn't bother to translate.

According to Saradet, he wasn't the only one dissatisfied. Issarapong's organisation was coming apart like a cheaply made shirt, as rival factions, kept in check by the father's legendary ability to inflict violence, sized up one another and prepared to make a move. Saradet wanted to get out now before the bloodletting started.

'You said there were two reasons he wanted you dead,' Chance said when Saradet finally finished talking. 'What's the second?'

Nattiya said nothing, flicked her boyfriend a nervous glance. Saradet nodded.

'Photographs,' she said.

'Of what?'

'Issarapong doing things of a personal nature.'

'You've got pictures of him fucking somebody? Doesn't sound enough of a reason to have someone killed.'

'That would depend on who it is.'

'Can you get hold of the photographs quickly?'

The woman nodded.

Nattiya was a savvy negotiator and Saradet seemed happy to let her do the talking. When they'd nutted out the details, Chance took his phone from the pocket of his denim jacket, keyed in Tavener's number.

'Where are you?' he said when the American answered.

'On my way to Huey's, as arranged.' The three of them had agreed Tavener and Kate would meet up at Huey's old bar, wait for Chance to show. If they hadn't heard from him in three hours they were to consider themselves on their own.

'Change of plan,' said Chance.

'What the hell you talking about?'

'No time for details, you're just going to have to trust me on this. I think I've got a way we can get out in front of this thing.'

Chance heard the American exhale loudly. 'Okay, what do you need me to do?'

Chance looked at his watch. Just past one.

'Do you know Thermae?'

An infamous bar on Sukhumvit, Thermae acted as a magnet for working girls from all over the city and stayed busy all night. Chance suspected the American would have come across it on his nocturnal travels around the city.

'Yeah.'

'Be there in an hour.'

'Pardon me for saying so, but now don't exactly seem like an opportune time to get my ashes hauled.'

'Saradet's girlfriend will meet you there, hand over a package. Be sure you're wearing that stupid fishing hat of yours.'

'What'll be in the package?'

'Money and photographs.'

Tavener started to protest but Chance cut him off. 'Take the package, head back to Huey's place. Call me when you get there.'

'What will you do?'

'Meet you there later.'

'What about Milo?'

'This works out, he won't be able to touch us.'

'And if it doesn't?'

'Just do what I ask.'

Chance checked his watch. He figured an hour should be enough time for Nattiya to get the photos and the money and meet Tavener at the bar, add another hour for the American to get to Huey's place and safety.

'If Saradet's girlfriend hasn't turned up by two, get out of there, get Kate, run. If I don't turn up by dawn, keep the money and the photographs, run. Anything seems out of the ordinary or wrong, run.'

'I hope you know what you're doing, son.'

'So do I.' Chance breathed deeply. 'And, Tavener, this goes

wrong, promise you'll look out for Kate.'

'Will do.'

Chance hesitated. 'You going to wish me luck, old man?'

'That's your problem,' replied Tavener.

'What?'

'You believe in luck.'

The terms of their deal were simple. Three hundred thousand dollars, half of the emergency escape fund Saradet had at Nattiya's condo, delivered to Tavener, seed money for the three of them to get out of Thailand and start fresh in another country. The photographs for added insurance. Once Nattiya made the drop, Chance would cut her boyfriend loose and the two of them would be free to spend the rest of their lives living in domestic bliss among the sand dunes and camels.

Chance glanced at his watch. Fifteen minutes until the deadline for Tavener to call. He perched on the bed, the pistol next to him, a semi-circle of butts on the floor around his feet, listened to muffled sounds of footsteps in the hallway, grunts and groans from the room next door.

Saradet had stretched out on the canvas in the middle of the ring, eyes closed, hands behind his head, grabbing rest while he could. Chance had worked with professional criminals who'd been able to grab shuteye right before a job, always wondered how they could do it.

He rolled his shoulders, heard bone and cartilage crack, looked at the Thai, wondered whether he'd be able to make good on his threat to kill him if the plan went wrong.

Chance heard more movement outside the room. The footsteps didn't continue down the corridor but stayed outside the door. Saradet heard it, too, opened his eyes, sat upright.

The girlfriend was the only person who knew they were here. There was no reason for her to come back. That meant someone else.

Saradet shot Chance a wary look. Chance put his hands up, shrugged. Saradet peered at him hard, nodded, climbed over the ropes around the boxing ring, glanced around the room. He picked up one of the leather stools, stepped closer to the door, the piece of furniture raised over his shoulder. Chance took up position on the other side, aimed the pistol with both hands at the middle of the door.

A tentative knock. They both tensed.

'Who is it?' said Chance.

'Me.'

Chance grabbed the knob, twisted it, opened the door. Tavener stood in the hallway, eye level with the barrel of Chance's gun, his face a mask of impatience. The American held a pistol parallel to his right leg.

'Put that away.' Tavener brushed the barrel of Chance's gun away, stepped into the room, noticed Saradet. The two men locked eyes until each decided the other was no threat.

'What are you doing here?' said Chance, closing the door.

Tavener did a slow sweep of the room, whistled. 'This sure is some fancy setup.'

'Tavener, why are you here?'

'She was followed.'

'What are you talking about?'

'His girlfriend, she was followed.' Tavener smiled at the disbelief on Chance's face. 'That's what happens when you put an amateur in charge of the store.'

The American reached behind his back, hitched up his polo shirt, tucked the pistol into his pants. 'So much for getting in front of things. Wasn't a complete waste of time,' the American wiped his mouth with his forearm. 'Got the money and the photos.'

'The photos, did you look at them?'

'Briefly.'

'The person Issarapong was with, was it a man or woman?'

'Just young.'

Chance grimaced. 'You sure you were followed?'

'Done it enough times myself, reckon I know when it's being done to me.'

'How many?'

'Two. That I saw.'

'Who are they?'

'How the fuck do I know. They were male, Asian.'

'Kate,' said Chance, a sliver of panic in his voice. 'Where is she? Is she okay?'

'Don't worry, she's safe and sound with Huey and the parcel.'

'How'd she get the parcel?'

'How the fuck do you think, Einstein? She came to the meet with me and I gave it to her.'

'You brought her to the meet? What were you thinking? How do you know the two men didn't follow her?'

'Because I made sure they followed me instead.'

'You've led them here?'

'No, I'm pretty sure I lost them.' Tavener wiped his mouth with his forearm. 'Now if you've finished playing twenty questions, get hold of yourself.'

Chance puffed his cheeks, blew out air. 'Okay.'

'Good.' Tavener hitched a thumb in Saradet's direction. 'Cut him loose and let's get the fuck out of Dodge.'

Chance and Tavener stood in the entrance of the hotel driveway, watched the Benz's rear lights grow smaller, disappear around the bend.

Bangkok's early morning sky was a soupy dark grey, the air rich with the smell of petrochemicals and rotting vegetable matter. The two men headed in the same direction as Saradet's car. They passed an old woman sitting in a dark stairwell, tiny red lights from a shrine flickering behind her, a vendor pushing a wooden food cart, a drunk Westerner, his arm over the shoulder of a hawk-faced bar girl.

Chance heard the whine of a motorbike like the buzzing of an angry insect in the distance. A bright light behind them cast their bodies in long shadows on the road. He glanced over his shoulder, was blinded by the hot glare of a headlight. Spots swam in his vision. He squeezed his eyes hard to clear them.

He felt a hand on his shoulder, opened his eyes. Tavener was guiding him toward an alley, pushed him hard into the blackness, just as the sound of automatic machine gun fire tore apart the night.

Chance tried to roll, cushion the blow from the concrete, only partially succeeded. He lay on the ground, one knee throbbing. He recognised the familiar noise of an AK-47, a series of sharp whip cracks, from his time in Afghanistan. Tavener grunted, seemed to freeze for a moment, dived after him.

The motorbike pulled up to the mouth of the alley, the shadows of the two men on the back outlined in the grimy half-light. Chance fumbled for his gun as Tavener fired several times in the direction of their assassins. The shots momentarily lit up the small corridor of brick. There was a moist tearing sound as the shadow on the rear of the bike fell backward, hit the asphalt with a thump

The driver gunned his machine, sped off. The noise of the motorbike receded, replaced by a chorus of enraged barking from the neighbourhood dogs.

'Tavener,' said Chance.

The American didn't move but Chance could hear his uneven, rasping breath, figured the fall had knocked the wind out of him. Chance's eyes slowly grew accustomed to the dark. He reached for what he thought was Tavener's shoulder, shook him gently.

'Come on, old man, no time to rest.'

Tavener groaned.

'The police will be here any second.' Chance shook him harder, withdrew his hand, felt a warm wetness on his fingertips. He dabbed one on the tip of his tongue, tasted blood.

The barking became more hysterical. Chance tore off his denim jacket, rolled it into a ball, pressed it hard against the part of Tavener's chest where he thought the blood was coming from.

Tavener emitted a moist cough, his breathing erratic. 'Ah shit,' he whispered. The words, filtered through the blood in his mouth, came out slurred.

'Don't worry, Lias, I'll get you out of here.' He reached under the American's armpits, tried to lift him toward the entrance to the alleyway, felt the man's body shudder in pain, put him down again.

'Reckon I've used up my nine lives.' Tavener's head rested in Chance's lap. 'Got to say, thought it would happen the other way around, you bleeding out on the pavement in a stinking Bangkok alleyway.'

'Relax, old man.'

Tavener shivered, went completely limp. Chance laid the old man on the ground, emerged from the alley and glanced down at the body of the man shot off the back of the motorbike. An AK-47 machine gun lay on the road next to him.

Chance leaned down, started to go through the man's pockets, when he sensed a movement behind him. He turned, just in time to see a blur of flesh speed toward his face.

Twelve

It was completely dark when Chance opened his eyes. A hood was over his head, the coarse burlap fabric rough against his skin.

He lay on his side on a smooth metal surface. Engine parts moved under him, the wheeze and sigh of a vehicle braking, the swish of air as traffic passed in the opposite direction. He slid across the surface whenever the vehicle turned or stopped.

His right knee throbbed, his head hurt more. He sniffed, got the acrid smell of piss, realised it was his own. He tried to move his arms but couldn't, his wrists tied tightly behind his back. He stretched his legs, probed the area around his feet. The tip of his shoe connected with something soft.

'Who's there,' he said weakly.

Nothing.

'Anybody there?' he said, louder.

A low-pitched moan was the only reply.

He remembered Saradet back at the hotel, resting while they waited for the phone call, knew there was no point struggling further. He had to conserve his energy for whatever came next. Chance rested his head on the hard surface, closed his eyes, let the vehicle's movement lull him back into unconsciousness.

Mottled daylight filtered through the hood and Chance felt the sun on his skin.

The traffic noise was replaced by a steady, metallic throb. The surface against his face rose and fell. A boat. He could hear water lapping against the sides. The equilibrium of the vessel shifted as he tested the bindings on his wrist. Still tight.

Chance heard men talk over the noise of the engine, a language he didn't recognise. He lifted his head. The voices stopped and something hard hit him on the side of the head, sent him tumbling back into the darkness.

He came to with a start. The light through the fabric of his hood was dimmer now. The engine had stopped. He heard water lap against the sides of the boat.

Strong hands took hold and lowered him into waist-deep water, let go. Chance fell forward, hit the water headfirst. He thrashed about under the surface, scared of drowning. Someone grabbed his hood, pulled him to the surface. Chance gasped for breath. Male laughter filled the air around him.

He was steered to shore, his feet making sucking sounds in the mud at the water's edge. He heard the crack of wood splitting in an open fire, the clink of metal, someone singing a Thai pop song, the thrum of a generator.

'Stop,' said a voice.

Chance felt a hand force the top of his head down, another push him forward. The remaining light faded as he was steered into position against a wall and forced to the floor. The ground was cool and damp, a dirt floor. He could sense his captors watching him for a moment, and then he was alone.

Hands still tied behind him, Chance was manoeuvred into a hard-backed chair. He closed his eyes against the flood of light as the hood was lifted off. The skin on his face and hands itched from where mosquitoes had feasted the night before, and his throat was dry.

Issarapong sat at a trestle table in front of him. The driver, Milo's minder, whatever Nareth was, stood next to him, arms folded across his broad chest, dressed in clothes similar to the ones he had worn when Chance first met him, with the addition of a machete in a scabbard, hanging from his belt.

Issarapong nodded absentmindedly. A wiry, dark-skinned man came into view. He held a plastic bottle to Chance's lips. Chance slurped at the bottle greedily.

The man doused Chance's head with the remains of the bottle. Rivulets of moisture dripped from his hair and cheeks, cleared away the grit and hessian fibres.

Chance shook his head like a wet animal, gazed at his surroundings.

They were in a large canvas tent, the sides rolled up to reveal a square of hard-packed red earth, several bamboo huts, surrounded in every direction by thick emerald green jungle that roared with insect life. A small satellite dish, several aerials, peeked out from the thatched roof of one of the huts. Smoke wafted from a campfire, chickens pecked at the ground, men busied themselves with tasks, high-powered weapons slung across their shoulders.

He focused on Issarapong. Even in the middle of a jungle Issarapong came off looking like he was on a corporate retreat, trainers, jeans, and a khaki shirt.

Issarapong tapped on the keys of a laptop open in front of him while he waited for Chance to get his bearings. The only other items on the table were an Akubra hat and a large, red semi-circle of plastic mesh. Flies buzzed over the cover.

'Saradet told me not everyone was happy with daddy's boy taking over the family business,' said Chance. 'But I didn't think you'd fallen this low, cowering from your enemies in the middle of the jungle.'

'Saradet?' Issarapong said the name as if it were unfamiliar. He reached over, lifted the red plastic mesh to reveal a bloated misshapen head. Chance dry-retched, nothing in his stomach to throw up. Flies danced in the air for a moment, descended in a frenzied swarm on Saradet's decaying flesh.

'Let me assure you, my presence here is merely a tactical retreat while I regroup to plan my next move against the dogs who have dared rise against me. As for you, thinking you could cut a side deal with that maggot Saradet.' Issarapong's voice trailed off in disgust.

'Who tipped you off, the girlfriend?'

Issarapong shook his head.

'Milo?' said Chance, trying to keep his voice level.

Issarapong's mouth contorted into a snarl. 'That half-cast fuck was as disloyal and treacherous as the others, tried to cut a deal with my enemies.'

'The men on the motorbike?'

Issarapong nodded. 'Gao's people.'

Nareth hadn't moved. It must have been him, spying for Issarapong the entire time. A loyal foot soldier, probably worked for the father, been passed on to Issarapong like the other possessions attached to the family business.

Issarapong noticed Chance staring at the man beside him. 'Do you think I'm so stupid that I'd hire thieves to do a job and not keep tabs on them?'

The crime lord stood, shouted something in Thai.

Chance noticed movement at the entrance to one of the thatched huts. A man emerged, arms bound behind his back, naked except for a filthy pair of Y-fronts, a hessian sack over his head. He was followed by another man with dark Afro hair, an AK-47 in his hands.

Afro prodded his captive forward with the barrel of his gun, brought him to a halt in the middle of the square. The other camp residents stopped what they were doing and watched.

The man trembled, glanced around, unseeing. His body was streaked with grime and covered in tattoos and deep purple bruises. Chance sensed something familiar about him.

Afro forced the man onto his knees, stood behind him, looked at Issarapong.

Issarapong made a cutting gesture in the air with his hand. Afro wrenched the sack off the man's head. Milo returned Chance's stare for a moment before a shot rang out and the front of his head exploded. He fell face down on the ground. The executioner spat on the ground next to the corpse, slung his gun over his shoulder, walked away. His audience resumed their duties as if nothing had happened.

'Now, what to do with you?' Issarapong turned to Chance. 'Pardon the pun, but I think the new face may have gone to your head, made you feel stronger than you really are.'

The crime lord chuckled at his own joke. 'I gave you that face. It's mine. Maybe I'll have Nareth peel it off you, make you watch as he feeds it to our pigs.'

Chance looked at Milo's body contorted in a ball on the ground.

'Aren't you forgetting one thing?'

'What?'

'The photographs.'

The colour drained from the Issarapong's face and he became serious.

'I don't know what you're doing in the pictures, but whatever it was,' Chance continued, 'must have been bad to kill Saradet over them.'

'Where are they?'

'Somewhere safe?'

'With your friend, the woman? My people in Bangkok are looking for her as we speak, she won't stay free for long.'

'Your people?' A sharp laugh escaped from Chances mouth. 'We have a saying in Australia, 'Don't shit a shitter.''

Issarapong's brow furrowed.

'It means don't lie to another liar. If you had the manpower to search Bangkok for my friend you wouldn't be hiding here in the middle of fuck-knows-where with your tail between your legs. You've got your hands full just trying to stay one step ahead of the mutiny, put your operation back together.'

Chance felt emboldened by the Issarapong's silence, locked eyes with him and breathed deeply to sooth the panic boiling in his chest. 'Way I see it, you have two choices.'

Issarapong leaned back in his seat, his hands forming a steeple in front of him. 'Go on.'

'Tavener may be dead but he's got friends in Bangkok. They've got a real mean streak. Not like me. They'll want pay-back, big time. Kill me, I promise, you'll jump on that laptop at some point in the next few days, see those pictures splashed all over the screen. That's quite apart from whatever else they have up their sleeves. You'll be fighting on two fronts.'

'Or?'

'Cut me loose. You'll never see me or my friends again and you can focus your energies on more pressing problems.'

Issarapong stared at Chance sullenly, inclined his head to Nareth and said something in Thai.

Like a robot suddenly activated by its master, Nareth walked around the trestle table. Chance squirmed against the binding around his wrists, tried to stand but only got halfway before Nareth had replaced the hood over his head.

Chance sat with his back against the bamboo wall. The piss smell was worse. Mosquitoes buzzed around him, bit his exposed skin at will. He was thirsty, hungry, and scared.

Someone entered the hut, hauled him up, and pushed him forward. He walked, the unseen hand prodding and turning him in different directions. Tiny shoots of fear grew inside him with each step, became thick vines, curled around his lungs and heart, until his breath started to falter. The camp noise faded, replaced by jungle sounds, insects, birds, the slap of branches and foliage against his face and body.

Eventually, the hand stopped him. The hood was lifted off. Chance stood in a shaded clearing, Issarapong and Nareth in front of him. Nareth unsheathed the machete, stepped behind Chance.

Chance felt the blade cut into the binding. He raised his arms. They were heavy, like metal. His wristwatch was missing, no doubt looted by one of his captors. The sun high overhead sent shafts of light through the tree cover. He guessed it was sometime in the middle of the day.

Issarapong removed his Akubra, ran a hand through his hair. 'What happens to the photographs if I let you go?'

'No one will ever seen them.' Chance flexed his fingers, rubbed his wrists vigorously to get the circulation back. 'They stay with me, insurance, just in case you change your mind, come looking for us or feel tempted to let slip to Gao's father where we are.'

'Did I say Gao's father had Long killed? That's right. I did, didn't I?'

'What are you talking about?'

'The e-mail I received, with that film, turns out it didn't come from Gao's people after all.'

Chance stopped rubbing, watched Issarapong.

'If it wasn't Gao that killed Mister Long, who was it?'

Issarapong closed his eyed, savoured his advantage over Chance.

'Dormer.' Chance answered his own question. 'Long must have told him where I was before he died.'

'I did a little work after our first meeting, wasn't easy but I managed to track the e-mail's source. The information technology degree my father paid all that money for wasn't wasted after all.'

'Where?'

Issarapong's face broke into a broad grin. 'Melbourne.'

All the time, sitting on the dirt floor of the hut in Issarapong's camp, Chance had thought about two things: finding Kate and getting out of Thailand. That plan was suddenly erased and a new one took hold.

'Deal's changed,' said Chance. 'In addition to everything previously specified, I want to know exactly where that e-mail came from.'

'As my father said, farangs are so predictable.' Issarapong produced a folded piece of paper from the pocket of his freshly laundered jeans, handed it to Chance. 'Now turn around.'

Chance saw a narrow trail cut in the jungle, descending toward a mass of fast moving brown water.

'Wait down there. A boat will come by shortly, take you across the border to Thailand.'

Nareth was already heading back along the path that had led to the clearing. Issarapong paused for a moment, followed.

'What happens then?' Chance shouted after them.

Issarapong disappeared into the riot of green without replying.

Thirteen

The light and noise of Soi Cowboy felt unreal after where he'd been. At the end of an eight-hour journey from the Thai-Burma border, most of it spent in the back of a flatbed truck full of migrants heading to Bangkok to find work, Chance found Huey sitting outside the same bar where they'd first met.

'You smell as bad as you look,' said Huey, as Chance sat next to him.

'I'm sorry about Tavener,' said Chance, taking the American's beer and draining it.

'Lias was a soldier. Soldiers get killed.'

The old guy had used what little juice he had left to get the authorities to release Tavener's body without too many questions, have the death ruled as the result of a robbery gone wrong.

'What about the other guy, the one on the motorcycle?'

'A Filipino national. Police weren't that concerned. Got more pressing issues, I guess.'

Chance had seen the front page of the main English language daily at a roadside news agency when their truck had stopped to refuel. The political protests were getting worse, rumours spreading of a possible military coup.

'Where's Kate?'

'Safe, along with your share of the money.'

'What happened to Tavener's share?'

'I'll hold onto it for expenses.'

'Is she still in Thailand?'

'Up-country. Nong Khai.'

Chance had heard of it, a town in the northeast of Thailand.

'Lias's funeral is tomorrow, you coming?'

'Yes.' Chance signalled one of the cowgirls for a drink.

The flames quickly consumed the mock wooden temple. Chance felt the heat from the blaze. Pieces of burnt yellow ribbon, flecks of ash mixed with the smoke fluttered and twisted in the air.

Huey stood next to him in a frayed charcoal brown safari suit, the only other mourner at the funeral. The old man stared at the pyre, his face more pinched and sickly than usual.

'Chanting monks aside, very Viking,' said Chance. 'Tavener would have approved.'

Huey said nothing, a slight quiver in his underbite the only sign he was annoyed by the comment.

'How long do we have to hang around?' Chance glanced at his watch. 'I've got a bus to catch.'

'A little longer, then you can buy me a drink or two.'

'Good, there's something else I need your help with.'

He left Bangkok later that afternoon, took an overnight bus straight to Nong Khai.

Kate was sitting outside her guest house room reading a thick paperback, gasped when she'd first laid eyes on his face, the bruises on his face still fresh.

She ran up, slapped him, followed it up with a long kiss.

'Is that what you call tough love?' Chance peered into her eyes. He'd forgotten how large and blue they were.

'I was worried about you.'

* * *

216

Outside, night had fallen and rain beat down hard on the tin roof.

Chance's mouth was full of her tang, his salty taste. He raised his head slightly, met Kate's half-closed eyes across the length of her stomach.

'No one said you had to stop,' she said.

'I'm getting a cramp.'

Chance admired the swirling tattoo letters on the smooth skin inside her left leg. 'Sean together forever,' he read aloud. 'I hope he got a matching one.'

She gave him a husky laugh. 'Yeah.'

'You never wanted to get it removed?'

'Never got around to it.' Kate grasped the back of his head, pulled him toward her. They kissed deeply.

'Besides,' she broke away, her large eyes looked up at him, 'doesn't it give you a thrill, fucking someone else's woman. Gao certainly liked it.'

'You have a very dirty mind, Miss Norliss.' She arched her back, sighed as Chance kneaded one of her breasts. 'Has anyone told you that?'

'Frequently.' She kissed Chance's neck. 'Christ, I've missed this. The last few days, I wondered whether I'd ever see you—'

Chance didn't want to go there yet, mashed his mouth roughly onto hers. She closed her eyes and allowed him to change the subject.

Chance hugged her from behind and kissed her neck, the skin slick with sweat.

He rolled onto his back, stared at the slowly moving ceiling fan.

'I'm going after Dormer.'

'Why?'

Chance felt her tense, the warmth drain away.

She cut him off as he started to speak. 'With the money we have, we could go anywhere. Is Dormer really that good? Can he find us wherever we are?'

'Yes. I mean, I don't know. Whatever, I'm not prepared to take the risk.' He let out a long breath. 'I don't know how much information is out there about my location, my new face.'

Chance reached for his tobacco, began rolling a cigarette.

'Those two men that came after Tavener and me in Bangkok mean Gao's people obviously know what I look like and that I'm in Thailand. For all I know, Dormer might, too. I have to move quickly, get to Dormer at least before he gets to me.'

Kate was silent.

'Listen. Do you think I want to spend the rest of my life with one eye over my shoulder, living in some rat-arsed caravan camp, like the one in Yass, a gun under the pillow and a go-bag next to the bed? It's no life, at least no life I want to live.'

'When will you leave?'

Chance exhaled a stream of smoke toward the low roof.

'As soon as Huey helps me with certain paperwork I need, a few days.'

'And, you thought you'd spend your remaining time in Thailand getting laid?'

'Kate, come on, it's not like that.'

Chance reached for her with his free hand. She shrugged him away.

'What exactly is it like then?'

'In case you don't remember, you made the first pass at me.'

'That doesn't give you the right to treat me as a bit of R&R between jobs.'

'Kate, come on.'

'Do you remember, back in Sri Racha, you asked me why I'd come to Thailand?'

'Yes.'

'I liked you, sure. But that wasn't the reason. It's because Thailand was far away from where I'd been and who I'd been. You were my ticket out of Australia and I'm not going back.'

'I could come back here, after I've finished what I—'

'I won't be here.'

'Where will you be?'

'I don't know.'

Chance stubbed his cigarette out in an ashtray on the bedside table. Kate lay with her head on his chest, ran her fingers through the fine dark hair.

'Do you know where he is?' she said.

'If my information is right, yes—'

Kate put a finger up to his lips, stopped him mid-sentence.

'I don't want to know,' she whispered, then kissed him hard.

GLOOMY CITY

One

Chance rubbed his forearm against the window, peered through the hole in fogged glass. The outline of abandoned factories hurtled past in the night.

The train carriage was packed, young Saturday night revellers headed to the city, undeterred by bleak weather, a few older people huddled into their clothing, eyes on books or smart phones.

On the seat opposite two cadaverous junkies engaged in foul-mouthed slow motion discussion about trying to score, oblivious to the people around them. Their clothes were filthy, their pale skin a patchwork of faded blue ink. One had a straggly beard, the other a badly shaven scalp, patches of hair where the razor had missed.

Chance got off at the second stop on the underground loop. On the escalator up to the street he checked his body for lingering symptoms of malaria. He no longer felt like sleeping all the time, the fever had faded and the ache in his muscles was down to a dull throb, similar to the sensation after a long run.

In Melbourne two weeks, most of it spent in his motel room bed recovering from the disease. The first symptoms had come on his last day in Thailand, intensified on the plane trip back. He thought he'd picked up some sort of bug but when the fever and sweats had become too much, he'd dragged himself to a doctor, slipped him several hundred dollars for an off-the-books diagnosis. The doctor had given him pills that seemed to work, cut down the symptoms, made him able to function.

He pulled his black woollen beany tight over his head, dug his hands into the pockets of his denim jacket to brace himself against the gloomy weather. After days of drenching his sheets with sweat, the cold shocked his system. It stung his eyes and slapped his cheeks. The wind, laced with moisture, created tiny squalls in the confined spaces between buildings, shook the skeletal trees along the footpath.

The city felt different after three years away. Familiar buildings and spaces were gone, whole city blocks empty or transformed with new structures. Chance paused in front of one of these spaces, had the sensation it was familiar, that he should know what had once been there, but couldn't remember.

A shaggy busker stood in a doorway, played an off-key version of Khe San to himself. Melbourne was a ghost town compared to Bangkok. Chance missed the press of people, the roadside food stalls, even the constant traffic. The smell and noise of a city that lived its life on the streets rather than huddling inside.

He missed Kate, too. He could sense their connection fading, the familiarity of her touch and smell. Another couple of weeks, he'd struggle to recall her face.

Chance found the building he was looking for, an old school pub situated between an office block and a shop selling golfing accessories, its peeling mustard façade at odds with the gentrification surrounding it.

He followed a hand-written sign, went up the stairs, handed twenty dollars to a woman sitting at a table outside the first room he came to, and went inside.

The harshly lit room was half full of florid, heavyset men in jeans, black T-shirts and black leather coats, equally tough-looking women. The crowd sat at large circular tables, jugs of beer and platters of fried food in front of them, listened to a slight man speaking into a microphone on a stage. He looked like a mid-level public servant or a school principal with his wire-rimmed spectacles, thinning hair and cheap black suit, an appearance at odds with the fiery tone of his oratory.

In a thick brogue he talked about the contribution of Aussie comrades to the independence struggle. He cracked a joke about kneecapping, which got a few shy laughs, went on to talk about the dire economic situation in his home country, the youth of Ireland, the country's best and brightest, leaving for jobs overseas.

Chance scanned the crowd, recognised a few faces, trade union hard men, a couple of minor underworld players, found Walsh in a knot of people by the bar.

The Irishman had the same short, dark hair, a flat face covered in dark stubble and softened only by a pair of sleek, almost feminine blue eyes. He was dressed in jeans and a leather jacket, like the other men, the only difference the trademark black and white chequered Arabic Keffiyeh around his neck. 'A gesture of solidarity with my Arabic brothers' was how he'd once explained his affection for the scarf.

Walsh leaned against the bar, a half-empty pint in his hand. Every now and again he shared an aside with an elderly man with a shock of thick grey hair, nicknamed 'Killer.' Chance had never found out why. Bored with the speech, the Irishman's eyes wandered around the room. His gaze briefly rested on Chance. Chance smiled, half-raised his hand to acknowledge the Irishman, stopped himself when he realised Walsh wouldn't recognise his new face.

Walsh's arrival in Australia pre-dated the Celtic diaspora lamented by the speaker on stage by more than a decade. When the ceasefire was brokered in Northern Ireland in the mid-nineties and the Provisionals cached their weapons, most of Walsh's comrades gave up the fight. A few joined the breakaway movement to continue the struggle. Walsh, a former IRA enforcer, was smart enough to know when politics ended and business started, went from kneecapping local crims to replacing them.

Chance and the Irishman had bounced at the same nightclub, clicked from the beginning, become good friends. He didn't know why Walsh had come to Australia, never asked.

Applause signalled the speeches were over. Chance nudged his way through the crowd that materialised at the bar until he stood next to Walsh.

'You looking at something, fella?' said Walsh, staring straight ahead. His voice had a hard Irish lilt. Walsh always accentuated his brogue when he wanted to appear intimidating.

'It's almost nine, Liam, and you haven't started a fight yet.'

Walsh liked a blue. Chance used to joke the Irishman could've started a fight in an empty room.

'Maybe you'd like to help me out on that score?' Walsh swivelled his head, locked eyes with Chance.

'What you going to do, Liam? Stash me in the cool room, like you did that stockbroker, give me a thrashing after closing.'

Walsh did a double take at the reference to an episode from their bouncing days, known only to Walsh and himself.

'What fucking nonsense is this shite,' said Walsh, looking closer at Chance. 'Gary Chance, surely not, is that you, comrade?'

'Live and in the flesh.'

'But your face. You always were an ugly fucker, but your face. I mean, what the hell happened?'

'Long story,' said Chance. 'Let's get out of here. I'll buy you a drink and we can talk about old times and a job you might be interested in.'

The two men sat in the front window of a Chinese restaurant, half-eaten plates of greasy noodles in front of them. Faded décor, shit food, even shittier service.

Chance gave Walsh a heavily abbreviated version of his life story since they'd last seen each other.

'You ask me, whoever did that to your face is the one you want to be going after,' Walsh said after Chance had finished talking.

The Irishman pushed his plate away, drank from his can of beer, joined Chance in looking at the street outside. It was crowded, gangs of young people, three and four abreast, shouting drunkenly at one another and passersby, Asian university students dressed like glam rock stars. The restaurant was on the Russell Street section of Melbourne's Chinatown, once the city's heroin capital. But if there was any action happening now, Chance couldn't see it. The junkies must have found somewhere else to score.

'You interested in the work or not?' said Chance.

'Let me get this straight. You want me to help you find this bloke who double-crossed you, what's his name?'

'Frank Dormer. Least that was his name the last time I met him. He was working with a woman called Sophia Lekakis. I've got a lead on where he might be. What I want from you is a bit of backup and some assistance getting around. My Melbourne geography is a little rusty and I don't have time to study up.' Chance looked at Walsh. 'Maybe some help when I find him.'

Walsh regarded Chance in silence, let the implications of the last part of his friend's statement hang in the air between them.

'How pissed are you at this fella?'

'How pissed would you be?'

Walsh acknowledged the point with a nod.

'I don't want to have to look over my shoulder for the rest of my life,' said Chance. 'And I want my share of the money.'

'What are you proposing?'

'A fifty-fifty split after expenses.'

'Sounds like a good bit of craic and I could use a break from construction work.' Walsh fingered the diamond stud in his ear, drained his beer. 'Why not.'

Two

Walsh arrived at the motel the next morning in a white Holden Commodore, like Chance had requested. The Irishman glanced around the cramped confines of Chance's hotel room, rolled his eyes. 'Aye, whoever said crime doesn't pay.'

Chance explained where they were going and why as they pushed their way through Melbourne's peak-hour congestion. He knew the only way to find the physical location of where an e-mail had been sent from was to hack into the internet server provider or get a court order for them to kick it loose. The best Issarapong had been able to manage was to pinpoint the street, a cul-de-sac in a new housing development not far from the city's main airport.

The cul-de-sac was lined with freestanding two-story houses separated by wooden fences, surrounded by a grassy field. It had probably been bushland once, now all that remained were a few gum trees. A 737 moved across the cotton wool sky as it came in to land at the nearby airport.

'The Paris end of Roxburgh Park,' muttered Walsh as he leaned on the steering wheel, peered through the windshield smudged and beaded with moisture. 'I can feel the mortgage stress from here.'

Four of the dwellings on the street were completed, the rest were in various stages of construction. Similar houses were going up across the field, Melbourne's outer urban sprawl expanding in all directions.

The two men sat in the warm vehicle at the mouth of the street, watched the houses for signs of life. Walsh spoke every now and again, updates about people they knew in common, what he was doing for work. He still bounced now and again, supplemented it with construction jobs. The construction industry suited him, the often paper-thin line between legality and criminality. You were either in the union or organised crime, or sometimes both. Just like being back in Ireland. Chance responded with one- or two-word answers, his attention on the houses. Walsh drained his polystyrene cup of coffee, dropped it on the floor at his feet.

'Doesn't make sense, your man Dormer living in one of these. Man doesn't steal several million in drugs and cash, live out here.'

Walsh was right. A white prefabricated two-story house, red-tiled roofs, hot off the plan, in the middle of Melbourne's outer suburban fringe, didn't feel like the kind of place Dormer would hole up in.

Then again, what Chance knew about Dormer would have fitted on the back of a postage stamp with space to spare. Ex-Australian Army, had worked in Afghanistan as a private security contractor. Chance had come across them during his time in the country, bullet-headed men with dark sunglasses, balaclava-obscured faces and secretive demeanours. They rode shotgun on supply convoys, stood at roadblocks, shot first, and asked questions later, if at all.

One thing Chance did know, Dormer was a professional, good at throwing out distractions and misinformation. Like the little horror film of Long, which he'd launched anonymously into cyber space to create maximum chaos and paranoia.

Chance felt a pang of anxiety. He'd come all this way to sit in the middle of nowhere on the say so of a Thai gangster with a pit full of snakes for a mind, who, for all he knew, was already dead, stripped to the bone by the former underlings who'd risen against him. Chance pushed these thoughts aside. Concentrated on the task ahead.

Over the next hour they watched people depart from two of the four completed dwellings, a man in a business suit, a backpack on his shoulder, and a harassed-looking woman and two young kids, driving away from each other.

That left two remaining houses.

'Fuck this for a joke,' said Walsh. He got out of the car, made his way along the footpath around one side of the cul-de-sac, put on a pair of surgical gloves as he walked, disappeared around the back of one of the houses no one had yet come out of. He returned ten minutes later, got back in the car.

'One hasn't been occupied yet, the other has been lived in but no one's home.'

'What do you mean?'

'We can sit around here while I try and explain it or you can have a look for yourself, Gary. Two men sitting in a car, we stick out like a pimple on a newborn baby's bottom. Won't be long before the peelers are round to check us out, then what? Either we call it quits or we check out this house now. What's it going to be?'

A few bits of basic furniture, bare walls, empty fridge, bare cupboards, bare everything. Chance flicked a light switch on the kitchen wall. The power was on, which meant someone was still paying the bills.

In a small room off the main living area there was a futon base and folded mattress. Next to it was a cheap computer desk, a power point on the skirting board nearby, but no computer.

Walsh appeared in the doorway. 'Found something you might want to take a look at.'

He followed the Irishman through the kitchen, into an adjoining laundry area, where a door led to a large windowless carport. Chance sniffed, a faint smell he couldn't identify, halfway between chemicals and cat piss. He looked around, realised it was coming from a large, blue plastic forty-five-gallon drum in a corner. Cardboard boxes and empty white plastic containers were stacked next to it. The drum was tightly sealed with a black lid. Chance kicked it. It was full.

Chance picked up one of the white containers. 'Certified lye,' he read from the label. 'What's that?'

'An alkaline solution used for cleaning,' said Walsh, grim-faced. 'Me ma used to use it to clean the drains back home. It has other uses.'

'Such as?'

'It's also good for dissolving bodies.'

'You're saying there's a body in there.' Chance said the words slowly.

'Maybe.'

'Should we have a look?'

'Nothing to look at, comrade.'

Chance raised his eyebrows, urged him to continue.

'Mixed with water, lye will liquefy a body in a few hours and God knows how long this baby's been brewing. All that would be left is a brown liquid the consistency of mineral oil, maybe a few bone fragments.'

Walsh's voice was monotone, like he was reciting a textbook. 'Acid is better, it'll get rid of everything, bones, teeth, the lot, but it's also more dangerous to handle and sales of strong acids are more tightly monitored because they can be used for bomb-making. But lye is one of the most commonly used chemicals in the world. You can purchase enough to dissolve an adult body from any farm supply store.'

Chance left Walsh to do one more sweep of the house, went outside, looked around the back yard, a square of unkempt lawn, big enough to build another house on. Against the back fence sat another forty-five-gallon drum, this one metal, the exterior covered in orange rust. It had been used as an incinerator.

Chance waded through knee high grass, peered into the drum, nothing but sodden ash. He rolled a cigarette, drew the smoke in deep, hoping to banish the chemical smell that clung to him from the garage.

He noticed a black and white shape in the moist weeds at the base of the barrel, picked it up. A tag of some sort. He swiped his thumb across the black plastic to remove the grime, saw the name "Sophia" in stylish gold letters.

The identification tag from the hotel she'd worked at in Surfers Paradise, where Gao had stayed.

If there was a body in the plastic barrel in the garage, he had a strong suspicion whose it was.

Three

'Charming playmates you've got, comrade,' said Walsh after Chance had explained his suspicions.

'This coming from a man who just gave me a lecture on how to dispose of a corpse.'

'Me?' Walsh shrugged. 'I'm just a sensitive New Age guy, knowledgeable about my cleaning products.'

'Did you check the mailbox?'

'Aye, rubbish, fliers for fast food, local tradies, an offer of a gym membership, all addressed to *the occupant*.'

Chance exhaled. 'Which means we're right back where we started.'

'Maybe.'

'What do you mean?'

'I had a look in the cardboard boxes in the shed, like you asked.'

'And?'

Walsh waited until they'd stopped at a red light, reached into the fold of his hoodie, passed something to his passenger. 'I found this.'

A business card, the name Touch of the Orient and a Western suburbs address—both in flowery pink letters on a glossy black matt background—a badly Photo-shopped image of a woman's arse and lower back.

Chance turned the card over, nothing. 'The business card for a brothel, so what?'

'There was an entire box of them.'

'Really?'

Walsh nodded, a grin plastered across his broad face. 'It's okay, Gary, don't fall all over yourself to thank me.'

Chance ignored him, looked at the card with renewed interest. 'You ever heard of this place?'

The mid-morning traffic was heavier as they approached the city. Walsh braked, came to a stop in front of a large semi-trailer. 'Do you know how many brothels there are in Melbourne?'

'Not counting all the illegal and fly-by-night joints?' Chance looked out the passenger's window, large furniture showrooms, hardware and office supplies shops as far as the eye could see. 'No idea, but it's a bit of a stretch to say Dormer is connected to the one we accidently stumbled across, yeah?'

'Normally, I say so,' said Walsh. 'But finding a cardboard box full of business cards in the same space as a barrel with a decomposed corpse, that's more than a coincidence, wouldn't you say, comrade?'

'Indeed I would, mate. Indeed I would.' Chance tapped the card on the dashboard. 'Fancy a trip to the Western suburbs?'

The address on the card was an abandoned two-story terrace house. Westgate Bridge, the link between the city and Melbourne's vast western suburbs, curved across the sky behind it in the distance, a concrete and metal rainbow in the clouds.

The terrace was painted pink, a faded sign, Touch of the Orient, also in pink, affixed to the front and another sign warning trespassers away. The windows were boarded up. To one side was a small car park. Weeds spouted from the cracked concrete.

Chance leaned against the cyclone wire fence surrounding the abandoned property, curled his fingers around the rings in frustration.

'Looks like business wasn't so good,' said Walsh, coming up

behind him. 'Don't reckon it had anything to do with the paint job, do you?'

Chance turned away from the building in disgust, started to roll a cigarette.

'It wouldn't be hard to find out who owned the title,' said Walsh.

'Just a name on a piece of paper.' Chance cupped his hands around his lighter and lit his cigarette. 'Same with the house. All we'd be doing is wasting our time.'

A wide grin spread across the Irishman's face.

Chance grinned back. 'You thinking what I am?'

'Indeed, comrade, great minds think alike.'

'You still in contact with our former employer?'

'Don't work her parties anymore, but I know people who do. I can set up a meeting.'

'Do it.'

Four

Half past five in the afternoon but darkness had already chased away all but the last few streaks of daylight. Chance threaded his way through the knots of office workers heading home, their neat, compartmentalised lives something he could scarcely comprehend.

Walsh had added his leather jacket to his layers, the ever-present Keffiyeh around his neck. Chance had a thick black woollen crew neck under his denim jacket but still felt the cold. He welcomed it as a sign he was getting the upper hand in the fight against malaria.

The two men turned into a narrow bluestone lane, the surface slicked clean by rain, stopped outside a black painted metal door. Walsh pushed a red button next to the door, smiled for the closed-circuit camera mounted above.

The owner of the building, all five stories, was a woman named Vera Leigh. She was a former working girl who'd saved her money, gone into business for herself, a high-class brothel, followed by a successful city nightclub. She'd settled into her dotage by running Melbourne's best-regarded S&M dungeons. Japanese rope-work bondage, air deprivation, whatever fetish or fantasy one desired, provided you had the cash to pay.

Walsh and Chance had bounced at her nightclub. On occasion, Chance had ferried clients from there to the dungeon, located in an anonymous brick building, once a textile factory.

He'd only ever got as far as the reception, where a blousy brunette behind the counter always greeted him like he was dropping in to buy bread and milk. The walls behind her were painted deep red, bristled with hooks holding an array of chains, handcuffs and leather bondage implements. The dull thud of techno trance always played from black speakers mounted on the wall.

He and Walsh had also done security work at some of the *invite only* parties Leigh held every few months in her apartment, a warren of stairways leading to different themed rooms. The two of them would pass the time celebrity spotting among the businessman and footloose rich engaged in a night of drug and alcohol-fuelled sex.

The black metal door opened to reveal a bulk of a man with long red hair tied back tightly in a pigtail, a matching beard. A swirl of tattoos peeked about the line of his black T-shirt. A dozen studs ran down his outer left ear, his eyes were hidden behind a pair of Ray-Bans.

'Walsh,' said the man. 'Been a while.'

'Angel. This is Chance.'

Chance could feel Angel's eyes stare at him behind the dark glasses.

'No offence, Walsh, but I got to pat both of you down.'

Walsh raised his hands, indicated for Chance to do the same.

Formalities over, Angel led the way into an oak panelled room dominated by a set of leather armchairs and sofas arranged on a square of Turkish carpet in front of a large open fireplace. Several logs burned, the flames crackled and spat. Above the fireplace hung a large, framed black and white photograph, Leigh hanging drunkenly off Mick Jagger at an after party during the Rolling Stones's Melbourne tour in 1973.

'Miss Leigh will be down in a minute.' Angel stood next to an old-fashioned metal drinks tray bristling with bottles of different shapes and sizes. 'She said to help yourselves to drinks.'

Chance waited until Angel left the room, picked up a bottle

of Chivas from the tray, poured Walsh and himself a finger each.

'He doesn't look like much of an angel to me.' Chance passed the drink to the Irishman. 'That some sort of S&M name?'

'It's his tattoos, a pair of huge angel wings on his back. Saw them once. Fucking incredible.'

Chance sipped his drink, smiled. Cheap scotch decanted into a Chivas bottle. There are reasons rich people are rich. Sometimes it's because they're smart, mostly it's because they don't spend their own money.

He scanned the room for the closed-circuit camera. The entire building was rigged with them. Leigh probably watched them now from her personal quarters on the fifth floor. Chance had been up there during lulls in her parties. Leigh, bored, would exchange pleasantries while he tried to ignore the images of squirming flesh on a bank of screens that took up an entire wall.

'The prodigal son returns,' said Leigh from the doorway. She grinned, stepped lightly into the room. Her tall, lean figure and mischievous smile helped hide the fact Leigh had left her sixtieth birthday behind long ago. Clad in black turban, tight-fitting black clothes with long red fingernails, and red lips, she reminded Chance of a large spider.

'Liam told me about your little, ah, cosmetic surgery.' She let Chance kiss her on the cheek, stepped back, held his chin in a taloned hand and surveyed his face over the tip of her electronic cigarette. Her sunken eyes, lined with shadow, shone with reckless energy, despite her advanced years.

'Rather an extreme makeover, but your Gaelic co-conspirator tells me the events warranted. I like it, makes you look cruel.'

'How's the S&M business?' said Chance.

'Booming, darling boy. Just booming.' Leigh poured herself a generous measure of clear-coloured alcohol, didn't offer to refill her guests' glasses. 'You'd be amazed at the amount of money powerful people will pay to be chained and whipped. It's like the businessmen's drug.'

'Speaking of drugs, you don't happen to have a real cigarette on you?' She put her drink down, looked at her electronic cigarette in disgust. 'I have to use these things, doctor's orders. Got to suck so hard to get the faintest trace of anything, feels like I'm giving a blowjob.

'You know, Gary,' said Leigh, taking the packet of tobacco from Chance and starting to roll a smoke, 'your face would work a treat in my dungeon, the punters would love it.'

'Maybe another time, Vera.'

'Yes, of course, you're here on far weightier matters. What can I do for you?'

'Information.' Chance fished the business card for Touch of the Orient out of his pocket. 'On the people behind this.'

Leigh blew out a stream of cigarette smoke, glanced at the card like it was a fresh turd.

'Positively reeks of low-rent sex, I can tell just by looking at it.' She handed the card back to Chance, gave him an indolent flick of her hand. 'Not the sort of place I'd be involved in.'

'But you can find out who is. Not just the public face, their associates. In particular, I want to know if there's any connection to an ex-Australian soldier called Frank Dormer, although he may not be using that name.'

'I don't get out as much as I used to, darling.' Leigh played with the large turquoise ring on one of her fingers, pretended to consider the idea. 'Old age and all.'

'Don't give me that. You've forgotten more about the sexual proclivities of Melbourne's wealthy residents than most people will ever know.'

'Never one to beat about the bush,' she said, obvious pleasure on her face at the backhanded compliment. 'Always liked that about you, Gary. So I'll reciprocate. What's in it for me?'

'Same as him.' Chance gestured in Walsh's direction. 'Money.'

'How much?'

'Enough.' Chance noticed the sharp look on Walsh's face. 'Out of my end,' he added for the Irishman's benefit.

'I suppose I could make one or two phone calls.'

'Walsh has given you my phone number.' Chance swallowed his remaining scotch, replaced the glass on the drinks tray. 'I'll expect your call.'

'Look forward to it, dear.' Leigh grinned. 'And remember, with that face I've got work for you, anytime you want it.'

Five

Chance untangled himself from the sheets, fumbled for the mobile phone. He glanced at the time on the illuminated screen, eleven in the morning, pressed 'answer.'

'I have some information,' purred Leigh into his ear. 'Come around this evening and I'll reveal everything.'

The line went dead.

Chance lay on the bed, stared at the cheap popcorn texture on the ceiling.

The fever had retuned something fierce last night, soon after Walsh had dropped him back at the hotel. Chance had no choice but to take his medicine, ride out the alternating waves of sweats and chills. He dozed off before dawn, serenaded by the sound of the couple fighting in the next room.

A slash of grey light came through a crack in the heavy curtains. He sat up, rubbed his chest and belly. The room was cold but his skin felt hot and clammy.

He lifted the phone above his face so the screen was looking down at him in the gloom, keyed in Walsh's number.

The city was deserted save for the last stragglers heading home from work. The Irishman was waiting on the corner of the laneway, fell into lock step with Chance as he turned and walked toward Leigh's apartment.

Angel answered the door sans Ray-Bans and his eyes were mean and beady. He patted them down without a word, led them up the stairs to the fifth floor.

Leigh reclined on a brown leather punch-button settee, bathed in the dull glow from the bank of closed-circuit TV screens. She sat up as the two men entered. Chance and Walsh sat on either side of her. Angel stood in front of a set of shelves crammed with books, his thick arms folded across his chest.

The screens beamed vacant spaces save one, a tiny black and white image of a male figure lying on a mattress in the middle of an otherwise empty room. Chance thought the figure had been dunked in black paint until he realised he was clad in a tight-fitting black rubber suit.

Leigh followed Chance's gaze, dismissed the image with a wave of her hand. 'Don't mind him. A business associate, likes to play breathing games.'

'I didn't know you provided on-site services.'

'Every now and again, for particularly high-paying clients who like the personal touch.' Leigh picked up a glass from a nearby coffee table, swirled the clear liquid around. 'As I suspected, the establishment you asked me to look into was a cheap and nasty fly-by-night operation. Women from Korea, Thailand, and Taiwan, brought out on student visas, treated dreadfully.

'The owner was a bottom feeder named Carl Feeney,' Leigh passed Chance a piece of paper, a photocopy of Feeney's driver's license. He looked like a pimp straight from central casting, sunken eyes, receding hair, a hooked nose and dark goatee.

'Carl's business only lasted a year or so.' Leigh drained her glass, motioned to Angel for another drink.

'My sources tell me just before he closed up shop, Feeney acquired himself a new business partner.' Leigh paused to accept a fresh drink, stared at Chance, a pencilled eyebrow cocked mischievously. 'Bit of a mystery man, this partner, a former Australian soldier, then worked as private security in Afghanistan. I hear he's cashed up and putting something big together.'

Chance looked at Leigh expectantly.

'Apart from that the well is dry.' She sipped her drink. 'Believe me, I had to call in quite a few favours just to get that.'

'Any idea where we can find Feeney?'

'If there's one thing I've learned from all my years in the business, it's that a hustler can always be depended on to be a hustler. It's in their blood. They can't help themselves. In addition to being a pimp, Feeney deals ecstasy at various house parties in the northern suburbs. There's a big one coming up this Thursday night, most likely he'll be there.'

'I owe you, Vera. But I need your assistance with two other things.'

'You do like to push, don't you?' Leigh sighed, flashed him a petulant look over the rim of her glass.

'I assume you still have contacts in the pharmaceutical business?'

'Yes.'

'Good. I need to talk to one of them. Someone discreetly.'

'If they associate with me, they're discreet. What else?'

'Can you lend us the use of one of your basement rooms?'

'I suppose so, but promise me no rough stuff.' Leigh grinned. 'Except when I'm not watching.'

Chance looked at the tiny black figure on the closed-circuit TV screen.

'I promise.'

They were parked in a narrow side street, a no man's land between the areas of the industrial past and its rapidly gentrifying future. Crash repair businesses and garages, a martial arts studio, factories and warehouses, everything covered in graffiti, including the two-story brick building where the house party was taking place.

Walsh dozed in the driver's seat while Chance watched the

flow of people in and out of the building. More leaving this time in the morning than coming in, the steady thump of house music mixed with the noise of crowds moving about in the street. The occasional reveller peered into the car on their way past, saw him stare back, kept walking.

Two hours and counting since Chance had followed Feeney up the stairs into a large space packed with people. The music, orchestrated by a DJ behind a turntable on a raised platform to the rear, made the entire building vibrate. Feeney moved through the crowded room like water on plastic. Several party-goers greeted the dealer like a long-lost friend.

After confirming the front entrance was the only way in or out, Chance left Feeney talking to a dreadlocked blonde on a sofa, went back to the car.

The radio was on, volume low. Late night talkback, someone complaining about the number of asylum seekers making it to Australia, their broad strine like the buzzing of an insect. He shifted his legs in the cramped space under the dash, tried to make them comfortable. He heard shouts, a bottle breaking against the footpath to the entrance to the party.

Walsh stirred, sat up. 'Anything happening?'

'This doesn't work out, we might be able to bag a job bouncing at gigs like this.'

Walsh yawned, stretched. 'No security?'

'None.'

'I thought that was illegal.'

'Yeah, the shit you can get away with these days.'

Chance was about to roll himself a cigarette when he noticed a figure exit the building and walk down the street toward them.

'Heads up, it's our man.'

'Too easy,' said Walsh as he got out of the car.

Six

The concrete floor was painted black and black plastic sheeting covered the walls. Chance carried an orange bucket seat from the adjoining room, set it down next to the double mattress, the fabric ripped and stained. He couldn't see the closed-circuit camera, but knew Leigh would be watching.

Walsh made the last adjustments to the full rubber body suit that now covered the unconscious man up to his neck, like he'd been dipped in wet tar.

'Shite.' Walsh stood up, grunted. 'Getting him into that suit was like wrestling with a greased pig.'

Chance sat, glanced at his watch. The chloroform would wear off any moment.

On cue, their prisoner groaned, moved his head from side to side. His eyelids fluttered, opened, became wide as he noticed the rubber suit, the two men in front of him. Muffled sounds escaped from under the ball gag strapped to his chin. He rocked from side to side on the grimy mattress, straining against the black nylon cuffs around his hands, his stifled shouts becoming louder.

Chance slowly rolled a cigarette, gave Feeney time to take in his predicament.

'Listen carefully, Carl,' said Chance as he lit up. 'It's not you we're after. You're small fry. It's Dormer we want.'

Feeney sat still, suspicion and panic battling in his eyes.

'Nod if you understand.'

Feeney shook his head vigorously up and down.

'Good. Now before we begin you need to understand there's no good cop, bad cop here. My friend here is bad cop.' Walsh stood at the end of the mattress, arms folded, looked down at their captor. 'I'm worse.'

Feeney nodded.

Chance exhaled. The smoke hung in air above the mattress. 'You tell us what we want to know, you won't get hurt.'

He held up a black rubber gas mask, Like WWII surplus, but instead of a filter canister, a limp black rubber bladder bag was attached to the mouthpiece.

'You don't, we'll put this on and play some breath-control games. You ever play breath-control games? The restriction of oxygen to the brain is supposed to lead to sexual arousal. The sound of their breath through the mask turns some people on. Others get their thrills by the eyeglass fogging up. Personally, I think it's a bit fucked up, but whatever. One man's pleasure and all that. Apparently, these things can be risky, even if you know how to use them. Not hard to lose consciousness and die.'

'Like that fella, the singer from INXS, what was his name?' said Walsh.

'Michael Hutchence,' said Chance.

'Aye, that's the one.'

'David Carradine, too.'

'What, the fella from Kung Fu?' Walsh looked at Chance askance. 'You're shitting me?'

'Police found him in his hotel room in Bangkok, hanging by a rope in the closet.'

'Never knew that.'

'Sad day when you don't learn something.' Chance returned his attention to Feeney. 'The unpredictability of the conse-quences, how it interferes with the body's basic requirement for oxygen, is supposed to be part of the kick. It's even more dan-gerous if you're panicked or scared. And it should never, under any circumstances, be tried if you have a weak heart or respiratory problems. Have you got a weak heart, Carl?'

Sweat popped on Feeney's forehead as he stared at the mask.

'Believe me, Carl, we strap this baby on and you die, we'll dump your body in a cheap hotel room, rig a belt around your neck, maybe throw in a few sex toys, a bit of porn for effect. No one will be any the wiser.'

Chance dropped the butt of his cigarette on the floor, ground it out with the heel of his boot.

'If you're happy to answer a few questions, nod.'

Feeney nodded.

Chance leaned over, undid the gag.

Feeney gasped for breath. 'Jesus fucking Christ, who are you people?'

Chance leaned forward.

'Carl, I ask the questions. Another outburst like that, you'll be wearing the mask.'

Feeney nodded. Chance smiled in return. He could get used to this S&M thing. Maybe a job in Leigh's club wasn't such a bad idea.

'Tell us about Dormer.'

'We met in Afghanistan. He was ex-army, doing private security. I was a construction contractor. We hooked up again when he got back to Melbourne.'

'What happened then?'

A wary look crept across Feeney's face. Chance could tell he was thinking about how much to tell.

'Don't even think of omitting anything.' Chance slapped the mask against his thigh. Feeney quivered at the sound.

'Look, man, like I said, we met briefly in Afghanistan. We hung out together in Kabul, hooked up again in Melbourne. Nothing else to it.'

Chance stood up, kicked the chair. It clattered across the room. 'Grab his shoulders while I strap the mask on.'

Walsh moved toward Feeney. The pimp squirmed, his body

taut against the rubber suit.

'Okay, man, fucking okay.' Feeney looked between the two men standing over him. 'He asked me if I wanted to go into business with him.'

'What kind of business?'

'Drugs.'

Chance noticed the flicker of alarm on Walsh's face, ignored it. 'Keep going.'

'He's connected with some towel head in Afghanistan, bloke named Rashid Jan, a warlord who runs one of the provinces outside of Kabul. Sounds like a movie, right? But it's true. Dormer said Jan was a wizened old guy in a turban, looked like you could blow him down if you wanted. But he'd been fighting for decades, first the Soviets, then the Taliban. Done a lot of bad shit.'

'How did Dormer meet Jan?'

'He was working security one night on a roadblock on the outskirts of Kabul. An SUV approached and wouldn't stop, so they fired on it. The passengers were some low-level Afghan official and his family. All dead. Turns out, the official is a distant relative of Jan's. Jan sends a minion to summon Dormer to a meeting. Dormer figures Jan's going to shake him down for compensation, but instead the old man starts going on about how soon all the Western soldiers will be gone from Afghanistan and it'll be back to the days of every man for himself. Jan needs money for guns and he's only got one thing to sell.'

Chance remembered walking through a valley of opium poppies back in Afghanistan, the pink flowers a blast of colour in the lunar landscape. In a country without even the most basic infrastructure or welfare services, poor farmers regarded opium resin as currency. It was easy to store and kept for years.

'Jan's been shipping heroin to Europe,' continued Feeney, 'but there's too much competition now, he wants to open up a new market.'

'In Australia?'

Feeney nodded, scratched at his face with his cuffed hands.

'He asked Dormer if he'd like to go into business with him. Only catch, Dormer has to provide seed money to fund his end of the operation.

'I wasn't crazy on the idea, competing with the established traffickers. I mean, those dudes play for keeps.' Feeney's sweaty, taut face glanced between his captors as he spoke. 'But Dormer's a fucking nut job. I tell you, the way he talked about Iraq and Afghanistan, dude enjoyed the war. I was worried what he'd do if I said no.'

'If Dormer's some sort of Jack Reacher, what's he need a low-life pimp like you for?' Walsh said.

'I have my uses,' Feeney shot back, his pride offended. 'He'd raised some of the money needed to finance his end of the drug operation, needed more. The proceeds from the sale of my business covered the gap. I've also got useful contacts, networks, you know, from getting girls out here.'

'How did Dormer bankroll his end?' Chance asked, already anticipating the answer.

'He ripped off some old gangster on a job they were doing together in Surfers Paradise.' Feeney's head swivelled between his two captors. 'I didn't have anything to do with it. Only reason I'm involved in all this is because he'd kill me if I said no, like he did the chick involved in the Surfers business.'

Chance knelt, leaned close enough to Feeney to smell his stale breath. 'You mean the woman whose body is decomposing in the barrel out near the airport?'

Feeney sniffed, on the verge of tears.

'Man, I swear, I didn't have anything to do with that. After the Surfers job, Dormer shot through to Afghanistan with the woman, stayed with Jan until things cooled down. She really didn't dig it. After they returned to Melbourne, she told Dormer she didn't want anything more to do with him and his business, so he had Ahmad kill her.'

'Who in fuck's name is Ahmad?' said Walsh.

'One of Jan's cousins. He came out to help supervise the Australian end of things. Dude's fucking scary, man. The two of them, Ahmad and Dormer, they hunted down this old Asian guy, some loose end from the Surfers Paradise job, tortured him, recorded it on film. Dormer smiled when he told me about it, said it was just like how the Taliban did it back in Afghanistan.'

Feeney licked his lips as he spoke, his voice becoming high pitched. 'Listen, you want my help to get payback? Just tell me what you need me to do. Anything. I'll do it. I just want to get out of this.'

Chance stared at the man cowering on the filthy mattress. He rolled a cigarette, heart beating hard in his chest as he processed the information. He glanced at Walsh as he lit up. The Irishman hadn't moved, but Chance could read the pissed-off look on his face. This was not what he'd bargained for.

'Do you know where Dormer lives?'

'Hell no, Dormer's weird about people knowing that shit. All I've got is a phone number. I need to talk, I call. He comes, usually with Ahmad in tow.

'Walsh, pass me Feeney's mobile. Carl here is going to make a call for us.'

Seven

'You know, comrade, if I had a piece of wood I'd beat some bloody sense into you for getting involved in this,' said Walsh, voice low to avoid being heard by other bar patrons. 'Then I'd use it on myself for agreeing to help you.'

'I believe Feeney.'

'Then you're even more of a fucking eejit than I thought.'

Chance and Walsh had stood silently while Feeney, still clad from neck to toe in the rubber suit, made the call to Dormer. Feeney played his part well. Chance's stomach churned as he listened to the faint sound of Dormer's voice on the other end of the phone.

Chance paid for the beers, downed half of his in one go. The mid-winter sky cast a shaft of dull light through the large window of the public bar. He was relieved to be out of the cramped, timeless confines of Leigh's basement.

He wanted a smoke, tried to distract himself by looking around the bar. Once one of the most dangerous pubs in the city, now transformed beyond recognition. Polished floorboards and smooth surfaces, the old menu—sausage and mash, rissoles and gravy—replaced by shared degustation platters and a lengthy wine list. The waterfront clientele long gone, in their place sharply dressed men and women. The only danger now, a heated argument about real estate prices.

'If it's about your money, don't worry,' said Chance. 'You'll get your share. Vera, too.'

'Ah, don't give me that shite. Sure I want the money, but I also want to live. Feeney's a pimp and a dope pusher, that's a mighty untrustworthy combination in my book. What's to say it's not a setup?'

A couple standing at the bar looked nervously at each other, moved away.

'Didn't you listen to him?' said Chance. 'He's scared and wants out. We're the only way that's going to happen.'

'Jesus Christ, whoever remodelled your face must have taken some of your brains as well. I mean, what the fuck have you become, man?' Walsh looked away, disgusted.

'That's rich coming from a former terrorist.'

'That was politics.'

'Right, just a few lads bombing pubs and knee capping collaborators between pints.'

'I wasn't involved in either.' Walsh's voice assumed a strong Irish lilt.

'Yeah, you just made people disappear in barrels of lye.'

'Jesus Christ, Gary, I signed on to help you locate your money.'

'You did and we are.'

'I didn't sign on to tangle with a drug dealing Afghan warlord and his cronies.'

'It's not like you to back away from a fight, Liam. Obviously, I'm not the only one who's changed.'

'A man should know his limitations.'

'What makes you think you know anything about my limitations?'

'You listen to me good, Gary Chance. I've dealt with some crazy fuckers in my day. Libyans, the Protestant paramilitaries, hell, some of the people on my own side, but none of it comes close to the kind involved in the drug trade.'

Walsh pointed at the Keffiyeh around his neck. 'Do you know why I wear this?'

Before Chance could reply, he pulled down the fabric to reveal the tail end of a jagged pink line.

'This is what I got for my troubles last time I tangled with drugs. Scrawny little thing she was, too. Accompanied her boyfriend on a buy. He was getting mouthy, I turned my back on her, when I turned back she had a blade in her hand, slashed me good.'

'Spare me the war stories, Liam.'

'I'm not afraid of a fair fight, comrade, and if you have any doubts let's go outside and I'll prove it to you.'

Chance needed Walsh, had come too far to run the risk of the Irishman pulling out. He had to keep him on his side.

'Liam, I don't like this any more than you,' he said calmly. 'The meeting with Dormer is set up for tonight. He has no reason to suspect it's a set-up, that we'll be waiting for him. We'll take him and he'll take us to the money.'

'What makes you sure he'll have the money and we'll be able to get to it?'

'He'll have the money close by and easy to get in the event he ever needs to leave town in a hurry.'

'What about the Afghan? What if he's tooled up?'

'Nothing the two of us can't handle.'

Chance wanted to get going, had things to organise before tonight. He placed a hand on Walsh's forearm, like coaxing a reluctant lover. 'We can do this. It'll work. Then you'll get your money and it'll all be over.'

Walsh drained his beer and placed the empty pot glass hard on the counter.

'I just hope you know what you're doing, comrade.'

The last person to say that was Tavener, and he was dead. Chance hoped it would be different this time.

Eight

Chance stood on the side of the road, watched the taxi pull away. His breath made tiny clouds in front of his face. The traffic flowed past, a blur of red and yellow lights, framed against the cobalt blue dusk sky.

He walked past a row of bare trees, turned into the motel's red-brick courtyard. Most of the windows were illuminated, travellers and the overflow from the local homeless service hunkering down for the night.

He paused outside his door, listened to the occupants in the next room argue while he fumbled for his key. He opened the door, navigated his way to his bedside table, felt for the light switch. The fluoro tube in the pelmet above the bed flickered to life.

Chance sat on the bed, his body exhausted but his mind a mess of emotions. Fear, anticipation, most of all, impatience and deep longing for the night to be over.

His stomach rumbled. He looked longingly at an empty pizza carton on the table on the other side of the room. He should have eaten at the bar. Now he'd have to make do with the vending machine near reception.

Chance didn't bother locking the room, went down the concrete stairwell. The glow of the vending machine was visible at the end of a corridor next to a sign with 'Exit' in red letters.

He ripped the top off the chocolate bar, ate as he walked

back. The light in his room had gone off. Not the first time. The wiring, like most of the fixtures in the aging motel, faulty. Chance swore under his breath. The last thing he felt like having to do was talk to reception, get someone up to fix it.

Chance closed the door behind him and was halfway across the room when he noticed a smell cut through the stale air, a female scent, like vanilla. He froze. The light flickered back on. A woman sat on the bed with her back against the exposed brickwork, propped up with pillows, regarded him with strong, dark eyes.

Chance stared at the woman, aware of sounds around him, shouting from next door, traffic. Her clothes, knee-length brown boots, designer jeans, a black roll-neck jumper and parka, looked expensive. She held a pistol level with his stomach.

'What a fucking dump.' She grimaced as she spoke. 'Do the couple next door always argue like that?'

'Yes.' Something about her was familiar, Chance couldn't tell what.

'Gives me a bloody headache,' she added.

As his surprise receded, he remembered his Sig Sauer under the Bible in the bedside table drawer, wondered if there was any way he could get to it before she could kill him.

'Looking for this?'

With her free hand she reached into the pocket of her parka, produced his gun, let it dangle from her middle finger for a moment, and placed it on the bed next to her.

'Sit, Mister Egan.' She used the name he'd checked in under, mimed a smile. 'Or whatever the hell your name really is.'

The smile, it came to him where he'd seen it. The TV news he'd watched in the hotel in northern New South Wales. The female cop at the press conference about Gao's murder. She flashed the same humourless smile at the media pack.

'You're the cop.'

Her mouth opened and the barrel of the pistol dipped slightly before she regained her composure.

'In the news report just after Gao was killed,' Chance continued. 'And your voice, you were one of the people in the bush, outside the caravan park in Yass.'

He thought about using her surprise to go for his gun, but ruled it out, was more interested in finding out who she was and what she was doing in his room.

'Chance?' She stood up, looked at his face from several angles. 'It can't be, your face.'

'An operation, it's a long story.'

'At least that would explain why you've been so hard to find. By the way, whoever was responsible for your surgery did a shit job.'

'Thanks. You going to tell me what you're doing here miss-whatever-your-fucking-name-is?'

'Blake. Elyssa Blake.' She chewed her lower lip, kept the gun trained on Chance's midsection as she deliberated what to do. 'That night in Yass, I lost a cop. He just disappeared like you and the others. You wouldn't have any idea what happened to him?'

'Maybe he ran away, joined that circus camped next to the caravan park.'

'Viljoen? I don't think so. Not the type.' She shrugged. 'Doesn't matter, didn't much like him anyway.'

Chance watched her eyes, reading her for clues.

'Okay, I'll play ball,' she said. 'Your trail went stone cold after Yass. But I did some digging, unearthed some leads on the other two people involved in the Surfers job, Dormer and his girlfriend, Sophia Lekakis.'

The image of the blue plastic barrel and its rotting contents flashed through Chance's mind.

'According to my information, after what happened in Surfers, Dormer and Lekakis went to Afghanistan for a while. They came back here a month ago. No sign of her, but through some contacts here I discovered Dormer is still in town. He's hooked up with an ex-brothel owner called Carl Feeney. I've been keeping tabs on Feeney off and on for weeks.' She shuddered. 'Weeks, freezing my arse off, trailing him around various house parties. It's made me tired and very grumpy.

'So, imagine my surprise when in the early hours of this morning, I see you and your big mate, Walsh, bundle Feeney into the back of a car. I followed the two of you to that place in the city, the apartment building.

'Your Irish mate, Walsh, he's got a little bit of form with the local cops, an even more colourful history back in Ireland. But you, you're a real mystery man. I've been following you all afternoon. Interesting tour it was, too, a secondhand white goods store, followed by a boat charter business in Williamstown. Planning a little trip?'

'You could say that,' said Chance.

'Your turn to spill. What are Feeney and Dormer cooking up?'

'You may have nothing to lose telling me what you're doing here, but why should I tell a cop anything?'

Her eyes glittered mischievously and she smiled, genuine humour in it for the first time. 'Who said I was still a cop?'

Chance felt the atmosphere in the room shift as the comment hung in the air. He realised he still held the chocolate bar, took another bite.

'In that case, put the gun down,' he said, chewing. 'We have a lot to talk about.'

Nine

The thin whispery rain was illuminated against the blackness in the tent of light from a nearby streetlight. The moisture on the windscreen cut visibility, made the world outside appear like it was melting. On the plus side, anyone looking in would find it hard to see the two of them sitting there.

Chance cracked his window, lit a rollie, his eyes never leaving Feeney's Commodore parked on the other side of the small square of park. Renovated terrace houses faced the park on three sides, a strip of shops, cafés, boutiques separated by a two-lane road on the other. Chance had spent his time in Melbourne north of the Yarra, always felt uneasy crossing the river to gentrified, affluent suburbs on the southern side of the city, like he set off against an invisible trip wire.

Just after two and the place was deserted. If Feeney was on the level, Dormer should appear any moment.

He started to go over the plan once more with Walsh, got nothing but grunts and dark looks from the Irishman for his trouble.

The arrangement, at least the part Walsh knew about, was simple. When Dormer appeared, Feeney would get out of his car to meet him. Feeney's excuse for meeting? He was nervous, wanted assurance that whatever Dormer was planning, everything was under control. Dormer might get pissed, but before he could do anything, Chance would be out of the car and walking across the park, the Sig Sauer in his hand. They'd get Dormer to take them to where the money was stashed. End of story. Chance particularly emphasised that Walsh was the wheelman on this job. Any rough stuff, Chance would take care of it.

The two men fell into a tense silence until Walsh turned to his partner, eyebrows raised. A light blue Toyota turned off the main road. The two men pushed themselves down against their seats, watched, eye level with the bottom of the window as the vehicle prowled around the park, disappeared back onto the main road.

'False alarm,' Chance murmured, ground his cigarette out in the ashtray, just as the Toyota re-appeared, turned onto the street.

'Doesn't bloody look like it,' said Walsh.

The Toyota parked half a dozen cars behind Feeney's Commodore and cut its headlights.

They watched the pimp get out of his vehicle, a newspaper over his head to shield from the rain, walk toward the new arrival, get in the passenger's side.

Chance felt the pistol in the pocket of his jacket, made sure that the safety was off, was just about to make a move when he spotted a tall figure walking along the footpath on the other side of the park.

Chance strained to get a better look. 'Someone walking the dog?'

'What kind of bloody eejit would walk their dog in this weather?'

Chance winced, a sharp sensation in the pit of his stomach. 'You're right, something's wrong.'

Chance got out of the car, blinked as the rain hit his face.

'You stay here,' he said, slammed the car door.

Chance wiped the water from his eyes, eased the pistol out of his pocket as he cut across the park.

The tall figure stopped next to the Toyota, disappeared into the back as the headlights came back on and the engine started.

Chance broke into a run as the car started, pulled away from the curb.

Chance stopped, doubled back. Walsh already had the engine idling, turned to Chance as he climbed back into the passenger's seat.

'What was that about a simple fucking plan?' said Walsh.

'Don't lose him.'

The Irishman grunted, followed the Toyota's red taillights down several side streets into a main thoroughfare heading to the city, weaved through the early morning traffic in an attempt to maintain their proximity.

'Don't lose the bugger, Liam, but don't do anything stupid,' said Chance. 'We don't want to get pulled over by the cops.'

Walsh flicked him a murderous look. Both cars slowed down as they hit the city. Taxis lined the roadside. Knots of people stood on the sidewalk or queued to get into nightclubs and strip bars.

The driver of the Toyota had to know he was being followed, but was disciplined, kept to the speed limit through the city. At several points, they got close enough for Chance to see the three figures illuminated in the Toyota's interior, before their quarry pulled away.

The Toyota turned into a stretch of road Chance knew would take them to the lightly populated sprawl of port facilities, refineries and container terminals at the city edge of the Western suburbs.

The rain stopped as they crossed back over the Yarra. On one side of the road, a rail yard with lines of idle freight cars on the tracks. On the other, the lights on the huge cranes that were used to pick up containers off visiting ships in the nearby port.

The Toyota sped up. Walsh put his foot down hard on the accelerator, passed a slow-moving semi-trailer, followed. With a squeal of tires, the Toyota entered a maze of deserted streets lined with container facilities. It swerved, came to a sudden stop twenty metres in front of them.

A man appeared over the top of the car. He had a bearded, gaunt face creased in concentration. He reached one arm across the roof, his hand wrapped around a metallic shape.

'Jesus Christ, he's got a gun,' yelled Chance.

Walsh spun the steering wheel hard right, as Gaunt Man fired. Chance heard the ping of metal being impacted, braced himself as a chain-link fence on the side of the road reared up in front of them. The car bounced as it hit the curb, came to a stop on the nature strip.

Chance gave the Irishman a quick glance. He was unhurt. Chance turned in his seat, the Toyota framed in the rear window. Gaunt Man, still leaning over the roof, sighted them with his pistol. Chance fumbled with the seat belt clasp, heard the sound of an approaching vehicle.

Gaunt Man heard it, too, swivelled his head in the direction of the noise, as a black four-wheel-drive roared out of a side street. The big car swerved just as its rear connected with the side of the Toyota. The force of the impact sent Dormer's vehicle onto its side. The four-wheel-drive did a hundred-and-eighty-degree turn and came to a standstill, its front stoved in. The sound of the collision lingered in the air.

Chance and Walsh stepped onto the nature strip, walked cautiously toward the wreckage. Shattered glass crunched under their feet. Someone moved about in the cabin of the four-wheel-drive. A woman climbed out, stood unsteadily, as if she were facing a heavy wind. There was no sign of movement from the overturned Toyota.

'About time you showed up,' said Chance.

Elyssa Blake bent over slightly, one hand on the bonnet, the other on her hip, looked up at Chance from under several strands of long black hair that had come undone from her ponytail.

'Fuck you and the horse you rode in on,' she said and breathed deeply. 'I just totalled a brand new rental car, saving your arse.'

Walsh shot Chance a confused look. 'Do you know this doll?'

'Who the hell you calling 'doll,' Paddy?' Blake put both hands on the small of her back, stretched.

'I'll make the introductions later,' said Chance over his shoulder as he walked toward the overturned car.

Gaunt Man lay on his back on the road surrounded by a pool of dark liquid. Dormer's Afghan business partner. His dusky skin, etched with lines, bushy eyebrows, coarse beard tinged with white, reminded Chance of the local men he'd seen around the Australian base at Tarin Kwot. There was no doubt he was dead, the lower half of his body crushed under the car. His dark eyes stared lifelessly at the night sky, his arms stretched, Christ-like. One hand still gripped the pistol.

'Ahmad's down,' said Chance. 'What about the others?'

Blake crouched on the ground next to Chance. 'Feeney's dead, broken neck.' She stood stiffly. 'Wasn't wearing a seat belt.'

'Walsh, what about Dormer?'

'Aye, we're in luck, bugger's alive.'

Dormer moaned as the Irishman helped him upright. A patch of Dormer's straw-coloured hair was matted with blood, one of his arms hung stiffly in his black leather jacket.

'We can make a deal.' Dormer appraised his three captors. 'I've got money.'

Chance smiled. 'I'll bet you have.'

Blake and Walsh sat in the front, Chance in the back with Dormer.

The initial offer of a deal rebuffed, Dormer spoke only to give directions. He had a broken wrist, the arm immobilised in a crude sling Blake had fashioned out of a T-shirt they found in the boot of Walsh's car. Although Dormer looked too banged up to be a threat, Chance rested the Sig on his knee just in case. He avoided eye contact with Dormer, stared instead out the window at the empty streets.

It was still dark when Walsh pulled into the driveway of a double-fronted house, one of a long row of identical dwellings.

Walsh pressed the button on the remote control they'd found on Dormer. The garage door crept up slowly. He drove in, closed it behind them. No barrels, no boxes, just smooth concrete surfaces and a door.

Chance placed one hand on the doorknob, the other on the grip of the pistol protruding over the belt of his pants, looked hard at Dormer.

'Don't worry, Rambo, there's no one else home.'

They moved through a sparsely furnished house into the main bedroom. Dormer nodded at a chest of drawers, sat on the bed, the pain from his broken wrist etched on his pallid features. He watched as Walsh moved the piece of furniture, pulled away a section of the carpet to reveal a trap door with a small latch. Blake looked over Walsh's shoulder, face tight with expectation.

Chance stood back, picked up a framed photograph from a nearby shelf. It was a group shot, young men in T-shirts and khaki pants, posing against a desert backdrop. A much younger Dormer was unmistakable, despite the wraparound sunglasses.

Dormer noticed Change looking at the photograph.

'Iraq. Simpler days.'

'Not if you were in Iraqi,' said Chance.

Walsh pulled up the trap door, reached inside, withdraw a small black daypack, passed it to Blake, who opened it and tipped the contents on the bedspread: bundles of cash in Euros, Australian and U.S. dollars, several passports, a mobile phone, a small, compact automatic pistol in a holster, several clips of ammunition.

'Looks like a go-bag to me.' Blake fixed Dormer with one of her humourless smiles. 'Not much use now, is it, Frank?'

Dormer shrugged, said nothing.

'Lot more where that came from,' said Walsh as he lifted out a garbage bag, then another. He untied one of the bags, took out a bundle of hundred-dollar bills, fanned the air in front of his face with them.

'I think my days on building sites are over.'

Blake's eye became wide. She reached in, withdrew a bundle, examined the notes carefully.

'That's it for me.' Chance put the framed picture back on the shelf, started repacking the go-bag.

'What shite are you talking?' said Walsh, unsure what was going on.

'There should be enough for you two, plus make sure Vera gets her cut.'

'Sure, mate, but what about your share?'

'Look after it for me,' said Chance, re-zipping the daypack. 'I've got other business to attend to. I'll need your car.'

'What are we going to do?'

'Get a taxi.' Chance smiled. 'It's not like you can't afford it.'

Blake, on both knees on the carpet, searching through the contents of the sports bag nearest to her, didn't look up, already knew what Chance had planned. Walsh started to speak, stopped himself, handed Chance his car keys.

Chance slung the daypack over his shoulder, tapped Dormer on the shoulder.

'Get up, you're coming with me.'

Dormer grimaced as he stood, the pain from his wrist getting worse.

'Am I going to see you again, comrade?'

'Probably.'

The two men hugged. 'Take care,' said the Irishman.

'Sure,' said Chance. He pushed Dormer toward the garage.

Ten

Dawn broke cold and pink, the bottle-green ocean completely still. Williamstown was a streak of uneven white behind him. To the stern nothing but open sea. The only sound was water gently lapping against the hull.

Chance shook his head to clear away the exhaustion, sipped from a half-full bottle of Teachers he'd found in the cabin. He shivered. A whisper of malaria or fear, he wasn't sure which.

His passenger stirred against the gunnel, the last of the chloroform wearing off. There was a brief flash of panic on Dormer's face as he took in his surroundings, the length of rope tied around his ankles. He raised his arms, grimaced in pain from his broken wrist, tried to move his feet. The rope tightened as it strained against whatever it was connected to under a faded tarpaulin next to him.

'The money you and your friends took, that's going to piss off a lot of very dangerous people,' he said.

Chance watched a gull cruise on a current in the sky.

'Are you at least going to tell me who you are?'

Chance had another hit of whisky, deliberated whether to respond.

Dormer shrugged, motioned at the bottle with his good arm. Chance passed it to him.

Dormer brought the bottle to his lips, drank. 'If you're not going to tell me who you are, at least tell me how you found me.

Not as though I can do anything about now.'

'Got lucky. Discovered the house near the airport, the body in a barrel. Also a box of business cards for that brothel Feeney owned. Connected the dots from there.'

A flicker of recognition flashed across Dormer's face. He tilted his head, as though a different angle might jog his memory.

'Always knew Feeney was unreliable.' Dormer smiled. 'As for the house, I told Ahmad to clean the place up. My fault for trusting the job to a man who'd spent most of his life in a mud hut. He couldn't read. Hadn't even seen a photograph of himself until a few years ago. Where's Ahmad?'

'Dead.'

Dormer's shoulders slumped and he let out a long breath.

'You don't sound very cut up about your partner.'

'Partner?' Dormer snorted, 'I suppose that's one way of looking at our relationship.'

Dormer passed the almost-empty bottle back to Chance.

'So what happens now?'

Chance finished off the bottle, dropped it on the deck. He grabbed one corner of the tarpaulin, pulled it off to reveal a small bar fridge, speckled with rust, connected to the rope around Dormer's ankles.

'That's how it's going to be?'

'Yeah.'

'My old man had a fridge like this one,' said Dormer wistfully. 'Weighed a tonne.'

'Mine too'.

'But first you're going to tell me it's not personal, right?'

'Like you said, Frank, the strong sharks eradicate the weak ones.'

Another flash of recognition, stronger this time, swept across Dormer's face. Chance picked up the bar fridge in both hands, dropped it over the side of the boat. It disappeared under the surface with a loud splash. Dormer looked for something to hold onto, but the fridge sank too fast, dragged him over the side and into the water. He opened his mouth but the sea swallowed his words.

Chance gripped the side of the boat hard as he watched the cloud of bubbles and foam explode in the green water and slowly disappear.

His hands trembled as he rolled a cigarette. The water was completely calm. His reflection no longer that of a stranger.

Chance slowly finished his smoke, looked up, aware of noise behind him. A vessel a couple of hundred metres away, a two-story cabin, packed with people, men and women, laughing and drinking from cans. Some of them wore sombreros.

One reveller waved. He waved back. Several partygoers cheered, saluted him with their drinks and went back to their festivities.

Chance watched the boat pass by. When the dance music faded, he pulled up the anchor, started the engine and pointed the boat in the direction of open water.

ORPHAN ROAD

Coming in 2019

One

Chance ignored the pain gathering force in the back of his skull, concentrated on aping the looks of joyous ecstasy plastered on the faces of the surrounding cult members.

The young woman next to him, Shannon, a model-thin former legal secretary from Sydney, squeezed his arm, smiled as she swayed. Chance grinned back, swept her up in his arms in what he hoped would be interpreted as a gesture of abandon. She hugged back harder.

Around a hundred people occupied the circle of cleared forest that served as the venue for Cornelius's regular soul cleansing sessions. Chance battled his headache for the name of tonight's subject. Wetzler. A stockbroker in his mid-forties. He sat on the ground, Cornelius squatting behind him, arms holding the overweight man, as if helping him give birth.

Tonight Cornelius claimed to be channelling the spirit of Siphon, a nine-thousand-year-old Atlantean wizard. The cult leader's deep voice was audible above the new age synthesiser music that blared from speakers affixed like beehives to trees around the clearing. Tears streamed down Wetzler's chubby face as the crowd chanted at him to confess his spiritual impurities.

Chance had to hand it to Cornelius. He knew all the tricks: switching between abuse and intimacy, subliminal messaging. In another life he would've excelled as an army interrogator, like those Chance had met during his tour in Afghanistan. The setting helped, the middle of the forest 'to bring us closer to the spirit world,' as Cornelius put it. A brilliant yellow moon partly obscured by wisps of cloud, a roaring log fire that cast flickering shadows across the crowd as it shrieked and moved in time to the music.

When Tremont had first suggested robbing a cult, Chance imagined something like the Manson Clan or a bunch of backwoods Christians who stockpiled guns and slept with each other's wives. New Atlantis was more like a rave party meets *Lord of the Flies*.

Chance broke away from Shannon's embrace, scanned the crowd. What he wouldn't give for a cigarette. One of the many items forbidden by Cornelius because they made the human body unsuitable for re-occupation by the Atlanteans, who, according to him, would soon emerge from their ocean home to reclaim the planet. Cornelius didn't exactly come across as prime real estate for a returning Atlantean spirit. Clad in a faded denim shirt and black jeans, eyes hidden by ever-present dark sunglasses, he struck Chance as a cut price Jim Morrison, his body, all bone and sinew, skin stretched and weather beaten.

Lilith on the other hand, Chance could well imagine an Atlantean spirit being at home in her form. One of the group's 'Elders,' watching Lilith had been one of the few pleasures in New Atlantis not forbidden by Cornelius. In her late thirties, if the faint wisps of grey that crept into her shoulder length black hair were any indication, tonight she wore narrow-cut black cotton pants that showed off the contour of her strong legs, and a loose purple overshirt that accentuated her cleavage. Her suntanned skin looked caramel in the firelight.

Chance gripped the little finger of his left hand. The digit, taken off at the knuckle with a pair of garden shears years ago, had been replaced with one of his toes by a plastic surgeon in Thailand. Remembering he played with it whenever he was nervous, he suddenly let go, as if worried he was giving himself away.

Lilith met Chance's gaze, held it. Chance felt sharpness in his gut at the possibility she was on to him. Without taking her eyes from him, she inclined her head, said something to the bald man next to her. Swain, another of the group's Elders. Swain was tall and well-muscled, but Chance wondered what the Atlanteans would make of the white supremacist tattoos that peeked out from under the long sleeved black tops he always wore.

A cry drew everyone's attention back to the centre of the clearing. Wetzler had broken. Head nestled against Cornelius's chest, he blubbered out his spiritual impurities—a selfish material life, fucking his secretary, tax evasion. Cornelius stroked Wetzler's thinning hair, leaned close, whispered in the man's ear. The stockbroker immediately became calm, his eyes fixed on a point in the night sky only he could see.

The music stopped, the signal that the ceremony was over. The cult members paused like a bar crowd when the lights come on, reluctant for the night to end. Chance joined them as they drifted towards the dormitories, watching from the corner of his eye as Cornelius and Lilith lead Wetzler in the opposite direction. He knew from Tremont that a soul cleansing was always followed by a one on one debrief during which Cornelius counselled the individual concerned about the uselessness of worldly possessions now they had reached a heightened stage of spiritual consciousness.

At first sight of the dormitories, Chance ducked behind a large gum tree. He waited until the last of the crowd had filed inside and made his way around the perimeter of the compound, pausing now and again to make sure he was not being watched. He found the spot he was looking for, scooped away the dirt, unearthed the zip lock plastic bag he'd buried soon after arriving in New Atlantis, took out a stainless steel wristwatch and a flashlight. Two more items banned in New Atlantis. He peered at the tiny green dots on the dial. Ten-forty-five. Tremont would wait until two am.

Cornelius lived in an old wooden farmhouse on the property.

The door was unlocked, the threat of excommunication for anyone caught near the house, the only security Cornelius needed. Chance whistled softly as the beam of light moved across the main living area. Sleek metal and leather furniture competed for attention with Asian-themed wall hangings, rugs and throws. A large plasma screen television stood against one wall, a well-stocked liquor cabinet by another.

The trap door was under a rug in the bedroom. He pulled the latch, put a hand in, felt smooth, cool wood but nothing else. He withdrew his hand as though he'd received an electric shock.

The money was gone.

Chance crouched in the darkness. The hairs on his arms and neck bristled. Had Tremont doubled crossed him? There was no way his partner could have made it onto the property and stolen the money without being detected. That left two other possibilities. Tremont's information was wrong or someone else had taken it.

He stood up only to be thrown back to the ground. The circle of light from the dropped torch illuminated his assailant's booted foot, the rest a grunting shadow. He wrestled with the figure. A blow cut deep into Chance's upper lip. Fireworks went off in his vision and his mouth filled with the taste of his own blood. His assailant used the seconds while Chance recovered to roll on top of him and try and pin him to the ground.

Chance threw several punches, found only air. He jabbed again, heard a wet crack that was his fist connecting with his assailant's nose. Chance tried to leverage himself up but a blow snapped his head back onto the wooden floorboards.

The pain became more distant with each blow until he felt nothing.

Chance's last job had left him broke and on the run. Working a long haul prawn trawler out of Cairns had seemed an ideal way to avoid the authorities. At first he'd welcomed being at sea, no external contact except a tanker that delivered food and fuel and took away the catch. Until he got to know the crew: a captain whose idea of letting off steam was to fire a shotgun at sharks trying to get the catch; a deckhand who got his kicks playing practical jokes with the chemicals used to freeze the prawns; another whose standard reply to anything was 'What happens on the boat, stays on the boat.' But the worst part was going through the nets. You had to sort the prawns without gloves to feel for the soft and broken ones. His hands were still scarred from the cuts. Not to mention the various lethal creatures that got caught in the catch, all of which had a ferocious attack or defence mechanism. Or both.

He'd been in the northern New South Wales town of Byron Bay two weeks, waiting on a call from a man named Loomis. A cut out for Vera Leigh, working girl turned Melbourne business-woman, Loomis dealt with anything messy or illegal, which in Leigh's business—owning a nightclub and one of Melbourne's best-regarded S&M dungeons—kept him busy. He also connected people with jobs. Leigh took a cut of everything he helped put together.

When Loomis's call finally came, the raspy voice, which sounded as if it emanated from a place farther away than Melbourne, gave him contact details for Carl Tremont. They met in a backpacker bar in town. Tremont came across as a middle-aged hustler, heavily tanned skin, long greying hair tied in a ponytail, his white shirt unbuttoned to reveal a chunky Buddha amulet on a gold chain around his neck. A self-described cult buster, Tremont had set up shop a decade earlier in Byron Bay, a place where the remnants of the seventies counter culture faced off against pastoralists and hard-core Bible thumpers.

On their second meeting, Tremont was accompanied by Celeste, an animated, curvy woman with a head of frizzy ginger hair. After drinking for a couple of hours, the three of them ended up on an L-shaped black leather couch in the family suite of the motor court Tremont called home. Celeste chopped up lines of coke on a glass coffee table, eighties stadium rock low on the stereo, while the cult buster told Chance about New Atlantis, a hundred-hectare property cut out of rain forest near the town of Mullumbimby, north of Byron.

'It was established by a bloke called Terry Cornelius. Claims he can channel the spirits of Atlantean wizards who died when their city was wiped out by an alien invasion thousands of years ago.

'He preaches humanity is just a transitory stage, we are merely minding our bodies until the Atlanteans return to reclaim them.' As Tremont spoke, Celeste did a line. 'The faithful will be elevated to a higher level of existence while the rest of humanity is destroyed. Something like that.'

'Do people actually believe that shit?' said Chance.

Celeste paused mid-snort, shot Chance a wounded look. 'It's not shit, Gary.'

'Celeste, not now,' said Tremont with a tight smile.

'Carl, baby, just saying, what Cornelius preaches about us just being the keepers of our bodies until the Atlanteans return, it's not all—'

'Honey, I get it, just not now. Okay?'

Celeste went silent.

Tremont put a hand on her shoulder. 'Would you go get Gary another beer, love?'

Tremont shook his head, looked to the ceiling after she'd gone.

'Nice lady, great in the sack, but a half a sandwich short of picnic if you know what I mean.' He winked at Chance. 'It's the same with a lot of cult survivors. The experience leaves them a little fucked up.'

Chance glanced in the direction of the kitchen, then back at Tremont, his eyebrows raised.

'Her old man paid me five grand to get her out of New Atlantis. Our contract didn't say nothing about what would happen afterwards.' Tremon shrugged, flashed Chance a sly grin. 'Can I help being a charming bastard?

'Anyway, Celeste was Cornelius's missus for a time and he was real open with the pillow talk, all the details of his operation, including where he stashes his money.'

Tremont leant forward, did a line, pinched his nose and indicated for Chance to do the same. Chance shook his head, rolled a cigarette.

'The coke is for down time only, Gary' said Tremont, noting the look of disapproval on Chance's face. 'I'm clean when I work.'

Tremont sat back on the couch, sniffed, swiped his forearm under his nose. 'New Atlantis has all the features associated with your garden-variety, nut job cult. Isolationist. Obsessed with the end of the world. Run along strict hierarchical lines, etcetera. But while the foot soldiers grow organic vegetables, those who've been spiritually purged and are loyal to Cornelius have a higher calling, tending the high-grade ganja he sells to dealers along the northern NSW coast.

'Their product is good, it's a cash business and Cornelius doesn't trust banks. What's more, its April, growing season's almost over and I hear they've sold most of the latest crop.' Tremont rubbed his hands together. 'Now does that sound sweet deal or does that sound like a sweet deal?'

Chance fired up his rollie from a novelty hand grenade lighter on the table, thought about the mechanics of the job, energised by the prospect of working again.

'What about security?'

'A couple of heavies to keep the local rednecks at bay.'

'If the money is so lightly guarded, there's nothing to stop us from just going in and getting it, right?'

'No. Guys like Cornelius are conditioned to expect someone to come at them from outside, cops or a rival grower.'

'Or someone like you.'

'Correct. But he'd never expect trouble from within. Believe me, I know what I'm talking about. I've been dealing with people like him for years.' Tremont looked around the motel room, sighed. 'With the money from this score I can get out of this game, do something else.'

'So, what's your plan?'

Celeste returned, passed a can of beer to Chance. Tremont put an arm around her waist, smiled up at her. 'Celeste, baby, tell Gary about life in New Atlantis.'

The New Atlantis minivan came into Mullumbimby for supplies every few days. It wasn't hard to spot. Tremont told him to look for a vehicle with the traditional symbol of Atlantis, a cross in concentric circles.

Chance tried striking up a conversation with the driver, an older woman in a caftan called Connie. He told her he was an ex-independent contractor gone bust, just come through a bad divorce, depressed, looking for a different path.

When that didn't get him anywhere, he disabled the van's clutch sensor while Connie was in the toilet, then offered to fix it when she returned and couldn't start the engine. Lilith accompanied Connie on her next visit, asked Chance whether he was interested in coming out to have a look at New Atlantis. On his second visit he was invited to stay.

Chance rang Tremont before he left, made a plan to meet him, with the money, in seven days.

The first thing Chance felt was pain. He remembered the beating, and the lead up. Then he noticed the smell, a cloying organic aroma.

He was cheek down on a wooden floor, four sets of feet at eye level. He inclined his head. Lilith and Cornelius, Swain, another man, short, broad shouldered with a head of blond hair, all backlit by a single globe hanging from a corrugated iron ceiling. Short Man glared at Chance, dabbed his fingers at the dried blood around his nostrils. Cornelius was dressed in the same clothes he'd been wearing at the soul cleansing but Lilith had changed into old boots, jeans, faded red cowboy shirt.

Cornelius nodded and Swain and the Short Man hauled Chance roughly into a wooden chair. Short Man propped him up, dug his strong fingers into Chance's shoulder while Swain tied plastic rope around him. When they were finished the two men resumed their position on either side of the cult leader.

The walls were lined with tin foil, plastic chemical containers stacked against one wall. In the doorway behind his captors hung a row of drying marijuana plants. Chance's eyes came to a standstill on a metal workbench where a selection of knives lay neatly arranged on a black canvas pouch, alongside a metal cylinder that looked horribly like a blow torch.

Cornelius adjusted his dark sunglasses, ran spidery fingers through his hair, sighed.

'Where's my fucking money?'

Stripped of the theatrics his voice had a brutal, authoritative tone.

'It was already gone when I got there.' Chance heard his own voice waver.

'Figured as much.' Cornelius scratched at the stubble on his face. 'No sense you stealing the money and coming back to an empty cubbyhole. But the thing is…' he lost his train of thought, looked at Lilith. 'What's this guy's name again?'

'Bell. Lawrence Bell.'

'The thing is Mister Bell or whatever the fuck your name is, you were trying to steal it all the same, so you must know something, follow my meaning?'

'Maybe he's a jack,' spat Blond Man.

'Shut up, Dobbs.' Cornelius flashed his enforcer an annoyed look as he picked up the metal cylinder from the workbench, twisted a valve at one end of it. There was a hiss and a tongue of blue flame came to life.

'You must be a pretty crappy messiah to have to resort to something as old fashioned as a blow torch to get answers.' Chance tried to sound braver than he felt.

'Don't be disappointed, son.' Cornelius's smile exposed a line of yellow teeth. 'There's so many people claiming they're Jesus, Satan or whoever, more people lining up to believe them. Way it's always been, way it always will be.'

'Sounds like you've been smoking too much of your own product.'

'Never touch the stuff.' Cornelius brought the flame close to Chance, ran it along his bare arm and took it away. Chance flinched at the proximity of the purring heat, focused on trying to control his bowels. The smell of burning hair mixed with the aroma of the drying marijuana.

'I'm working with someone on the outside,' Chance said quickly. 'A man called Tremont.' He noticed Cornelius's brow furrow at mention of the name. 'He gets people out of places like this, one of them told him about the money.'

Chance looked at Lilith as he spoke. She gazed back at him, her face blank.

'He hatched the plan, recruited me to work it from the inside. I was supposed to steal the money, meet him at the front entrance at midnight.'

'Swain, Dobbs, take the van, go and pick up this Tremont fuck. Do it quietly. Don't wake the sheep.' Cornelius stared at Chance as he spoke. His glasses reflected the flame from the blowtorch. 'Bring him back here,' he yelled after them. 'Alive.'

Within moments of the men leaving, Chance heard a vehicle splutter into life, drive off.

'Now, what to do with you, Mister Bell?'

Lilith stepped towards the workbench, picked up a shorted bladed knife. 'Terry, I reckon I can think of something.' She stood next to Cornelius, held the knife in front of his face.

The cult leader smiled, licked his upper lip. 'You're full of surprises, ain't you?' He turned off the blowtorch.

Lilith slashed the knife across Cornelius's throat, stepped back. Blood poured through Cornelius's fingers as he clutched helplessly at the wound. He swayed like one of his followers during a spiritual cleansing, fell backwards onto the ground, squirmed a few moments and went still.

Lilith stared at the body, her breath coming in short gasps. She shook her head hard, glanced at Chance as if noticing him for the first time.

'Whoever you are, we've got to move quickly,' she said, cutting the binding. Chance stood, rubbed his wrists for a moment, grabbed Lilith's knife hand by the wrist, twisted it behind her back, put his other arm around her neck.

Lilith dropped the knife and yelped in pain. 'What the—'

'I don't know what the hell's in the water around here—' Chance spat, '—but before we go anywhere I want some answers.'

'You're hurting me.'

Chance twisted her arm further.

'Okay, okay,' she stopped struggling. 'I stole the money.'

She uttered a husky laugh at Chance's silence. 'What, upset I crashed your party?' Her voice had regained its confidence.

Chance cursed, let her go, angry his reaction had been so easy to read.

'How much?'

'I haven't had the chance to count it but enough.'

'Now you got a partner.'

Her large blue eyes glared at him. 'Why the hell should I throw my lot in with you when your last partner is probably having his teeth kicked out by Swain and Dobbs as we speak.'

'I'm not the one who just killed a man.'

'Believe me, mate, that wasn't originally on tonight's agenda. I could've just left you here, let Cornelius slowly barbecue you.'

'And I appreciate it,' he said, staring at Cornelius, who lay face up, surrounded by a balloon of dark liquid. His sunglasses had slipped off, the whites of his eyes staring up into his skull.

'Besides, my partner's safe for now. Unless Cornelius's thugs went in the opposite direction to the one I gave them.' Chance scanned the room as he spoke, fixed on a pile of tools on the floor. He stepped carefully around the blood, selected a large spanner, tested its for heft.

He glanced at his watch. Less than an hour to get the money and meet Tremont. He quickly explained the plan to Eva.

'Now where's the money?'

Her brow furrowed as she weighed up her options.

'Don't fuck around,' Chance snapped. 'The money, where is it?'

'I hid it.'

Chance fought a wave of exhaustion. His face throbbed. 'Where?'

'Behind the farmhouse.'

The night was clouding over and a wind had whipped up, rustled through the canopy, as Chance crouched in bushes near the farmhouse. The woman had been gone almost ten minutes He turned the spanner over in his hands, starting to think he'd been an idiot to trust her, another criminal, suspecting that she'd taken the money and run, when he heard a movement in the bushes.

'Lilith?'

Without a word, a figure stepped towards him. Its shape wasn't right, shorter and thicker. A male. Chance didn't hesitate, lunged towards the figure, swung the spanner as he moved. The figure went down. Chance hit him again to make sure, peered at the body, recognised Dobbs.

'Got it,' came a female voice behind him. Chance, his mind racing and blood simple, twisted around, raised the spanner, ready to strike.

'Whooa, boy, it's me.' She raised one hand palm out in front of her. The other clutched a canvas bag. She noticed the body on the ground.

'Dobbs.'

Chance breathed deeply, nodded.

'Which means—'

'Yeah. Swain isn't far away.'

He took the bag, unzipped it, and looked inside. Twenty and fifty dollar notes, some tied with rubber bands, the rest loose. Nowhere near the million Tremont had promised but at least he wouldn't walk out of the job with nothing. He zipped the bag shut, slung it across his shoulder.

'Who nominated you for bag duty?'

Chance glared at her, started walking.

They ducked and weaved through the thick undergrowth that surrounded the New Atlantis compound, emerging onto a flat stretch of pasture. The moon was now almost completely covered in cloud, the wind stronger.

'Has anyone told you your timing sucks?' she said as they walked.

'All the time.'

'Two fucking months, pretending to chase Atlantis with the rest of the crazies, trying to keep Cornelius's paws off me long enough to score the cash and get out.'

Chance, realising that talking was her way of coping with the fear, was happy to play along.

'The name change, all that stuff about channelling an Atlantean priestess, that your idea?'

'Cornelius's. He said most people were prepared to believe any old crazy shit you fed them, as long as you gave them the courtesy of putting on a show. And, boy, did that son of a bitch know how to do a show. I almost believed him myself.'

'So your name's not Lilith?'

'No. It's Eva.'

The moon was almost completely covered in cloud, the wind becoming stronger.

'Bell's not your real name is it?'

'No.'

'You going to tell me what it is?'

He hesitated. A show of trust now would work in his favour. 'Gary. Gary Chance.'

'I always thought there was something suss about you, Gary Chance. The way you were always watching me. I thought you were onto me.'

Chance looked behind them. Still nothing. Picked up his step.

'Tonight was going to be my last in that place. The it was goodbye Australia and hello Fiji, white sand beaches and cocktails.'

'You can still do that, though you might have to forgo plans for that first class plane ticket.'

They reached a strip of dense scrub, plunged through it, emerged onto a dirt road, the shape of Tremont's station wagon visible in the gloom a couple of hundred metres ahead.

The engine kicked into life as they approached, the head-lights illuminating the stretch of dirt road in front of it. The driver's door opened, Tremont got out, stood by the car

'Whose your friend?'

Chance tensed, alerted by the forced casualness in Tremont's voice, his lack of surprise at Eva's presence.

'Introductions later.' Chance tightened his grip on the span-ner. 'We need to go.'

'Sorry, mate.' Tremont flashed a weak smile, lifted two palms towards Chance. 'Plan's changed.'

Swain emerged from the undergrowth at the side of the road, stood next to Tremont. He pointed a pistol at Chance and the woman.

'Put the bag and the spanner on the ground and stand back.'

Chance dropped the bag on the ground, let the spanner fall after it, tried to estimate whether he'd get to Swain before the man could pull the trigger.

'Don't even think about it,' said Swain, reading his mind. 'Big man like you, I figured you spilt your guts too quickly. So when Dobbs and I found nothing at the front gate, I wasn't surprised.' Swain switched his gaze to Eva. 'But it was back at the drying shed, Cornelius bled out and no sign of you, that's when the alarm bells really went off. Tell me. Which of you did the boss?'

Eva smiled.

'Not that I care but always told Cornelius he shouldn't trust you. Pity he was too busy trying to get down your pants to listen.'

'You jealous, Joe?'

'You're not my type.'

'What, not Aryan enough?'

'Enough bullshit.' Swain gestured at Tremont with barrel of his pistol. 'Check the bag.'

Tremont came forward, knelt and unzipped the bag. His eyes widened at the sight of the money.

'Bring it here,' said Swain.

Swain took the bag in one hand, couldn't help himself, peered inside. Chance seized the opportunity, launched himself rugby tackle style around Swain's stomach. It felt like hitting a brick wall. Swain grunted as the air was knocked from him. The gun skidded into a gully at the side of the road, the bag dropped to the ground. Bills spilled out, quickly picked up by the wind.

'Don't just stand there,' grunted Chance as he wrestled with Swain on the ground. 'The bloody gun.'

Tremont and Eva glanced at each other, had the same thought. Tremont moved first. Eva tripped him up as he grabbed the bag, kicked him in the side of the head. More bills flew out as he fell.

Chance and Swain were off the ground, circling each other, looking for a weakness to attack.

On the edge of his vision, Chance saw Eva reach into the side of her boot, withdraw something and throw it. Swain howled as the knife she'd used on Cornelius bit deep into his shoulder, lurched towards the shadows at the side of the road.

Chance stood stunned for a moment. Tremont lay groaning

on the ground. Chance thought about helping him, dismissed the idea as Swain re-emerged, the pistol in his hand. He swayed like a drunk, his face set hard against the pain, aimed unsteadily at Chance, fired.

The shot went into the bushes behind him.

Chance made a desultory attempt to grab at some of the loose bills blowing in the air.

'Forget the fucking money,' shouted Eva from the driver's seat of the car. 'Get in.'

Swain fired again. A rear passenger window shattered.

Chance dived into the back seat. Eva slammed her foot on the accelerator. Several more shots sounded in the darkness behind them.

'Where'd you learn to use a knife like that?'

'Let's just say I had a misspent youth.'

'Lucky for me.'

'That's the second time I've saved your arse tonight,' she said.

Chance brushed window glass off the back seat with his hand, stretched out. 'How will I ever repay you?'

She smiled, not taking her eyes from the road. 'We'll figure out something.'

ACKNOWLEDGMENTS

Thanks to David Whish-Wilson, Eva Dolan and David Honeybone for reading the manuscript of *Gunshine State*, and to Chip Henriss, Jeremy De Ceglie, and Liam Farrelly for sharing their stories. I am also grateful to Eric Campbell, publisher of Down & Out Books, for giving this book second life.

Finally, this book would not have been possible without the love, patience and thoughtful advice of my partner, Angela Savage.

Andrew Nette is the author of one previous novel, *Ghost Money*. His short fiction has appeared in a number of print and on-line publications, most recently the anthology *The Obama Conspiracy: Fifteen Stories of Conspiracy Noir*. He has contributed reviews and non-fiction to a wide variety of publications and is co-editor of *Girl Gangs, Biker Boys, and Real Cool Cats: Pulp Fiction and Youth Culture, 1950 to 1980*.

PulpCurry.com

BOOKS

On the following pages are a few
more great titles from the
Down & Out Books publishing family.

For a complete list of books and to
sign up for our newsletter,
go to DownAndOutBooks.com.

Shakedown
Martin Bodenham

Down & Out Books
978-1-946502-13-1

Damon Traynor leaves a glittering career on Wall Street to set up his own private equity business. When it is the winning bidder in the multi-billion dollar auction for a government-owned defense company, his firm's future success looks certain. But soon after the deal closes, Damon makes an alarming discovery—something that makes the recent acquisition worthless. Facing financial ruin, he investigates the US treasury officials behind the transaction and finds himself locked in a deadly battle with the leader of the free world.

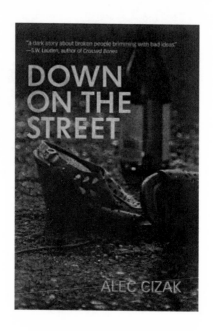

Down on the Street
Alec Cizak

ABC Group Documentation,
an imprint of Down & Out Books
978-1-943402-88-5

What price can you put on a human life?

Times are tough. Cabbie Lester Banks can't pay his bills. His gorgeous young neighbor, Chelsea, is also one step from the streets. Lester makes a sordid business deal with her. Things turn out worse than he could ever have imagined.

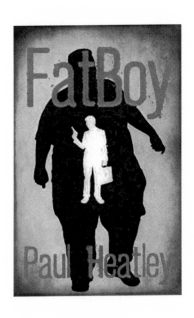

Fatboy
Paul Heatley

All Due Respect, an imprint of
Down & Out Books
978-1-946502-94-0

Is Joey Hidalgo really as angry, as volatile, so close to constant violence, as ex-girlfriend claims he is? No, Joey thinks, of course not, the real problem is money—or lack thereof. Joey's a bartender, always struggling to make ends meet, unlike his most vile regular customer, the rich and racist fatboy. So Joey hatches a plan to get his family back by taking him for all he's worth.

But the fatboy isn't going to make it easy for them. Neither is Joey's temper. Things are going to get messy, and it's gonna be one hell of a long night.

Slaughterhouse Blues
A Love & Bullets Hookup
Nick Kolakowski

Shotgun Honey, an imprint of
Down & Out Books
978-1-946502-40-7

Holed up in Havana, Bill and Fiona know the Mob is coming for them. But they're not prepared for who the Mob sends: a pair of assassins so utterly amoral and demented, their behavior pushes the boundaries of sanity. Seriously, what kind of killers pause in mid-hunt to discuss the finer points of thread count and luxury automobiles? If they want to survive, our fine young criminals can't retreat anymore: they'll need to pull off a massive (and massively weird) heist—and the loot has some very dark history...

CPSIA information can be obtained
at www.ICGtesting.com
Printed in the USA
LVOW10s1824270218
568056LV00004B/898/P